"Karin, you know what I want."

She knew.

Oh, God, she knew.

She wanted it, too.

But this was wrong. She had a job. He had a case. They were going to have to work near each other, at least for a while. What was she thinking? Even if they weren't working near each other, this could go absolutely nowhere. TJ Vasquez was not the man for her.

He was not the man for any *one* woman.

"TJ, I don't think—"

"Shhh." He shook his head slowly, firmly, and stared deep into her eyes. "Woman, you think far too much." He moved closer, until she was drawing her very breath from his.

She wasn't thinking now.

She was feeling....

Dear Reader,

This is officially "Get Caught Reading" month, so why not get caught reading one—or all!—of this month's Intimate Moments books? We've got six you won't be able to resist.

In *Whitelaw's Wedding,* Beverly Barton continues her popular miniseries THE PROTECTORS. Where does the Dundee Security Agency come up with such great guys—and where can I find one in real life? A YEAR OF LOVING DANGEROUSLY is almost over, but not before you read about *Cinderella's Secret Agent,* from Ingrid Weaver. Then come back next month, when Sharon Sala wraps things up in her signature compelling style.

Carla Cassidy offers a *Man on a Mission,* part of THE DELANEY HEIRS, her newest miniseries. Candace Irvin once again demonstrates her deft way with a military romance with *In Close Quarters,* while Claire King returns with a *Renegade with a Badge* who you won't be able to pass up. Finally, join Nina Bruhns for *Warrior's Bride,* a romance with a distinctly Native American feel.

And, of course, come back next month as the excitement continues in Intimate Moments, home of your favorite authors and the best in romantic reading.

Leslie J. Wainger
Executive Senior Editor

Please address questions and book requests to:
Silhouette Reader Service
U.S.: 3010 Walden Ave., P.O. Box 1325, Buffalo, NY 14269
Canadian: P.O. Box 609, Fort Erie, Ont. L2A 5X3

In Close Quarters
CANDACE IRVIN

Silhouette

INTIMATE MOMENTS™

Published by Silhouette Books

America's Publisher of Contemporary Romance

SILHOUETTE BOOKS

ISBN 0-373-27148-4

IN CLOSE QUARTERS

Copyright © 2001 by Candace Phillips Irvin

This edition published by arrangement with Harlequin Books S.A.

Visit Silhouette at www.eHarlequin.com

Printed in U.S.A.

Books by Candace Irvin

Silhouette Intimate Moments

For His Eyes Only #936
In Close Quarters #1078

CANDACE IRVIN

The daughter of a librarian and a sailor, it's no wonder Candace's two greatest loves are reading and the sea. After spending several exciting years as a naval officer sailing around the world, she finally decided it was time to put down roots and give love another chance. To her delight, she soon learned that writing romance was as much fun as reading it. Candace believes her luckiest moment was the day she married her own dashing hero, a former army combat engineer with dimples to die for. The two now reside in Massachusetts, happily raising two future heroes and one adorable heroine—who won't be allowed to date until she's forty, at least.

The more I learn, the more I realize
how little I truly know. My deepest thanks
to the following folks for loaning me their expertise
in an effort to mask my ignorance:
Special Agent Dennis Leahy, ATF;
Dr. Sandy Norton, USN-MC;
Dr. Harold L. Crossley, DDS, Ph.D.;
Ms. Debby Delany, RN;
Ms. Marie Provenzano, MS, RN;
and Mr. Jason Lizot, NREMT, ORT.
I'd also like to thank my critique partners
CJ Eernise Chase and Sharon Cline
for their eagle eyes, razor pens and unstinting honesty.
And, as always, my husband, David,
for his unfailing support.

For Helene Beharry,
a nurse of the highest caliber. As a woman,
she soars even higher. Sis, you're still my idol.

Chapter 1

Her career was over.

Karin slumped down into the swivel chair at her desk, staring at the single typed sentence screaming up from the sheet of paper in her hands. *Class twos are walking.* Oddly enough, she was stunned more by what the words didn't say than what they did. She flipped the sheet over and examined the back.

Nothing.

No name, no signature.

Not a single identifying mark on either side to even hint at the sender's identity. Against hope, she grabbed the matching envelope off the stack of manila folders on her desk and slipped her index finger into the torn end as she tipped it upside down.

Empty.

She slapped the envelope back down, sucking in her breath as her own name stared up, mocking her. *Lieutenant Karin Scott, MD.* Good God, why her?

And why now?

Rap, rap, rap.

Karin shot straight up in her chair as the knock on her door reverberated through the office. Who…? What…?

No time.

Her heart hammered against her ribs as she wrenched up the cover of the ten-pound *Physician's Desk Reference* she'd dumped beside the files and crammed the incriminating note inside. She heard the door to her office swing open behind her just as she slammed the cover down.

"Eric?"

She knew that voice. God, no.

She couldn't help it. Her stomach bottomed out. Nausea surged into its place. She staunched the wave in the nick of time. Of all the officers she had to run into on her first day, why him? Come to think of it, it was actually fitting. After all, the bastard had taken a crack at ruining her career himself. Two deep breaths, a quick glance to make sure the note was firmly hidden, and she was ready.

She twirled the chair smoothly about and nodded. "Doug."

"*You?*"

Judging from the disgust darkening the man's eyes, Doug Callahan was even less thrilled to see Karin than she was to see him. Funny, she wouldn't have thought it possible. But as Doug's tan bleached down to rival the collar of his white Navy uniform, she realized something else, and she smiled. "You didn't know."

The sleaze recovered quickly, slicking his hands through the barely regulation surfer waves on his head before locking his arms across his chest. "Sure, I did."

Karin ignored the blatant lie and smoothed the skirt of her own whites as she tipped back in her chair. "Of course, the fact that you didn't just proves you're not the golden boy you think you are."

A shrug, followed by a sneer. "I just figured you'd fall off the side of your ship on the way to the Persian Gulf and save yourself the humiliation of washing out."

"Liar." She offered up her own shrug. "Not that I'm surprised. You do have a knack for it. Or rather, you did...until me. Tell me, Doug, how many other women have you had to stoop that low with? Five? Ten? Every woman you've ever dated or, rather, tried to date?"

He didn't answer.

But the color was revving back into his face, only to stall at his taut cheeks. He tried covering by stepping into the office and stalking down the line of steel bookshelves on her right. It didn't help. Mottled fury was still riding high on his cheeks as he bypassed the pair of file cabinets and the X-ray reader to hook his hind end onto the edge of the desk cattycorner to hers.

She couldn't help it.

She grinned.

Hell, maybe the next two years of residency wouldn't be as bad as she'd expected. Not if she'd be able to break up what were bound to be eighty-hour workweeks with an occasional jaunt down to the pharmacy just to irritate the hell out of— *Pharmacy?*

The note.

Panic slammed back up her throat, strangling what was left of her smirk. She sucked in the remains, damn near choking on them as she fought the urge to double-check the armload of reference books and files she'd lugged in from her car, and the envelope Mr. Anonymous had secreted into the stack of paperwork already awaiting her arrival.

She needn't have bothered.

Doug jerked his chin toward the teetering pile on her desk. "Already in over your head, eh?"

He couldn't see the damn thing, could he?

The nausea returned. It must have shown.

"By God, you are."

She stared into his now-gleaming gaze, at the blue rapidly turning black with triumph. Or was that satisfaction?

Almost as if... Oh, Lord, why hadn't she thought of it before?

Had he sent it?

The mere thought was worse than petty. It was cowardly and underhanded, as well as thoroughly reprehensible.

And it was right up Doug's alley.

She drew herself up in the swivel chair and stared right back at him. "Don't you have someone else to harass?"

Triumph or satisfaction—whichever had caused his own smirk—went up in flames. "You were ordered not to use that word in connection with my name ever again."

Despite the panic still thundering through her veins, she relaxed enough to let her eyes widen. "Oh, did I mention your name? You probably misunderstood me. A nasty habit of yours. Then again, maybe it's your guilty conscience—Oops, I forgot." She leveled a equally steely gaze on his. "You don't have one."

"Lieutenant Callahan, please dial seven-five-three-two."

She could have sworn that was relief edging out the fury in his eyes as he jerked off the edge of the desk to respond to the hospital's page. He turned toward the door.

She couldn't help it. She grinned again. "Leaving so soon? There's a phone right here."

Idiot.

Why was she still baiting him? She needed Doug out of here so she could think. When she'd first opened the envelope, she'd assumed the accusation was true. Now she wasn't so sure. Yeah, she definitely needed to think.

Alone.

Doug's sneer was firmly in place as he turned back. "No thanks, it's a bit too frigid in here for my taste."

She caught herself a split second before she stiffened. Didn't matter—he'd already turned to the door. She waited until his hand was on the knob, the door halfway open.

"Doug?"

He glanced back as he stepped into the hall. "Yeah?"

"I should have gelded you when I had the chance."

His sneer evaporated as the door slammed in his face. She didn't even pause to savor the victory but spun the chair around to her desk to stare at the telltale strip of white poking out from the cover of the desk reference, instead. It didn't matter that the words weren't visible. They were burned into her brain.

Right along with the implication behind them.

Class twos are walking.

If that note was right, someone at the hospital was stealing prescription narcotics. She raked her fingers through her newly cropped curls, groaning as she slapped her forehead onto the tome's cover. Yup, her career was definitely over. There wasn't a damn thing she could do about it.

Unless…

She stiffened. No way. She was not calling him.

Anyone but him.

As if TJ Vásquez would even care.

Okay, so he might. But it would be on a purely professional basis. She'd nipped anything personal in the bud too hard and too long ago. Hell, TJ hadn't even dropped by to see her ship off. And he certainly hadn't been around when it had come back.

That only left one option.

Her best friend's husband, Reese.

Reese and Jade shouldn't have left for the airport yet. She snapped her gaze to her watch, hoping the time hadn't gotten away from her in her shock. It hadn't. In fact, Reese might still be at work. Technically she didn't begin her anesthesiology residency for another two weeks. Her friends would be back from their belated honeymoon by then. If Reese thought he could help, she could take two weeks leave and pretend she hadn't read the note until he and Jade returned.

Call him.

And do it now, before you're forced to crawl to TJ.

That image made up her mind.

A quick glance over her shoulder assured her the door

to her office was still sealed shut, before she reached for her wallet to rummage through for the number Jade had given her the week before. A number she never thought she'd use, let alone need. She grabbed the phone and stabbed the buttons, only to wait through four excruciatingly long rings.

The line was finally picked up. "Drug Enforcement Administration. How may I direct your call?"

She took a deep breath and just did it. "This is Dr. Karin Scott. I need to speak to Special Agent Reese Garrick."

"Yo, Vásquez!"

TJ did not bother glancing up from the stack of files splayed across his desk. He simply raised a hand and waved his fellow agent over as he continued to read. But moments later, as two more folders landed atop the report he was studying, he was forced to sever his concentration.

"Gracias."

"De nada." Joaquín's wide grin greeted him as he cuffed the black motorcycle helmet from the spare chair, his gaze sweeping the DEA office discreetly as he sat.

TJ knew full well whom his friend was seeking.

She was not here.

Joaquín covered his disappointment well. "What are you still doing here? You know what they say—while the cat is away, the mice should—"

"Stay." TJ chuckled as his friend's grin wilted. "A joke, my friend. Go home. Your assignment tomorrow will make up for this."

The grin was back. "A finer temporary boss I have never had. But what of you? You should be taking off as well, no? You are last to leave—again." His smile faded once more as he leaned forward to tap the preliminary autopsy reports he had dumped onto the desk. "The girls are dead, Tomás. Much as I dislike admitting this, a few hours more will not make a difference."

TJ's swivel chair groaned as he leaned back to stretch

his legs and rub his eyes. Joaquín was right. The girls were dead. A few hours more would not change this. But he had already dropped Reese and Jade at the airport. If he left now, there was naught left to do but go home and listen to his phone. A phone that had refused to ring.

For six days.

Once again he suppressed the sigh he had been holding throughout the week. "Soon." He tapped the new folders. "I must review these first."

A frown. "She has not called then."

It was not a question. It also required no response.

"I am sorry."

TJ shrugged.

"Have you eaten?"

He shook his head.

"There is this new seafood spot on the Embarcadero. Perhaps we should visit a club after?"

"Joaquín, I thank you, but no." The San Diego waterfront would not be wise tonight, nor would it be for some time. *Dios mío,* had he not gazed his fill of the empty ocean these past months?

And a club?

He sighed. Joaquín knew full well he did not do this anymore. But then, for all his friend's attempts at distraction, neither did he.

Another sigh. This one belonging to his fellow agent as he thumped the helmet onto the reports, then leaned back to withdraw a slip of yellow paper from the front pocket of his jeans. He flicked it beside the helmet. "Gina handed this to me on her way out, said to give it to you."

TJ retrieved the message slip and unfolded it, sucking in his breath as the neat script ripped into him.

Madre de Dios! It was not possible.

Or was it?

He tore his gaze from the memo to stare at the now-taunting folders scattered across his desk as his mind raced his heart. It was a tie. He shot up from his chair. "When did Gina take this?"

"I do not know. Why?"

He grabbed his leather jacket from the back of the chair and shoved his arms into the sleeves. By the time Joaquín had shot to his feet, as well, TJ had cuffed his motorcycle helmet.

"Tomás, what is wrong? Is it—"

He did not hear the rest, because he had already left.

Karin stared at the LED clock on the back of the stove and frowned. Seven-fifteen. If Reese didn't return her call soon, he wouldn't get the chance. Not for two weeks, anyway. In half an hour the flight he and Jade had booked to Hawaii would be leaving. Come to think of it, the plane was probably already boarding. She plunked the copper teapot onto the rear burner and sighed. Now what?

What about—

She might have a remaining option or two, but calling TJ Vásquez was not one of them. She'd just spent six months purging the man from her mind. There was no way she was letting him back in. Not until she was forced to, anyway.

Damn, it wasn't even fair.

She'd never even dated the man.

All she'd done was spend two lousy months planning a wedding for their best friends with him. Unfortunately it had been enough. The man's pull was that steady, that strong.

That inescapable.

Hell, who was she kidding? TJ had hooked her the moment they met. Charming, smooth and way too sure of himself, Special Agent Vásquez had arrived aboard the *USS Baddager* as Reese's backup at the tail end of an undercover operation designed to flush out a heroin dealer on the ship—and he'd damn near left with her heart. Except, it wasn't her heart he'd been interested in, was it?

At least not permanently.

The proof had slapped her in the face less than a week later. TJ had thrown a party at his weekend place just south of the Mexican border to celebrate Reese and Jade's engagement. She'd been leery about attending, mainly because she hadn't been able to get the party's host out of her head in the preceding days, but Jade had begged her. Not one for parties to begin with, her friend had been nervous about being thrust into a house full of DEA agents with whom she had absolutely nothing in common except that she was marrying into their tight group.

She should never have succumbed to Jade's pleas.

In the hours that followed, she'd gleaned more about the DEA in general than she'd ever wanted to know...and about one special agent in particular. While TJ was showing her the courtyard, she'd overheard two of his fellow agents laying odds that she was his next conquest. Even more appalling was that they couldn't agree on what number to assign her. Both held an opinion and both exceeded civilized comprehension. Humiliated, she'd turned to TJ and asked if there was any truth to his reputation.

To her horror, he'd said yes.

Of course, he'd promptly sworn it was behind him.

Right. *Under* him was more like it.

Either way, it didn't matter. She wasn't into one-night stands. And even if she was, she was no match for that level of experience. No match at all.

And yet...those eyes.

Six months and the mere memory of that dark smoldering gaze could still send smoke whispering through her body. Worse, even now, knowing the man for the hound he was, deep down she still wanted to believe the shame and regret she'd seen on his face that day in his courtyard had been real.

But of course, they weren't.

Nor was the promise that had come with them, that insidiously magnetic pledge that always came with those eyes. One sultry look and TJ could pull her right in, have her believing that no matter how many women he'd had in his past, she was the only woman he wanted in his future.

But that was a lie.

His behavior at the wedding had proven that, hadn't it?

She dragged the copper teapot to the front burner of the stove and toggled the corresponding switch to high. Okay, so there was no way she was calling TJ. Next option?

For the life of her, she couldn't think of one. Not one that would preserve her career, anyway.

Music. It always helped her think.

She spun back to the breakfast counter, dodging the pair of white heels that matched the uniform she'd yet to remove as she snagged the radio/CD remote from the counter. She aimed the remote past her mother's latest gift to the wall unit beyond. A saucy voice she hadn't heard in months filled the apartment.

''—hoping to get to the airport on time, it's not looking good. I-5 north is still backed up from the Coronado bridge to Hawthorne due to a serious four-car collision earlier this evening. Ambulances have cleared the scene, but it could still take an hour or more to sit through the cleanup. Seek an alternate route. That's it for now. In the traffic center, this is Country 99.5's Candy O, saying—''

Karin punched the remote again, slapping the remote on the counter as a jazz CD kicked in. At least now she knew why Reese hadn't returned her call. He and Jade had obviously heard about the accident and left early. Maybe it was for the best.

Chances were, the note was all some stupid joke.

Someone at the hospital was probably trying to get a rise out of her. Maybe Doug Callahan, maybe not. Heck, for all she knew, every other first-year resident would be getting the same note when they checked aboard. No doubt it was some sick rite of passage. Maybe even a drill of some sort. The Navy was big on them.

But what if the accusation was true?

She rounded the breakfast counter to scoop up the note.
Class twos are walking.

No. This had to be a prank.

If someone was stealing narcotics from the base hospital, wouldn't she have been given a bit more to go on? Like a specific drug? Or a suspect? At the very least, a point of contact?

Well, she hadn't.

And that was because this was a test. Someone obviously wanted to see if she was on her toes. Maybe even evaluate her integrity. Probably because of Doug.

Thump, thump, thump.

The knock on her door startled her so swiftly, she dropped the note. She grabbed the sheet of paper as it fluttered down, snagging it inches before it reached the cream carpet.

Reese?

Not unless their flight had been delayed along with the traffic. Hoping against hope, she refolded the note and slipped it into the breast pocket of her uniform as she headed for the door. Rising on her tiptoes, she peered through the peephole—and gasped.

Impossible!

But as she stumbled away from the door, she knew it wasn't. Even from his backside, there was no mistaking that shock of straight black hair falling well below those broad shoulders. She had a special agent standing at her door, all right, but it wasn't Reese Garrick.

It was his partner, TJ Vásquez.

She recovered quickly, creeping back to the door to tiptoe up and peer out. It was him all right. He still hadn't turned around, but there was no doubt in her mind. That sleek six-foot-plus muscular frame could only belong to one man. As usual, he was wearing snug black jeans and his matching black leather jacket. The one that smelled just like him.

Half a year and a door between them, and she could still

smell that jacket. The most incredible mix of leather and spice, with a tease of fresh air. Of course, the clincher was the equally black helmet cuffed under his arm. The one that matched the satin paint on his motorcycle. According to TJ, not just any motorcycle. A 1949 Indian Arrow. A classic.

All she knew was the bike was as dark and sleek and dangerous as he was.

Any hope she'd held out that it wasn't him crumbled as he turned to glance down the hallway. At least he wasn't facing the door. Six months was a long time. She blessed each and every one of those months as she reacclimated herself to the sight of that dusky skin, proud nose and prominent cheekbones. She also doubly blessed the three inches of solid wood between them. It gave her something to hold on to. And then he turned.

In profile, Tomás Juan Vásquez was handsome.

Head on, he was downright devastating.

Even through the glass, the force of those deep-brown eyes and thick brooding brows punched her stomach straight through to her toes. She tried sucking in her breath one shallow gulp at a time, only to discover he'd knocked the air from her lungs, as well.

He stepped forward to rap on the door again, this time hard.

Damn. What the devil was she supposed to do?

If Reese didn't know about the note, there was no way TJ could, either. So what was he doing here? And how had he gotten by the doorman? Peter had been known to turn away veteran cops, unless they had an official warrant—

Official?

Panic streaked through her as she zeroed in on the chilling explanation. But as TJ shifted the helmet to his left hand and raked his right through his hair, she realized the fear wasn't irrational after all. It mutated to full-blown terror as she finally noticed the lines that had set in about his mouth, the tension threading through his gaze, as well as gripping his shoulders. It would take a direct blow to TJ's heart to put that look there.

Jade. Reese.

The accident.

She grabbed the security chain and yanked it across the metal track, wrenching the door open as it popped free. ''Oh, my God, how badly are they hurt?''

Chapter 2

TJ blessed his reflexes, catching Karin instinctively as she hurled her petite curves at him, firing questions faster than he was able to empty the magazine in his Glock. What was she talking about? Who was she talking about? Then he knew.

Reese. Jade.

The flight.

Madre de Dios, what had happened?

His helmet landed at his feet as panic swamped him. Lifting Karin by her arms, he scooped her back into the apartment, releasing her as he scanned the entertainment unit that spanned the wall opposite him—but if there was a television behind one of the whitewashed doors, it was off now. He spun back around, straining for the sound of late-breaking news on the radio.

Nada.

All he heard were the muted notes of a jazz instrumental.

Frustrated, he turned back to Karin, wrapping his hands around her arms as he pulled her close again. This time, he

was not sure if he was steadying her or himself. "*¿Cariño?*
What has happened? Was there something on the news?"

Karin stared up at him, obviously stunned, her huge blue
eyes growing even larger. "You mean you haven't heard
anything? But I thought…" She shook her head. "Why
else would you be…" She shook it again, then pulled away
from him to rub her temples as she sighed. "TJ, what are
you doing here?"

The panic fled as quickly as it had come.

Reese and Jade were fine.

He stared at Karin as she folded her arms across the shirt
of her Navy uniform. The panic in her eyes had ebbed as
well—only to be replaced by determination. She was waiting for an answer.

Unfortunately he did not have one to give.

Not at this moment, anyway. And not when it was all he
could do to simply stand here in the middle of this room,
with his arms dropped to his sides—with them not locked
about her, squeezing her for all she was worth. For all he
was worth.

Six months.

It had been six months since her ship had pulled away
from that concrete pier. Six months since he had last feasted
his gaze on this tiny golden fireball of perfection standing
before him. Six months, six days and ten and a half hours,
if he had been counting. Not that he had.

Sí, so he had.

Unable to stop himself, he reached out and tipped the
heart-shaped curve of her chin, clenching his fingers as she
jerked away. He swallowed his hiss of disappointment before it could escape and firmly tucked his hands into his
jacket pockets to keep from touching her again.

He had told himself he was not going to do it.

He was not supposed to touch her.

But then, he was not supposed to be standing this close
to her, either. He was close enough to smell the whisper of
vanilla that always clung to her. Close enough for those

mesmerizing dimples to swallow him whole, the ones that were so deep, even her current frown failed to contain them. Close enough to trace the bottom curve of her full, pink lips.

No, he was definitely not supposed to be this close.

He had to move. Pronto.

Before he drowned in the blue ocean of her eyes—and told his good sense to go straight to hell. Or worse, ripped his fingers from his pockets and dug them into those golden curls.

Those *short* curls.

He stared hard. "You cut your hair."

Her hands were halfway up her neck before she stiffened. She pulled them down and folded them across her chest as her chin kicked up. Not much. Perhaps a fraction of an inch.

It was enough.

It told him more than her silence. Even more than the ice now frosting her gaze. She had cut her curls to spite him.

Dios help him, he was pleased.

Her chin hitched another notch. "Like it?"

"I do not."

But he did. It accentuated her eyes, made them appear larger, bluer.

Her maddening dimples deepened. "Too bad. I do." With that, she twirled smoothly about, her white skirt revealing a most enticing length of calf as she slipped away. When she rounded the breakfast counter, he assumed she was simply putting her usual distance between them—until she reached the stove. The shrill whistle and steam shooting from the copper teapot finally pierced his stupor. As she flicked off the burner, he turned back to the apartment, this time really looking.

He had known this woman had money. After all, she drove a Jaguar. And there was the Cartier on her wrist. But not even that—nor even the chunk of gray marble some might call a sculpture in the lobby—could have prepared him for this.

And the fact that it was so very…white.

Everywhere.

From the gauze draped across the tops of the towering windows down to the carpet, the entire room was white. The leather couch was white, the pair of overstuffed chairs flanking it were white, the lamps were white. Even the wall unit, the dining-room table and the chairs beyond were some sort of colorless wood washed with…well, white.

Suddenly he was twenty-four again, reaching for the brass knocker on those enormous double doors. They yawned open. And then *she* was standing there, looking down her perfect nose at him. He could not help it—he glanced down at his jacket, then his T-shirt, jeans and boots, half-afraid his mere presence had rubbed off, leaving a great dark stain in the middle of this virgin room. Thankfully, he had not.

Yet.

He turned back to the kitchen, to Karin, and was once again confronted with white. This time, though, it was her.

She arched her brows. "Well? Are you going to tell me or not?"

He blinked.

She sighed. "What you're doing here? I've figured out by now they weren't involved in the accident."

The accident? What— Ah, the freeway.

No wonder she had been frightened. He shook his head. "No, they were not. It came through on the scanner when it happened. I dropped Reese and Jade off an hour and a half ago by way of another route. From the way you threw yourself into my arms, I thought you had heard something about the plane."

She flushed.

Not much.

Just the tips of her ears.

Most odd. He had always thought her so cool, so col-

lected, so in control. But with her curls off her ears, he now
knew she was not. Fascinating. He wondered if she knew.
He caught the panic flitting through those deep-blue eyes
as he stared, and knew.

She did.

She turned away quickly and headed back to the kitchen.
This time he labeled her action for what it was.

Retreat.

He masked his smile as she turned back, the high counter
once again firmly between them.

"You didn't answer my question."

He shook his head. "I did not."

"Well? Are you going to? Or did you just drop by for
dinner, unannounced?"

"Would you dine with me if I had?"

"No."

He glanced down at the counter, at the empty yogurt
container with the spoon still inside, at the orange rind piled
beside the remote control, and tsked. "You could use a
good meal, no?"

She did not answer. Nor did she need to, for her narrow
gaze spoke for her. She finally severed that frosty glare and
scooped up the rind and carton before she turned her back
on him to head for the trash compactor. He waited until
she had opened the steel drawer and dumped them inside.

"You called Reese today."

The drawer slammed shut.

She continued to stand with her back to him for a moment, then slowly turned around. "Yes, I did. I called
Reese."

He shrugged. "You got me."

"I don't want you."

If she thought it took one of her neurosurgical colleagues
to figure this out, she was mistaken. "This I know. But me
you have. Why did you call?"

"You know, I don't believe it's any of your business."

If it involved what he thought it did, it was very much

his business. It was also his case. But there was no way he could tell her this. At least, not until he was certain.

He sighed. *"Cariño—"*

She held up a hand. "You can stop right there, Agent Vásquez. First of all, I told you months ago, my name is Karin, just Karin. Not carino—or however you keep pronouncing it. Second of all, my phone call had nothing to do with you or your agency. I just told you—I called to talk to Reese, not you. As you damn well know, Reese is married to my best friend. I needed to discuss something with him. Something personal. If your boss is so straitlaced you guys can't even receive a brief personal call on the job, I'm sorry. I'll apologize to Reese when they return."

"Are you finished?"

Pink washed the tops of her ears. "Yes."

"Good. Now, I am aware of the fact that you called to speak to Reese and not to me." Painfully aware. "But you also left a message. A message that said…" He made a show of searching the pockets of his leather jacket for the yellow slip Joaquín had handed him before he had torn out of the office. "Here it is." He did not need to read the words, but did so, anyway. "Dr. Karin Scott called. It's business."

"I know—personal business." She raked her fingers through her curls. "How many times do we have to go through this?"

"Until you tell the truth."

She stiffened. "Just where the hell do you get off showing up at my apartment, giving me the third degree about a personal call and accusing me—"

The rest of her words were severed as he rounded the counter and reached out to touch the tip of her ear. It was tinged with pink for the third time that night.

She swallowed.

Evidently he had made his point.

Several moments passed before she honored it. "Okay,

I've been busted. What are you going to do about it? Cuff me and drag me down to the nearest station?''

Oh, he would like to.

But if he ever got a set of cuffs on this woman, jail was the last place he would be taking her. He slipped his finger down, tracing the outer curve of her ear until he reached the tiny lobe. He dipped his finger beneath her jaw, reining in his thudding heart as her eyes widened. What he would have given for the flaring in these dark pupils to have been caused by passion. For him.

But it was not passion, nor even desire.

It was fear.

He forced his attention back to the reason he was here. Why had she called Reese? He tipped up her chin. "Are you in trouble?"

She tried to look away, but he refused to let her. He moved his head until he had again captured her stormy gaze.

"*Cariño,* you must tell me. I can help."

She closed her eyes.

The action pained him more than he cared to admit.

Reese, she trusted. Him, she did not.

"Please." His voice was low, hoarse, but he did not care.

"Don't. You can't help. No one can, not even Reese." She sighed and finally opened her eyes. "I'm sorry. I shouldn't have called him. Dr. Manning was right."

He brushed his thumb across her bottom lip. "This thing which troubles you, this Dr. Manning knows it?"

"God, no. At least, not yet." Again the pink found her ears. Though for some reason, he felt the cause was not the same. But before he could question her, she stepped back. "Oh, hell, you're already here. And I don't think you're going to give up." There was a wealth of hope in those rising brows. "Are you?"

He shook his head firmly. Not when she was this upset.

She sighed again. "I thought not. Well, you'd better have a seat, then. It's a long story." She tilted her head toward the teapot sitting on the stove. "I'd offer you some, but..." Her gaze swept his clothes. "You don't look the tea type. Coffee?"

He nodded. *"Gracias."*

"Cream? Sugar?"

"Black."

A ghost of a smile curved her lips, dipping her dimples as her gaze traveled his dark length again, this time leisurely. "Somehow, I'm not surprised."

She was teasing him. Karin Scott was teasing him. The realization ricocheted off his brain and headed straight for his heart, snapping a grin back up his throat before he could prevent it. Jade, she teased. Reese, as well. She had even teased Reese's mother within minutes of meeting her—this he knew, for he had been there. But Karin had never, ever, teased him.

Until now.

He sobered.

She was upset indeed if she could not remember she disliked him. But at least she would trust him. For now, he would settle for this.

Relief washed through him as he stepped around the counter to give her room to work. On the ride to her apartment, he had not been certain he could convince her to confide in him. If she had refused, there was naught he could do to force her.

Even with his suspicions.

He would have been left with little option but to call Reese once his plane had landed and ask him to phone Karin back—from his belated honeymoon. Not his first choice.

TJ crossed the carpet and stared at the couch and matching chairs. Though they appeared comfortable enough, he was reluctant to sit. They were so white. Admittedly he was not one for decorating. But even he could see the room needed color—any color. Desperately.

And what was that odor?

It was faint, so faint he could not quite place it. In fact, he had not even noticed it until Karin had taken her whisper of vanilla back into the kitchen with her. He glanced across the room as a grating whir cut through the air.

Beans?

She did not cook, but she ground her own coffee beans?

TJ bit back a low whistle. He turned to face the wall unit and stared at the whitewashed doors as the minutes dragged by. What secrets did those doors conceal? Her music collection? The final notes of the jazz instrumental that had been playing when he arrived had long since died out. What else would he find in there? Beethoven, Mozart, Bach? Or would she surprise him with salsa?

Doubtful.

Whatever lay behind those doors, he would wager it was white. The Beetles' White album most likely.

"TJ?"

He spun about, wincing as he nearly upset the twin mugs of coffee in her hands. At least the mugs were yellow.

Pale yellow, but it was a start.

She held one out and nodded to the chairs. "Have a seat."

He accepted the mug and took the couch, instead, in the hope that she would join him.

She did not.

He squelched his disappointment as she lowered herself into the chair next to him, then settled himself as far back as he dared and took a sip from his mug. He glanced up as the distinct flavor of vanilla swirled over his tongue, taking the edge off the familiar bite of coffee.

"Do you like it?"

He nodded.

"Good." She slid a coaster across the table.

He stared at the white disk a moment, then rested the mug on his thigh. At least if he spilled it there, the stain would not show. He waited until she had taken a few sips

of her own before prompting her. "Reese? You were to tell
me why you wished to speak to him?"

Setting her cup down, she sighed as she retrieved a
square of paper from the pocket below the row of ribbons
on her uniform shirt. She unfolded the sheet and passed it
to him.

He took it and read the short, typed sentence.

Class twos are walking.

Dios mío, he was right.

Somehow he managed to do naught but lift a brow as
he glanced up. "Nothing to do with me—or my agency?"

She stiffened. "Not necessarily."

He shook his head. "*Cariño,* since when does the theft
of class-two prescription narcotics not involve the Drug Enforcement Administration?"

"When it's a joke."

He flipped the note over, taking care not to contaminate
it with further prints. It was blank. Someone had gone to
the trouble of concealing his or her identity. If this was a
joke, he was not laughing. He stared at the slender fingers
knotted in her lap. Nor was she.

He placed the sheet on the table. "This note, who sent
it?"

"I don't know. But it doesn't matter. It's a joke."

No, it was not.

Unfortunately he would also wager this sparse message
was connected to the thickening files on his desk—and the
autopsy reports Joaquín had dumped there. But why had
this woman been singled out for involvement, and why
anonymously? He glanced at the sheet. "You received this
how?"

"It was in my in-box." She retrieved her mug. "You
don't know this, but I'm not attached to the ship anymore.
Not as of this morning, anyway. I was accepted into the
Navy's anesthesiology program. Only, when I checked into
the main hospital this morning, I learned my residency

starts two weeks from today, not today.'' She paused to draw another sip from her coffee.

He waited patiently.

This much he knew from their mutual friends. But he was not about to confess he had been attuned to Jade's every word at dinner this past evening, waiting for the woman to mention what her friend was up to. Thankfully Jade had done so without his asking. But she had failed to reveal enough to satisfy his constant thirst for information about this lady.

Of course no one could satisfy this need but Karin herself.

Until now, however, she had volunteered naught.

It did not help to know precisely why she had refused to date him in the months before her ship departed. Nor did the knowledge that he had only himself and his shameful reputation to blame. A reputation he freely admitted to cultivating in the past. But it was in the past. Surely six years of abstinence was enough to have earned even the most devout of monks his absolution?

At first, he had thought it possible.

Until the engagement party.

Though he himself had never truly expected to find forgiveness for his sins, he had been astonished at the depth of his own reaction—to hers. The shock, the horror. These he had anticipated, had even prepared himself for. But not the other.

The disappointment. In him.

Logically he should have realized this would happen. And perhaps, in some way, he had. But until that moment she had turned to him and asked him of his past, he had not truly understood how deeply another's pain could cut. More deeply than he had ever thought possible.

When he had recovered, she was gone.

She had caught a ride north, back across the border with another agent. And the pain had begun anew. But this ache was different. For it was a product of the waiting. His heart already snared, there was naught left for him to do but bide his time. Patience was his only recourse. Two months he had waited, the ache growing stronger with each passing day, with each meeting he and Karin shared as they helped to plan their mutual friends' wedding. But through none of them had he noticed a difference. Not so much as a fissure in her resolve.

Until two weeks before her ship deployed.

On the eve of his marriage, Reese had spoken to her. He would have been furious with his friend except the next day Karin had finally accepted his invitation for dinner, right there at the wedding. Right there in the church. But then, hours later, following their sole dance at the reception, she had rescinded. No argument, no explanation—*nada*. She simply said she had changed her mind and would not be changing it back. Ever.

Why?

"TJ?"

Startled, he glanced up, then drew another sip from his own to cover as he forced his attention back to the hospital, back to the note—where it should have remained all along.

"Anyway, when I checked into the hospital, I was given the option of taking two weeks' leave. I was considering it when I picked up the stack of paperwork already waiting for me in my in-box." She nodded toward the note. "That was inside the stack. I made up my mind to take the leave when I read it."

"Why?"

She glanced up, startled. "Why what?"

"Why would you need the time? I know you, *Cariño*. You are not one to conceal something such as this. There is more."

"Excuse me? You don't know the first thing about me."

She was wrong. But now was not the time to upset her further by arguing. He simply inclined his head—and let her read the motion how she would.

She slumped back in her chair. "This is all so frustrating.

I never should have chickened out. I should have marched into Dr. Manning's office and shown him the note as soon as I read it."

Dr. Manning again.

Though he knew full well who this man was, he was not supposed to. "Dr. Manning?"

"The head of anesthesiology."

"And why did you not show him the note?"

"Because I wasn't looking forward to kissing my career goodbye so soon into starting it."

Now he was confused. Unwilling to juggle the mug a moment longer, he set it on the table next to the note and leaned toward her. "I do not understand. Why would your career be over? You know as well as I this cannot affect you, because you are not involved." He was certain of this. Stealing surgical opiates was not in her nature.

Her lips curved—briefly. "I appreciate the vote of confidence, Agent Vásquez, but I'm afraid it's a bit more complicated than that. Actually—" a slight, but unmistakable wince "—it's a lot more complicated."

He waited as she reached for her mug, suppressing a wince of his own as she took a sip. At best, it was lukewarm by now. His was. She drained the rest, anyway.

"I'm sure you're familiar with the concept of three strikes you're out?"

"*Sí.*"

"Well, I don't know about the DEA, but in the Navy you only get two—and I've already got one."

Again, he waited.

Finally he was rewarded with a shrug.

"About a year ago I was asked out by one of the lieutenants at the hospital. I admit, I was leery. He wasn't a doctor, so I wasn't sure he'd understand that my schedule as the *USS Baddager's* doctor came first. But he assured me he did, so I accepted."

TJ retrieved his mug, if only to give himself something

to hold as he prompted her about dating another man. "What happened?"

"You know, I'm still not really sure. We went out a few times, and while he seemed nice enough, it just didn't click. At least, not for me. Anyway, I decided to break it off. I invited him over for dinner, thinking it would be better to tell him in private." She frowned. "In retrospect, it wasn't a bright idea."

"Why is this?"

"Let's just say, he didn't take it well." Something new and dark entered her eyes and caused his blood to run cold. She masked it quickly, but he had already seen it.

"*Cariño*, tell me this man did not—"

She shook her head sharply. "No, nothing like that."

"Then what? What did this man do?"

"He didn't *do* anything. It was more of a suggestion. Hell, at first I thought he was joking. But he wasn't." She paused for a moment, then took a deep breath before focusing her stare somewhere past his left shoulder. "He suggested a trade of sorts. My…favors…in exchange for his help in securing a slot for myself in the next class of anesthesiology residents."

"And when you told him no?"

Her gaze snapped to his.

TJ refused to dignify her surprise over his certainty with a comment.

"He left," she replied.

Gracias a Dios. He eased out the breath he had not known he had been holding. "I still do not understand. His offer, how could this mark your record? Especially since he left once you refused."

"Because that wasn't the end of it."

He set his mug down. Carefully.

She shrugged. "Maybe he was afraid I'd squeal, or maybe he just wanted to get even, I don't know. All I do know is he stopped by Dr. Manning's office the next morning and confessed that one of the residency applicants had invited him over for dinner, and that she'd tried to use sex to ensure her slot in the class.''

TJ sucked in his breath as he shot to his feet and strode to the windows. He stared at the string of palm trees lining the kidney-shaped pool ten stories below as he worked to control his growing fury. It was useless. His blood was no longer running cold. It was hot. Searing. And there was but one way to cool it. He would find this man who had slandered his woman and wrap his hands about the bastard's neck until he no longer breathed. TJ locked his stare on the pool, certain that if he turned, all the undercover skills in the world would not keep her from reading the intent in his heart.

"Who?"

"I don't understand—"

"Who did this to you?"

"Why? I doubt you know him, even if you are DEA."

"Who?"

He heard her sigh. "His name is Doug Callahan. He's the hospital's—" She broke off again as he whirled about.

It mattered not. She was wrong.

He did know this man. He knew the name, anyway. As he should. In fact, he would say he knew Doug Callahan exceedingly well—considering he had spent the better part of the afternoon studying the man's official military record. But apparently there were a few assessments missing from his officer fitness evaluations. For not only was Lt. Callahan a first-rate pharmacist, he was a first-rate bastard, as well.

But this was not all.

Doug Callahan had just become his number-one suspect.

Chapter 3

Karin stepped out of her car, smoothed the skirt to her Navy whites and snagged her briefcase off the leather seat before slamming the door. TJ would be furious if he knew where she was and what she was about to do.

Too bad. It was her career, not his.

So what if she'd agreed to let him nose around?

Yes, as a DEA agent, he could backdoor the hospital's records. Yes, he could check with the distributors and see if the pharmacy had been ordering an unusually high number of narcotics. He could even discover which types. If the right numbers had gone up, they'd know there was truth to the note she'd received. That it wasn't a joke or another nasty link in Doug's chain of petty revenge.

But it *was* a joke.

The more she thought about it, the more she realized it had to be. In fact, she'd lay odds Doug was rubbing his grimy paws together in anticipation right now. He'd probably slipped the note into her paperwork, hoping she'd run to Dr. Manning the moment she read it, screaming the sky

was falling. Doug knew better than anyone that when they
combed his pharmacy records and found nothing amiss,
she'd come off worse than Chicken Little—more like a big
fat sitting duck. And that's when he'd take aim and blow
her career right out of the water.

Well, she sure wasn't handing him the gun.

Not when she could do something about it.

And she *could* do something.

She shifted her briefcase into her left hand and shoved
the hospital door marked Staff Entrance open before march-
ing down the corridor. Besides, TJ wasn't being totally honest with her either. She was sure of it. She might not have
concrete proof he'd held something back on her last night,
but she didn't have to. Her instincts were pretty darn good.

They were right about him.

Tijuana Jones.

God, she hated that nickname, almost as much as she
hated the man's reputation. She wasn't stupid. She hadn't
missed the not-so-subtle allusion to Indiana Jones.

What a crock.

It wasn't the man's sultry looks, either. It was his personality. TJ Vásquez was no self-effacing Harrison Ford.
But then, it wasn't his personality his fellow agents had
been attempting to immortalize when they'd baptized him
with the moniker, now was it? And while she didn't doubt
that a number of his DEA exploits had taken on the legendary feel of an action hero's, she had a feeling the topic
those two agents she'd overheard betting on her was closer
to the real reason behind the name.

Yes, the man was irresistible.

Unfortunately he also knew it—and he abused it.

She reached the end of the corridor and took the left that
led to her office. Tijuana Jones her tush. His buddies should
have nicknamed him Don Juan. He probably had women
lined up outside his apartment, waiting their turn.

Well, she wasn't standing in it.

Karin stopped in front of the door to her new office and

grabbed the knob, but as she twisted, something made her jerk her hand back and blink. She grabbed the knob again and turned it again, opening the door a crack so she could peer inside.

She couldn't see anything, but there it was again.

That noise.

Someone was scraping open the drawers of the desk across the room. *Her* desk. But all she could make out as she craned her neck around the door were broad shoulders encased in Navy whites and the back of a blond, barely regulation haircut. It was enough.

Doug.

She slammed the door open and stormed in. "What the hell do you think you're doing?"

An equally loud string of curses blasted back at her when, closing the top drawer of her desk, he smashed his fingers. Then he turned. She stared up into a pair of deep-green eyes. Not blue.

And not Doug's.

The lieutenant quirked a sheepish brow. "Looking for a pen?"

She closed her eyes, certain her humiliation had seared off the tips of her ears. But mercifully, the man was smiling sheepishly as she reopened them.

He stuck out a hand. "Dr. Hunter—Eric. And you must be Dr. Scott, my new office mate."

She returned his easy grip. "Karin. Look, I'm sorry. I had no right to startle you like that."

Eric shook his head as she withdrew her hand. "No apology necessary. And I swear, I don't make a habit of going through people's desks. I just needed a—"

"Pen—I know. And really, I am sorry. Look, I had a rough night. It's not an excuse, I know. But I'm sorry."

He grinned as she dumped her briefcase on the desk. A friendly open grin that didn't churn her stomach into a mass of quivering nerves.

Thank God.

She opened the briefcase and pulled out her basic office supplies, including the ghastly silver nameplate her mother had just engraved for her.

Eric nodded. "That's right, you just got back from the Persian Gulf, didn't you? Having trouble sleeping without a ship rocking beneath you, eh?"

She smiled. "Among other things."

"So what are you doing here, anyway? I thought the new class didn't start for another two weeks."

"We don't. You know how it is—just wanted to get in, catch up on a few medical journals, maybe nail down a detailed layout of the hospital while I'm at it." She pulled a pen from the inner pocket of her briefcase and held it out.

Eric took it, slipping it into the breast pocket of his whites. "Thanks—I owe you. Hey, how 'bout joining me in the cafeteria for lunch? I'd take you someplace nicer, but I'm on call today—obstetrics. I'll give you the grand tour afterward." He was smiling again, a charming smile, in a safe friendly kind of way.

Not like TJ's.

God, why did she have to compare every man to him?

She was about to accept, out of spite if nothing else, when the door opened.

"*Perdóneme.* I will come back."

She stiffened. "TJ?"

It couldn't be.

She spun around.

Stunned, she stared at the uniformed janitor standing in the doorway. It was TJ, all right. She wasn't fooled by the way he'd pulled his hair into a low ponytail and capped it with that worn blue baseball hat. Nor was she fooled by the matching blue coveralls or the cart of cleaning supplies in the hall beyond.

Then it hit her. TJ was undercover.

And she'd blown it.

Or would have if he hadn't covered quickly. He shook

his head smoothly as he strolled forward. Her mouth was still gaping open as he reached for her hand. He tugged it toward him, his dark hooded gaze smoldering into hers as he bowed over her hand and grazed her flesh with his lips. "Believe me when I say, señorita, this TJ is a lucky man to know such beauty as you. But alas, I am not he, for I would remember meeting you. José Rodríguez at your service." His breath feathered over her hand as he kissed it again.

A shiver of warmth stole up her arm and into her stomach, sparking a fire that threatened to consume her on the spot. She couldn't move, couldn't talk. Hell, she couldn't breathe. All she could do was stare into those dark bottomless eyes. Into that dark seductive soul.

TJ hadn't dared to loose the full brunt of his charm on her since the afternoon of Jade's wedding. It was a damn good thing, too. Because just like that, he snared her heart. Snared it, softened it and shaped it—sculpting it into something she didn't want. Let alone want to have for him.

A cough, and suddenly the spell broke. The remaining pieces shattered as someone cleared his throat again.

Eric.

Oh, Lord, how could she have forgotten he was here?

Easy. TJ.

Dammit, he'd done it to her again, and she hated him for it. She clawed through her mind until she found the face from long ago. Her father's face. She slapped it over TJ's confident one. Amazing how the two could look so much alike. One might be dark and the other light. But they both used the same smooth overpowering charm to get what they wanted.

And they'd both used her.

She ripped her hand back, stabbing TJ with a glare as she shrugged. "Sorry. My mistake." Still humiliated, she faced Eric.

Thankfully, he laughed. "Guess you weren't kidding

about not being able to sleep. You're seeing things—or, rather, people.''

She was saved from a response when his beeper went off.

Eric tugged it off his belt and stared at the readout. ''Damn. Sorry, Karin, it looks like we'll have to take a rain check on that lunch date. My patient just shifted into hard labor, apparently without any relief from her epidural.''

''Yikes, you'd better go rethread her anesthesia line before the woman unthreads your esophagus.''

Eric chuckled. ''You know it.'' He nodded to TJ as he reached the door. ''Hey, José, if you find any pens, leave 'em on my desk—and don't touch the paperweight. The last guy broke my old one.''

TJ hunched his shoulders slightly as he tipped the bill of his cap. ''*Sí,* señor.''

The second the door closed, he straightened.

''What the hell do you think—''

An iron hand clapped over her mouth, cutting off the rest of her tirade. She waited none too patiently as TJ quickly reopened the door and hauled the cleaning cart inside. He snapped the door shut and shoved the cart up against it, then flipped on the radio at the edge of Eric's desk.

Soft rock filled the office.

She glared at his coveralls. ''Nice cover, José.''

He folded his arms and shrugged.

She did her damnedest not to let her gaze linger at the rolled sleeves hugging his dusky biceps as she continued to scowl. ''Perhaps you'd like to tell me what you're doing in that outfit—and what you're doing here?''

''Why am I here? Perhaps we should start at the beginning, no? Why are *you* here?''

''I work here, remember?''

''A good try, *Cariño.* But you yourself told me you did not start for two weeks. You came to confront him, no?''

''Doug? Of course not.''

A single dark brow rose.

She ignored it. "Look, all I did was stop by to drop off some stuff and check out a few medical journals. I'm way behind in my reading. I was out of the country for six months, you know."

"This, I know. I also remember seeing a stack of journals on your kitchen counter last night."

Damn. Busted again.

She shrugged. "So I'm missing a few. I like to read them in order."

He shook his head, actually chuckling as he stared at her ears. "*Cariño,* if you intend on persisting with these lies, you may want to consider growing your curls again."

Oooh, she really did not like this man.

So why did her heart have to start thumping erratically as he leaned back against Eric's desk? And why did she have to notice the way the muscles of his chest strained against those blasted coveralls as he leaned over to pick up the crystal paperweight?

Undercover—ha! Suiting TJ Vásquez up like a janitor was tantamount to slapping a collar on a panther and passing it off as a newborn kitten. His arms flexed as he tossed the crystal globe in the air. He caught it neatly, then stared into it.

"This man, you know him?"

"Who? Eric?"

"*Sí.* Eric."

"I met him two minutes before you walked in."

He glanced up. She could have sworn he was startled. "And yet you date him?"

What the...? "No, I'm not dating him. I told you, I just met the man."

"But you agreed to have lunch with him, no?"

"He asked, I accepted. Then he canceled. Are you finished with the third degree?"

"Why?"

She blinked. "I beg your pardon?"

"Why did you accept?"

What the devil was he getting at? And why was he staring into that stupid crystal again as if it could divine the future of the world? "Because he offered."

"I have…offered."

That was what this was about?

Perversely, she smiled. "His was interesting."

Liar.

TJ flipped the crystal into the air again, waiting until the last possible moment before catching it. His gaze narrowed as he studied the clear depths. "This lieutenant, have you considered he may be involved?"

"Because he asked me out? Thanks. That says a lot about your own invitation if you're so sure he had to have an ulterior motive." But she remembered Eric's hands—*in* her desk. "Besides, I want to help. I need to. Not only that, someone obviously thought I could. *If* the note's even real. Maybe if I get to know Eric and some of the other residents, something will click."

"What?"

"I don't know. Something."

TJ tossed the paperweight a final time before setting it back down on the desk. He folded his arms across his chest, his gaze dark and brooding as it met hers. "*Cariño,* I must ask you to stay away from the hospital for a few days. Take your vacation, visit your mother."

She frowned. "My mother lives an hour away in La Jolla."

"Visit her, anyway. You have been gone awhile. Or go to the beach, read your journals. Just stay away from here."

"Why?"

"Just do it. Please."

"No."

He sighed.

"I mean it, TJ. If you want to get rid of me, you'll have to do better than that. Tell me what you're holding back— and don't tell me you're not keeping something from me.

What is it you said about the note last night? Oh, yes, 'Most likely this means naught, but I will look into it.'"

At least he didn't pretend to misunderstand. "It was necessary."

She stared at his coveralls. "Necessary to poke your nose in this deep or necessary to lie to me about it?"

"I did not lie."

"Oh, no?" She jerked her chin toward the cleaning cart. "I suppose that's your idea of looking into something discreetly?"

"The situation has changed."

"That much is obvious or you wouldn't be so damned anxious to get rid of me. What I want to know is how? Exactly how has the situation changed and what was it like to begin with?"

He glanced over his shoulder at the door, then turned back. "Not here. Meet me later. We will speak then."

Dammit, she knew he'd been holding out on her. And from the look in those deep-brown eyes, whatever he was holding on to was something big. It figured. Another he-man who just had to take care of the little lady—for her. Well she wasn't bowing to it.

Not with him.

She shook her head firmly. "You'll tell me now, or I'll do what I should have done yesterday. I'll— Oh, God. You told Dr. Manning, didn't you?" She slumped onto the edge of her desk and closed her eyes, as she watched her short career flash before them. The coveralls, the cleaning cart. Suddenly it all made sense. "That's why you're here. Manning knows I found the note."

"No."

She opened her eyes.

TJ shook his head.

"But he does know you're here, right?"

Again he shook his head.

"You mean to tell me, you came in here undercover and

you didn't even clear it with the head of anesthesiology? What *did* you find out about Doug?''

TJ tugged off his ball cap, staring at the bill as he curled it.

''Just tell me.''

Dread slid down her spine as he continued to study the cap. He finally sighed and looked up. ''I do not know if this Señor Callahan is involved or not. Three days ago—well before you got your note—my office received a call from San Diego General. Two teenagers were brought into the emergency room just after midnight. They were dead when they arrived. Drug overdose.''

Oh, God.

Class twos are walking.

The dread reversed its track, snapping back up her spine and slamming into the base of her skull. She rubbed the resulting knot. ''It was morphine, wasn't it?''

''Fentanyl.''

''Fentanyl? But that's…'' She couldn't even finish.

He nodded. ''Much deadlier.''

''But…teenagers?''

Another nod.

She wrapped her arms about her chest, desperately trying to ward off the sudden chill swamping her. ''You think it's related to the note, don't you? You think the fentanyl came from this hospital.''

''Perhaps. I do know it was surgical quality, definitely not street, because they still had the glass ampules on them, but the stock numbers were etched off. When you showed me the note, I had hoped to check around a bit more before I came in undercover. To be sure the ampules were from this hospital.''

''Then why didn't you?''

But she knew.

His frown deepened, confirming her suspicions. ''There was another overdose last night. 2:00 a.m. She was sixteen, perhaps seventeen. I cannot be certain because I have not yet been able to identify her.''

Karin bypassed her desk and slumped straight into her chair with a thud. "So young."

"*Sí.*"

Sixteen years old.

A sophomore in high school.

She should be going on her first date, learning to drive a car, looking forward to college. She certainly shouldn't be out at 2:00 a.m. on a school night, shooting up a drug that was seventy-five times more potent than morphine. The girl had to have suffocated within minutes. Where the hell had she gotten it?

"Doug."

TJ hunkered down in front of her, reaching for her hands as she locked her fingers together and stared at them.

In a way, this was her fault. She should have nailed Doug Callahan's ass to the wall last summer when she'd had the chance. But no, she'd kept her mouth shut. She'd been so damn worried about making waves for fear she'd lose her slot that she hadn't even tried to turn him in—not to mention the fact that her stepfather would find out—that all she'd done was deny the charges. Without proof, it was Doug's word against hers. When hers finally won out, no doubt aided by her stepfather's reputation, Doug had even had the gall to call her up and warn her that someday he'd get even.

Well, it looked like someday was here.

She really should have gelded him when she'd had the chance. She glanced up as TJ squeezed her fingers. "If Doug is behind this, I want his head on a pike. You just tell me what I have to do to get it there.''

"Dine with me."

"Excuse me?" Of all the requests she'd expected, that was not one of them. At the very least, she was sure he'd be telling her to leave town again.

"*Sí,* dinner. I want you to sit down with me tonight, go

over the list of names I have. Doctors, residents, interns, nurses. As the *USS Baddager's* doctor these past two years, you had to have consulted with some of them, no? I must learn as much as I can about each one. Information that will not be in their files, information you may have."

She nodded. "Anything you want."

"Good. Then after dinner, I would like you to pack your suitcase. I want you to visit your mother, *Cariño,* and leave the remainder of this case to me."

She'd do anything, all right.

Anything but that.

He was late.

Karin kicked off her heels and stalked across the kitchen tiles in her stockings, stopping just short of the cordless phone on the wall. She glared at the chunk of silent plastic before wrenching her gaze back to the clock on the stove. No, TJ was worse than late.

He was dead—or he'd better be.

He'd stood her up.

Why she was even surprised, she didn't know. But she was. Correction, at six-thirty, when he was still just half an hour overdue, she was surprised. Perhaps even a little worried. But now? At ten o'clock? She was beyond worried.

She was livid.

Karin ripped the refrigerator door open and stared inside. The bottle of wine she'd left to chill in the middle of the empty shelves taunted her. She slammed the door and turned back to the stove. Back to the clock. Back to that damned silent phone. Not only had the rat stood her up, he hadn't even had the decency to call and let her know. As if he would.

They never did.

Not the smooth ones.

Oh, no. They just cruised in, hours late, flowers in hand with a new lie dripping from their lips. No doubt his would be a doozy. Probably twenty-five with long brown hair and

legs even longer. Not that he'd phrase it quite like that.
Lord knew TJ was experienced enough to couch it better.
He'd have been running late, there'd been an accident, he'd
stopped to help. Or maybe he'd been called out on a case.
Hell, given his past, he probably had a hundred prime ex-
cuses stocked inside some corner of that philandering brain,
each just waiting its turn.

Well, it didn't matter.

By the time she was five years old, she'd heard them all.

She spun around and jerked the refrigerator door open
again, this time reaching for the bottle of wine. But as she
thunked it onto the counter and opened the drawer to grab
the corkscrew, she froze as the enormity of her actions
slammed into her.

What the hell was she doing?

She swung her gaze back to the bottle. To the goblet she
hadn't even realized she'd placed beside it. How many
times had she seen her mother with a goblet and a bottle
just like this one, on a kitchen counter just like this one?
And how many times had she sworn that no man would
make her do the same?

Disgusted, she slapped the corkscrew back into the nest
of utensils and slammed the drawer home. She turned back
to the oven and yanked the door open. Removing the still-
warm containers of Luigi's legendary take-out linguini, she
dumped them into the trash compactor. Finally she added
the unopened bottle of wine to the top. She was not recy-
cling that bottle—because it was exactly where it belonged,
along with any chance of ever dining with TJ Vásquez
again.

In the garbage.

Then she turned on her heel and went to bed.

She was going to be angry.

TJ stood at Karin's door, his motorcycle helmet resting
gingerly in the crook of his left arm, the knuckles of his
right hand poised, inches from knocking, as he acknowl-

edged the truth. No matter how much he had tried to deny it on the ride over, he knew Karin was going to be angry.

And that was if she let him past the door.

He pulled his hand back. Perhaps this was not a good idea. *Dios mío*. He knew it was not. Unfortunately he needed to see her. Tonight. For several reasons. The least of which was the message she had failed to get.

Then there was the other.

He knocked.

As ten raps became twenty, he increased his force—and his worry. Where was she? Had she not left the hospital as he had asked this morning? Had she confronted Doug Callahan, instead, even though she had promised she would not?

He refused to believe she would be so foolish.

He chose to believe she was safe.

Sí. Most likely, she had grown tired of waiting for him to arrive and had packed as he had requested. At this very moment she was no doubt tucked between satin sheets at her mother's home in La Jolla. He was about to pick her lock and make certain when he heard a noise from within. The scraping of a chain sliding across its track.

The door opened.

Karin's beautiful face, heavy with sleep and heavier with anger, greeted him. "Good, you're alive."

The door slammed back in his face.

He waited a moment, then knocked again.

And again.

"*Cariño*, open the door."

"I did. Now go away." The words were muffled, but soft they were not.

He sighed and cursed as he shifted the helmet, growing heavier by the moment, to his right hand. "Five minutes, this is all I ask, *sí*?"

"No."

"*Cariño*—"

"I said no. Now go away before I call the police."

"I am the police."

"Wrong. You're DEA, and I'm smart enough to know the difference. Now *leave*."

He stared at the door, then up and down the dimly lit hallway. "I will go—after we talk. Unless you would like me to knock loudly enough to wake your neighbors?"

"You wouldn't."

But he would.

And evidently she knew this. Because the door reopened. A crack. Her huge blue eyes filled the space.

"May I come in?"

"Don't press your luck."

"Five minutes, no more. I give you my word."

Her gaze narrowed. "No, and you have five seconds."

"Cariño—"

"It's two in the morning, Agent Vásquez. You want five minutes, come back at nine."

He sighed. If he had but five seconds, he had best get started. "I am sorry I missed dinner."

"Apology accepted. Good night."

Dios mio. She was *furiosa.* Definitely angry enough to slam the door in his face again. He wedged a boot into the narrow opening just in case.

"Get your foot out of my door."

"Un momento, por favor."

"Now."

It was late and he was tired, or he would have caught the warning fire in her eyes—and heeded it. Certainly before she whipped the door open and slammed the heel of her palm into the pocket of his shoulder.

He stumbled back to absorb the blow, grunting at the shaft of pain that stabbed through his shoulder before slicing across his chest and down his arm. He was dimly aware of her answering gasp, and then she was standing before him, shoving his leather jacket aside and gasping again.

"Oh, my God, Tomás, what happened?"

He stared down at the spare T-shirt the paramedic had

given him, at the scarlet stain seeping through the gauze beneath and rapidly spreading into the white—and groaned.

Madre de Dios.

He was going to do the one thing he had sworn he would not do. He was going to bleed on that damned white carpet.

Chapter 4

Karin snatched back every vile curse she'd leveled at TJ during the past eight hours as she waited on him yet again—this time for an answer. When he didn't speak, she ripped the hem of his T-shirt from his black jeans, determined to get the answer herself. Unfortunately his hands closed over hers, stopping the shirt halfway up his chest.

"*Cariño,* I am fine. A minor knife wound, nothing more. I was on my way to the hospital, but first stopped to—"

"*Knife?*" She swallowed the surge of fear that followed, or thought she had, until his free hand came up to cup her cheek.

"A graze, I swear."

She jerked her chin from his palm and tugged his shirt the rest of the way up. *Graze, her ass.* That gauze swathed around his chest was damn near soaked with blood—inches from his heart. "Inside."

"But—"

"Now." This time she didn't leave room for argument as she wrapped her fingers around his good arm and hauled him into the apartment. She slammed the door behind them and threw the chain home. "Don't bother stopping at the couch, either. Head back to my bedroom—past the kitchen on your right. Take off your shirt and lie down while I grab my bag."

She didn't wait for another argument, but sprinted across the apartment, instead. Along with her bedroom, her study was the only other room that had escaped her mother's redecorating wrath. That meant she might actually be able to find her doctor's bag without tearing the room upside down. A rifled desk, rummaged closet and storage chest later, she wasn't so certain.

Calm down, dammit.

She was a doctor, for goodness' sake.

Surely she could find one simple suture kit and use it to stitch up one Latin lothario, without that same lothario realizing she'd spent half the night sitting up in bed worrying about him. She hit the closet again and made another pass through the clutter. Where was it?

There.

Five seconds later, her black bag firmly in hand, she was back in the living room. Unfortunately so was TJ. The man hadn't moved a blasted inch toward her bedroom, and he was still holding that damned helmet.

Oh, Lord, he wasn't going to faint, was he?

She wasn't taking any chances.

Karin grabbed the helmet and dumped it on the breakfast bar, easing out a sigh as she studied his face. His pupils looked good—not fixed and dilated. Other than exhaustion, he seemed okay. "Aren't you supposed to be lying in my bed?"

Nope, those pupils were definitely not fixed. If anything, they were flaring. "*Cariño,* I—"

"—said move. And I meant it." She planted her hands in the muscles of his back and nudged him through the open bedroom door. This time he complied without argument. What the hell—she pressed her luck and tacked on another order. "Strip."

Leaving him to the task, she quickly skirted the rumpled bed and dumped her bag on the nightstand before clicking the reading lamp to high. That done, she started in on the covers, glancing up as she peeled the floral sheets down to the brass spindles that made up the footboard—and groaned.

TJ was still standing just inside the doorway, still staring into the room, or rather at the room. He was also showing signs of shock now, or rather surprise.

Okay, so she was a slob.

Sheesh. It wasn't as if she'd been expecting company. At least not in here. Besides, if the man was looking for a sterile environment, he should have headed for the emergency room. Come to think of it, why hadn't he?

Unless the cut was so severe, he hadn't had the time.

She rounded the bed. "Tomás, will you please hurry? You'll need a transfusion at this rate."

He came out of his stupor, suppressing a grimace as she helped him shrug off his leather jacket. She tossed the jacket over the stack of clothes on the chair that had made it off the ship but not quite into her closet, then helped him ease off the still-mostly-white T-shirt. And promptly wished she could say the same for the gauze.

She nudged TJ down into a sitting position on the bed and sucked in her breath as she bent to unwind the saturated strips. Whoever had wrapped him had done a damned good job, leading her to believe the person knew something about medicine. But as soon as she was down to bare seeping flesh, she cursed the person a thousand times, because he never should have let TJ leave without stitches.

"What happened?"

"I told you, I was cut."

That much she could tell by the four-inch slice riding his left pectoral. This was no graze. It was, however, superficial. The muscle beneath his skin was firmly intact. All he would need were stitches and those she could do here. She sent up another round of thanks and pressed a wad of the clean gauze over the laceration. "Who cut you?"

"You want his real name or his street name?"

"Are you telling me you got this during a drug bust?"

Several strands of dark hair slipped past his shoulders as he nodded, shadowing the side of his face. She ignored the urge to brush them back, squelching the spurt of disappointment when he did it himself. "I tried to tell you at the door. The agent I filled in for had a major heroin buy lined up for tonight. Joaquín was our point of contact. Unfortunately he fell ill. My friend tried a new seafood restaurant on the Embarcadero last night and received food poisoning for his patronage. We were fortunate, though, for while Joaquín came by referral through one of his informers, he had not yet met the dealer face-to-face. And since we resemble each other well enough…" He shrugged.

The silence that followed told her that was all the explanation she was going to get. She wasn't even annoyed. Because he hadn't stood her up. But he could have called.

His thumb scorched the curve of her jaw as he tipped her face down slightly and captured her gaze. "My message telling you this, you did not receive it?"

"No."

"From your reception, I thought not." His frown deepened. "But surely you did not believe I forgot?"

She glanced past that probing gaze—and the hurt lurking within. Unfortunately she had a feeling the heat searing the tips of her ears had given her away, anyway.

"You did." A sigh. One honed so deeply by disappointment it cut straight through her. *"Cariño."*

She ignored the gentle rebuke, focusing on the wad of gauze until she was mesmerized by the heady contrast of her own light skin pressing into his dark.

Don't let him get to you. Stay cool.

But her body betrayed her. First her fingers trembled, then her entire hand. She stared at it in shock. That hadn't happened since med school, and then only out of nerves. To make matters worse, she was suddenly, acutely, aware of his musk. Subtle and seductive. Her panic must have masked it when he'd arrived, but it was definitely there now. His scent drifted dangerously close and then it was swirling into her lungs, up to her head, edging out every other thought in her brain.

Good Lord, why TJ?

Eight hundred men on her last ship, and not one of them had ever affected her like this man could.

Focus. Check the bleeding. See if it's slowed.

Then stitch this damned dusky chest back together and kick its owner out of your apartment. Out of your life.

She started to.

She did manage to lift the gauze, was relieved to see the bleeding had slowed to a trickle, was even about to round the bed again and grab her bag, when he stopped her. Before she realized what had happened, TJ had trapped both her hands in his, her bare thighs between his denim-clad ones, and he held her. Just held her. Well, he couldn't make her look.

She wouldn't let him. If she did, she'd be lost.

Since the day Reese and Jade had married, she'd known that standing this close to this man's dark eyes and sensual lips would be her downfall—and that was before she'd had his naked chest to contend with. She was so close she could feel the heat radiating off him, the desire.

She was not going to look.

"Karin?"

Dammit, she looked—and she was lost.

Somehow she'd known Tomás would kiss like this. He wasn't even touching her. Not with his mouth, anyway. But he was kissing her. With his eyes. He stared at her lips, searing them with that smoldering gaze, sliding the fire slowly across, then over the curve of her jaw and down her throat. She could feel his eyes igniting the pulse at the base of her neck until it throbbed. Until she throbbed.

But still, he didn't move.

He refused to douse the inferno he'd just lit. Six bloody inches of air between them, and he just stared.

Burning. Searing.

"Tomás?" Her voice was hoarse, clipped, and to her utter humiliation, there was no mistaking her own desire.

"Shhh."

He released her hands and brought his fingers to her face, gently cupping her cheeks. He drew her face down slowly, so smoothly she hadn't even realized she was holding her breath. Until his mouth grazed hers—and she exhaled softly. He caught the puff between his lips and she swore she felt him smile as he gave it right back, wrapped in his slow deep sigh.

The tip of his tongue followed closely behind.

Just barely enough to drive her insane as he traced first her bottom lip, then the top. Then again...and again. Slowly, lightly, steadily, until her lips were damp and hungry. Until she was hungry. And not just for this light caress of flesh, this whisper of heat. She wanted more.

She wanted him.

The realization slammed into her like an ambulance screaming down the freeway at full code. She jerked her head back and stared into his smoldering gaze.

What the hell was she doing?

How could she stand here and kiss this man? This was the same man who'd admitted to his own blasted reputation. Hell, even his best friend had confirmed it before he'd clammed up and told her to discuss it with TJ himself.

Why should she?

In addition to his reputation, TJ had proven himself a liar as well—and that, she'd seen on her own.

The reception.

She tore her mind from the memory and fused it to the gaping laceration on his chest. At least the bleeding hadn't worsened.

"*Cariño?*"

She took a deep breath and dragged her gaze up, only to stare into the one emotion she never thought she'd see in this man's eyes. Uncertainty.

Stick with what works.

She took another breath. "*Karin.* Sorry, Agent Vásquez, this time, you've been busted. I just heard you say it right." She pinned a brisk professional smile to her lips and nudged him down until he was lying on the bed. "Now, unless you plan on waking up the thoracic surgeon in apartment 506, you'd better get comfortable—and find something to hold on to, because this is going to hurt."

Hurt?

TJ stared at the cool smile that did not quite reach Karin's eyes. He clenched his fists and locked them to his sides to keep from reaching out and dragging her back as she rounded the bed to retrieve her supplies. Hurt? This lady did not know the meaning of the word. If she thought a couple of needle pricks could hurt him, she was wrong. This puny scratch did not hurt.

Not like that distant smile.

But that smile would be cutting much deeper if he had not just discovered what was behind it. He had thought his past had finally rendered her immune to him. But he now knew differently. Her facade was just that—*una ilusión.* Smoke. Somewhere over the past two days he had begun to suspect it. But that kiss had just convinced him.

That kiss.

No. Now was not the time to dwell on that.

Nor was now the time to touch those glorious sleep-tousled curls. It had taken nearly every restraint he possessed to resist digging his fingers into that mass of spun gold. And then it had taken every one of the rest not to tug the straps of that slip of blue silk right off her soft shoulders and down her hips.

He ripped his gaze from that same silk as the fabric skirted the upper reaches of her thighs and fused his stare to her busy hands. If she caught him looking, she would no doubt realize precisely what she was wearing—or rather, what she was not—and then, stitches or no, he could guarantee she would stop her ministrations long enough to find a robe to cover those enchanting curves.

Though how she would find a robe, he knew not.

He swept his gaze about the room as she squirted something cold and clear into his wound, only to soak it up again. He was not sure which surprised him more—the absolute mess surrounding them or the color.

The room was exploding with it.

Pink, green, yellow. From the flowers on her bedcovers to the brass bed and the light-blue walls, somehow she had managed to incorporate every shade of the rainbow. It did not make sense. Indeed, compared to the winter wonderland of the rest of the apartment, this was most baffling. When had this woman decided to suck the color from her life?

And why?

Because it had happened in that order. He had finally placed the faint odor still lingering in her living room.

Paint.

"Tomás?"

He returned his attention to her. He was fairly certain she had not realized she had used his given name again. Though oddly enough, on her lips the cursed name did not carry its customary sting. Progress on all fronts.

He smiled. "¿Sí?"

"This may hurt."

He flicked his gaze to the needle and syringe she was holding and nodded. "Begin."

She bit down on her bottom lip and bent her head. Several pricks later her gaze returned to his and she eased out her breath. "Okay?"

He nodded again.

"Good." She smiled softly and this time it reached her eyes, beautiful blue eyes that were still tinged with concern.

Most definite progress.

"I just need to give the lidocaine a chance to numb the

skin, and then I can start.'' She placed the empty syringe on the nightstand and reached into her bag again, this time removing a suture kit not unlike the one the paramedic had waved beneath his nose as the man yelled at him. The paramedic had ceased arguing once TJ had sworn he would stop by the hospital and see a doctor.

True, he had not made it to the hospital. But he was seeing a doctor, was he not? A competent and stunningly beautiful doctor at that. As Karin readied the supplies, he caught her glance stealing across his chest—and the softening in her gaze.

His breath stopped. She wanted him still.

Why, then, had they returned to this distant dance?

And why had she started it?

Not that first time at his home, but the second. Why had she accepted his invitation to dinner at the wedding only to reject it—and him—once and for all at the reception? The question had driven him nearly insane these past six months. And now he would finally get his answer. All he needed to do was bide his time until she was well and truly distracted. He settled back to do just that.

He waited as she took the first stitch in silence, and then the second. The third and the fourth followed. Still he waited. Again and again, stitch after stitch. Until finally she was three-quarters of the way through sealing his cut, and then—

''Why did you change your mind?''

She froze, for perhaps no more than a second. And then she resumed her stitching. She did not glance up as she tied that stitch and started in on the next, but neither did she ignore him. Nor did she pretend ignorance.

''The wedding.''

Somehow he managed not to flinch at the sudden, but not thoroughly unexpected, fist of chill that gripped his heart.

Surely she did not mean—

No.

Had he not already considered this? And many times. He had even thought to ask. But why? It was never wise to borrow more trouble than one already owned. And given his past, he owned more than enough with this woman. Besides, Consuela had cornered him in the unlikeliest of places. Nor had Karin behaved differently following his escape and return to the wedding dinner. True, he and Karin had been seated on opposite sides of the bride and groom, but he had most definitely been watching. Waiting. Praying.

Nothing.

She had even agreed to dance with him after the meal.

But she had been reluctant, had she not?

Again, the fist of dread.

Best he tread carefully. He cleared his throat. "The wedding?"

A sigh rife with exasperation filled the room as she tied off her stitch and moved on to yet another. "Yes, the wedding. Surely you haven't forgotten your date so quickly?"

"My date?" *Carajó,* this did concern Consuela.

Another cold fist.

And another stitch. But no words.

Yet another prayer as he prompted her again. "Did my cousin say something to offend?" Please to God, let this be all it was.

A long pause as Karin took the next two stitches and tied them off. Through both, she still refused to raise her head and meet his gaze. And then a sigh. Heavy. Rife with pain, with certainty. "Your cousin didn't have to say anything."

Madre de Dios, she had seen them.

Worse, she had taken the sight, unexplained, aboard her ship and on to her deployment. For six months.

He reached for her cheek. "*Cariño,* I am sorry you saw. But you must know I did not kiss Consuela. It was she who—" He closed his hand as she jerked from his touch.

At least her gaze had found his.

Unfortunately fire had consumed the blue. "Hogwash. I was there. So was the champagne, but *you* weren't. Silly me, I assumed you'd gone to squirt shaving cream on the car, or whatever it is best men do, so I slipped out of the reception hall to warn you that it was time for the toasts. But you weren't in the parking lot, either. Or back at the church. And when I saw the door to the minister's office ajar..."

Her brows lifted sharply.

The fire had cooled. But the hurt that replaced it burned him regardless. More painfully than the knife he had taken to his chest an hour before. "*Querida*, I swear to you—"

"Don't even bother. I saw you. Less than two hours after professing your undying and *sole* interest in me, I caught you performing deep throat on someone else." A bitter smile. "Hell, I've seen tonsillectomies that were less invasive."

"This may well be. But you did not see what you—"

"Yes, I did."

"Please, you must allow me to finish." He placed a finger on her lips to forestall further argument. The fire in her eyes reignited. This time flaring hotter, burning bluer, but she remained silent. He drew his breath in slowly. "If you had remained but a moment longer, it would have become obvious that Consuela was kissing me, not the other way around. Consuela is a distant cousin of mine, as well as a friend. I thought you knew this. She had broken off with her *novio*—her boyfriend—the week before. Since you would not attend the wedding with me, I had thought to cheer her up."

"Well, it looked like you succeeded."

She was truly jealous. Still.

He could not stop the hope that flourished within his heart, nor the smile that accompanied it. "*Querida*, I ended that kiss soon after it started and helped my cousin to realize why she had done it. Consuela was very angry with Roberto, hurting. Once she saw this, she also saw it was not me she wanted to kiss, but him." He smoothed his fingers down her cheek, tracing the angry tide as it receded, leaving her skin pale once again from lack of sleep. "Consuela and Roberto married a few months ago." He waited for his words to sink in, relieved when the flush fled altogether.

"I'm sure it was, ah, beautiful." She swallowed. "The wedding, that is."

"It was."

A pause.

"So...I am absolved?"

Another pause, this one longer. Then finally, a nod.

"Then you will have that dinner with me after all, *sí?*" His thumb found her lips as he waited yet again, as he willed her to say yes. This time, she did not reject his touch.

But she did refuse. "I don't think that's a good idea."

"Why?"

She did not answer.

He lowered his hand as the silence stretched out, somehow locating a teasing smile. He drew it across his lips, hoping it would mask the awkwardness—his hurt. "I asked for a date, *querida*, not your hand in marriage."

A mistake.

This he saw in her eyes, even before she pulled away. The barrier was back. But this time it was not forged upon *ilusión*. It was most real.

What had he done?

She shook her head firmly. "I'm sorry, I don't think it's a good idea. You have a case to investigate, remember? And I have a career to keep afloat." With that, she returned her cool gaze to his chest and resumed her stitching. She worked in silence for another few minutes, then finished off her work with a bit of ointment, a large rectangle of clean gauze and several strips of surgical tape. This done, she raised her head. "You'll need a tetanus shot if you're not current, and I can give you something for the pain if you want. Other than that, I'm done."

He nodded, hitching his elbows on the bed to rise.

"Where do you think you're going?"

"Home?"

She rose instead, suppressing a yawn as she stared down at him. "And ruin my handiwork by getting back on that damned motorcycle? I don't think so. You can sleep here for the night. Besides, we still need to go over those names. We can take care of it in the morning before you leave." She dumped the rest of her supplies on the nightstand, finally succumbing to her yawn as she arched her back and stretched.

May *Dios* forgive him. He stared at her. At her shapely thighs to be precise.

Somehow the whisper of silk she was wearing had ridden up her right thigh and gotten pinched into the lace of her matching blue panties. Panties that were now clearly visible. He strangled his groan before it could escape, but the sound betrayed him by sinking lower, rumbling from somewhere deep within his chest before he could prevent it.

"Tomás?"

He tried to tear his gaze away, truly he did. But his eyes, they simply would not cooperate.

"Are you okay? Is there another wound?"

Somehow he managed to shake his head.

Be a gentleman. Tell her.

"You...ah..." He cleared his throat. "That is, your...ah..." He gave up on speech and settled for pointing.

Her attention followed his finger. She flushed deeply as she yanked the hem free. "Thank you."

"*De nada.*"

Fool.

Once again the room was thick with tension.

"Your guest room, where is it?"

"I turned it into a study. Sorry."

"I shall take the couch then." And hope he did not bleed on it during what was left of this night.

"No, you take the bed. I've slept on the couch before."

She reached for the vial she had left on the sheets, her hand colliding with his as she found it.

He covered her hand. "We could share."

She tensed. He caught the corresponding flare of desire in her eyes before she masked it, as well. Despite denying him dinner yet again, she was tempted.

But still, this damnable tension.

Anything to break it.

He opted for teasing again. "Come now, you have scalpels and needles in that bag, no? Surely you can fend off one injured man." This time it worked.

Her smile was small, soft. But it was real.

And it renewed his hope.

Now, if he could only rattle that calm of hers.

"You're incorrigible. You know that, don't you?"

He grinned. *"Sí."*

"But the answer's still no."

He inclined his head, determined to accept her decision with grace. "But surely you would not refuse to help a patient undress?" He schooled his face to papal innocence as he glanced at his jeans. "Removing them could cause strain to your handiwork, as I am somewhat…stiff."

For a moment something he could not quite place entered her eyes, but then it was gone, once again drowned by a sea of cool, though still friendly, blue. She stepped up to the bed and offered her slender hands. "Okay."

He stared at her fingers. This was all?

Not so much as a protest?

"Well? Would you like to get comfortable or not? If so, hurry up. We've both got a long day ahead of us tomorrow."

He allowed her to take his hands, but used his own strength to rise, his surprise turning to shock as her fingers tucked into the front of his jeans and searched out the back of the stud. She did not appear flustered in the least. Did she do this often?

No, not given her reaction to his own sullied past.

This was bravado, nothing more.

Guilt finally overcame his desire to rattle her, and he closed his hands over hers as she worked the stud. "*Cariño,* I should warn you—"

Her husky chuckle lodged the remainder of the words within his throat. "Relax, buster. I've been undressing men since med school. Boxers, briefs, colors and patterns, hearts and hot-pink…" She sighed. "I've seen them all."

This may well be, but this was also not the point.

He sucked in his breath as she finally released the stud and latched on to the zipper's tab. "I wear none."

Her hands froze. "N-none?"

He smiled into the riot of curls atop her head. "None."

"Oh."

Several excruciating moments passed, during which he worked frantically to keep his body from reacting to the slender fingers still locked to his zip.

She finally swallowed. "Well, I…uh…imagine you'd prefer to turn around, then, wouldn't you?"

"I would." *Ha!* He turned regardless. "Perhaps I should finish the zip?"

"If you can."

He could do so much more than open his pants at this moment, but he suspected he was pressing his luck as it was. "Done." He folded his arms beneath the bandage on his chest and waited.

She would not do it.

Not that he blamed her.

At the very least, he deserved a slap for allowing this to proceed as far as it had. He reached down to zip himself up so he might turn and apologize, but he did not get the chance. Her hands reached his waist two seconds before his and less than one later, her fingers were gone—and so were his pants.

He sucked in his breath, digesting shock as the night air swirled about him. *Jesucristo.* He had been joking.

And now he was naked.

And hard.

Exceedingly hard.

The remainder of his body stiffened along with his *erección* at her sharp intake. He stood absolutely still in the silence that followed. So still, he could hear his heart throbbing, could feel her staring. *Dios* as his witness, this was the most erotic moment of his life. To stand stark naked two feet from the very woman he wanted more than the breath that was searing through his lungs and yet not turn around.

It was also more than he could take.

He clenched his fingers into fists and stared at the foot of her bed, counting the brass spindles as he willed his raging desire to ease. It did no good. By the time he reached the spindles at the head to count those as well, he could see her slender fingers locked about the inner two, feel her scented body arching into his mouth, hear her moan as he…

His body began to tremble.

Why was she still here?

She must leave. Now. Or she never would.

"Querida?"

"Y-yes?" He could hear the shock in her hoarse whisper, the desire. Just like that, the trembling stilled.

He smiled. "May I turn around?"

"Yes…uh, no. I mean, just a m-minute." She cleared her throat. "I need to grab something from my closet."

He heard the door slide open. A solid thump and a soft curse as she rummaged through what no doubt resembled the rest of her room, then the door sliding again, coming to rest.

"Well, ah, good night. I'll…see you in the morning."

She fled.

He felt her absence as keenly as he had felt her presence, and missed her more. His pent-up breath came out in a rush as he pulled up his jeans and turned to the bedroom door.

Closed.

He had expected no less.

Before he realized what he had done, he was standing at the door, his hand on the knob. He jerked his fingers back and crooked his arms up against the door, pressing his forehead to the wood as he cursed himself soundly. A shower spewed to life somewhere on the other side. He groaned, through grace alone managing to sear away the image that sprang to his mind as he drew another deeper breath.

Slowly. He must proceed slowly and carefully.

It was enough to finally know that no matter what Karin had said to him six months before, no matter what she said when she had retreated from his kiss tonight, she wanted him. She might yet be able to overlook his sins. Surely she would not have stared, much less lingered for so long, if she could not. The knowledge filled him with hope and with determination. He would find a way to bring this thing between them to fruition. She might as well accept it. Karin Scott was about to become his lady.

And it was going to happen soon.

Chapter 5

She was doomed.

Karin shoved her face into the steaming water jetting from the nozzle in her guest shower and groaned. Not only was she repeating her mother's mistakes one by one, she was plowing through them.

With a vengeance, honey.

She grabbed the shampoo bottle. She still couldn't believe it was happening. Despite all her efforts, TJ was getting to her.

A womanizer.

Oh, the man was smooth about it. Even smoother than her father had been. Of course, he'd have to be to get past her defenses. She'd spent too many years constructing them. She'd maintained them well, too. Constantly checking for cracks in the foundation and in the walls, looking for any hole tiny enough for some slick smooth-talker to slip through.

So Consuela was his cousin.

Big deal.

She'd give him that one. Mainly because she doubted even TJ would be arrogant enough to lie when she could easily double-check the story when Jade and Reese returned. Hell, even Daddy hated getting caught. Besides, there was still his past. If he was so repentant, why did he still go by that damned nickname?

Tijuana Jones. Lord, she hated that name.

So why couldn't she resist the man that went with it?

That kiss.

It had been almost reverent. How could a man kiss like that and not have some fidelity left in him? She could only thank her lucky stars she'd found the strength to pull back when she had, or she would have lost more than her sanity tonight.

Hell, she almost had.

That stupid nightgown.

What was it about this particular man that had her blushing like some virginal bride?

If the shoe fits…

She finished rinsing her hair, then hooked the body puff from the shelf beneath the nozzle and lathered it up. Satisfied, she scrubbed it across her face.

It was no use.

She couldn't scrub the man from her mind any more than she could scrub his scent from her lungs or his touch from her skin. She tossed the puff onto the shelf and twisted the knob off before stepping out of the shower. A few brisk moments with the towel and she was ready to don her armor. The silk teddy lay in a crumpled heap in the corner of the room right where it belonged. In its place, she pulled on her mother's latest gift.

At least this gift was one she wanted.

She tugged on the sweats and turned into the mirror behind the sink with a smile. A split second later it fled as she muttered a string of curses. It figured. She'd been so relieved to latch on to something fleecy and long when she'd hit her closet on the way out of her bedroom that she'd forgotten she hadn't actually tried the outfit on. She jerked the cropped sweatshirt down several times, but it didn't help.

Her midriff was still bare.

Well, there wasn't a thing she could do about it now. She was not heading back into that bedroom. Not after that stunt with his jeans. Another second, and TJ's confession wouldn't have mattered. She would have seen it all.

Not that she hadn't seen enough as it was.

She'd lay odds the last doctor TJ had bared his butt to so flagrantly was the one who'd delivered him. Once more he'd enjoyed every second of that damned display. She could hear it in his voice. The beast had actually gotten turned on.

So did you.

Hell, what woman wouldn't?

She might not have personal experience in that department, but she had plenty of professional. There was no doubt about it. As hind ends went, TJ's was exceptional. Firm, sleek and one-hundred percent pure male muscle.

Just like the rest of him.

And, oh, that body!

It had taken every ounce of professional training to just stand there and anchor her fingers deep into her palms—so that she couldn't use them to knead those solid shoulders, stroke them down his smooth dusky back and dig them into that absolutely *perfect* ass. She stared down at her hands, stunned to see her nails imbedded once again. Her dry mouth, erratic breathing and rapid heart rate had returned, as well.

Damn him.

It didn't matter if she wasn't the only doctor he'd bared his butt to. It didn't even matter that she wasn't the only woman.

She would never be the last.

And that made all the difference.

She took her humiliation out on the light switch and then

the bathroom door before she headed for the couch. Diving in feet first, she thumped her head back onto the spare feather pillow and hauled the quilt past her exposed belly button, right up to her chin.

Finally.

Not an inch of flesh was showing. Now all she had to do was get to sleep. And pray to God she woke first.

Something was wrong.

Karin didn't even have to open her eyes to know it. All she had to do was breathe. Either she'd died and gone to heaven, or she'd been grafted into an episode of *The Twilight Zone*. She smelled food. Good food.

From her kitchen.

But, of course, that was impossible. The only other person who had a key to her apartment was her mother, and she couldn't cook, either. Then she remembered.

TJ.

She opened her eyes cautiously, half expecting to find the man standing at her side, staring down at her body and the usual pretzel she managed to twist her covers into. She'd probably offered him a choice view of her belly button for the past ten minutes. But…he wasn't there.

And she wasn't on the couch.

She was in bed. Her bed. Her favorite pillow plumped beneath her head, her floral sheets and comforter tucked snugly about her body. There was only one way she could have gotten there. TJ had carried her.

She was going to kill him.

Karin ripped the covers off and vaulted off the bed, slamming the bedroom door behind her as she tore out of the room. She didn't slow down until she'd rounded the breakfast bar, but by then, it was too late. She barreled smack into his chest with a most unladylike *oomph*.

TJ compounded her humiliation by wrapping his arms around her to steady her and ended up pressing her face even closer in the process. Frankly she would have pre-

ferred landing in a heap at his feet than finding herself
plastered to this particular T-shirt-clad chest this early in
the morning. She was so close she couldn't even smell the
food anymore. All she could smell was…

T-shirt?

She snapped back as far as his arms allowed.

He was wearing one of her navy-blue *USS Baddager*
shirts. Only, on *his* chest, extra large looked extra small—
and more than extra snug. *"Buenos días, querida."*

"Just what the hell do you think you're doing?"

He glanced at his chest, as well. "The shirt will shrink
back."

"I could give a rip about the shirt." Besides, that scrap
of cotton did a heck of a lot more for him than it had ever
done for her. "You carried me."

"You did not wish to sleep in?"

She raked her fingers through her tangled curls and
groaned. "Don't you get it? I stitched you up less than—"
She flicked her gaze past his healthy biceps to blink at the
clock.

6:00 a.m.?

Had the man slept at all?

She glared back at his face. "Four hours ago. Mister, do
you have any idea how much I weigh?"

"You wish to tell me?"

"No! And that's not the point. The point is—"

He was smiling.

No, he was laughing. At her. Silently, but he was definitely laughing. His deep-brown gaze warmed her from the
inside out as it slid down her body, coming to a complete,
riveting halt at her belly button. At least he'd stopped
laughing.

"Enchanting."

"I'm glad you like it. You can thank my mother."

"I intend to—"

"But *not* before you strip."

She should have known better. Especially in light of last

night. He didn't even bat an eye as he went straight for the stud crowning those snug black jeans.

"No!" She lashed out, clapping her hands over his with less than a zipper to spare. "Not your pants, your *shirt*."

"Ah...*perdóneme*. I misunderstood."

The hell he had.

His eyes were gleaming with barely restrained mirth now.

She reached up and tugged the T-shirt over his head, lest he misunderstand again. It would serve him right if she stuffed the thing down his cocky throat. She would have too, if she hadn't had more important things to worry about than her sanity. Like his wound. She peeled the surgical tape back and carefully lifted the gauze dressing, leaning closer to inspect the line of neat stitches tracking up his right pectoral.

"Well?"

"There're a couple flecks of blood, but you'll live. You managed to keep them fairly intact."

"Then I am absolved?"

For what?

For nearly ruining her stitches? Or for looking this damned sexy in spite of them? She held up the T-shirt, praying he'd put it back on—and release her from purgatory while he was at it.

He didn't.

And damned if the gleam wasn't back.

He knew he was getting to her. The invitation smoldering alongside that gleam proved it. She turn her back on both, determined to ignore the man and his too-tempting offer, only to come face-to-face with the reason TJ was standing in her apartment to begin with.

The case.

Three manila folders were stacked next to his motorcycle helmet on her breakfast bar. A leather folder lay open beside them with several sheets of notes spilling out.

"You've been working."

"Sí." His gaze followed hers as he joined her at the counter.

"Did you get anywhere?"

"I did not."

It wasn't his answer or even the way he raked his hands through his hair and shoved it past his shoulders. It was the deep, bone-weary sigh that followed. She knew Tomás was dedicated to his job. It was one of the reasons she'd weakened in the first place and agreed to have dinner with him before she'd left on deployment. A man who was this committed, who honestly believed the world could be a better place if they all worked a little harder, just plain got to her. But this case went even deeper than that. She knew it.

"This one's getting to you, isn't it?"

"Cariño, they all do."

No, they didn't. Not like this.

She touched his forearm. "Tell me about it."

A lengthy pause and, finally, another sigh.

He reached for the folders, turning them around as he slid the files toward them. He tapped them. "These first two women? They were friends. She was twenty, the other nineteen. Young, but old enough to know better. Especially since they had already been through rehab three times between them. But the older one, her father resumed her allowance—and you know the rest." He slid the top two folders off the pile and stared at the third. "But this one..." This sigh was so heavy, it seeped into her.

"Is it because she was Hispanic?"

"Partly, but there is more. Her name was Magdalena. At least, I believe that was her name. It was written on the inside of her purse, under a flap. Other than an empty ampule and syringe, not much else was in the bag. The couple who found the girl run a diner just north of the border. The two had seen her around several months back, but not recently. No one could confirm her identity."

"A runaway."

"Most likely."

"Where did they find her?"

His eyes closed, and she had her answer before he spoke. "In a box, in the alley. They were bringing leftovers from the night to those who sleep there. They phoned 911 as soon as they found her, but she did not make it to the hospital."

Karin closed her eyes as well, mourning the unknown girl along with him. No, she wasn't totally unknown. Her name *was* Magdalena. The girl might not have had anything else, but she would have a name. At least from them.

She opened her eyes and stared at him. TJ was right. It didn't add up. "I don't understand. If Magdalena didn't have money, how could she possibly afford fentanyl?"

But she knew.

Prostitution.

He nodded.

Still, why not crack or heroin? Why fentanyl? It just wasn't your average street drug, even in its street form, China White. The first two girls—the wealthy ones—she understood. It disgusted her, but she understood. Two spoiled kids who already had it all and wanted more. She'd gone to private school with enough of them to see that one a mile away.

But Magdalena?

Had the girl even seen it coming?

She took a deep breath and held out a hand. "Give me the list. Let's see who I know."

It was shorter than she'd expected. After all, theirs was a teaching hospital. The list had been made even shorter as TJ had worked his way down, winnowing out at least ten of the suspects and crossing them off. That left about twenty.

She knew maybe five well enough to offer comments.

"You already know everything I do about Doug. I wouldn't put anything past him. But Lt. Walters is different. At least, he seems okay. I consulted with him a few times when I was on the *Baddager,* but I never saw him off hospital property, so who knows what he's really like or into.'' She scanned further and picked out two more names. ''You can probably cross off Lieutenants Zack Jacobs and Jerry Denton, or at least move them to the bottom of the list.''

''Why?''

''Well, Jerry's father is a physician actively involved with Doctors Without Borders. Denton Senior was still in Bosnia last I heard. Jerry and Zack used their thirty days' leave last year to fly out and assist his team.''

TJ nodded and retrieved the list to scrawl a couple notes next to the names. She leaned around him to glance down the rest, blinking when she reached the bottom.

Shelley Ryder?

What was Shelley doing in town, let alone on TJ's list?

''*Querida,* what is it?''

''I know her.''

His gaze followed her index finger. ''This one—Doctor Ryder? You know her well?''

''Yes. No. Well, kind of. I used to, anyway. We went to med school together. She was two years ahead. I knew her husband better. He was older, but he was in my class. It took him a couple of years longer than the rest of us to make it in and, well, he never made it out. Flunked out second year. Chuck and Shelley got married right after. It was...odd.''

''How so?''

She shrugged, feeling guilty for even thinking it, let alone voicing it. ''I always got the feeling Chuck was more of a social climber than really in love. Shelley didn't have money. But she had the degree, so the potential was there. After she finished her obligation to the Navy for picking up her loans, anyway. Last I heard, she was stationed in Maryland—Bethesda. They'd even bought a house. What's she doing out here?''

''Residency, like you.''

''Anesthesiology?'' No way.

But he nodded. "She just finished her first year."

"But that's impossible. All she ever talked about was Peds—pediatrics. Oh, right. Damn him."

"Who?"

"Her husband, who else? Chuck wanted anesthesiology."

"Let me guess."

"You already did. A hell of a lot of money on the outside. Shelley could do it, too. She's good. Rock steady and as sharp as they come. Still, I could have sworn her heart was with the kids."

"People change."

People did. But not Shelley.

Nope, she smelled a skunk, and she knew exactly what his stripe looked like. "Do you have their number?"

TJ's gaze narrowed. "Why?"

"I'll call her. I'll tell her I heard she was in town and decided to look her up and—"

"No."

"Why not? We used to be pretty close. Heck, I even went to her wedding. I'll invite her out. Shelley never could hold her wine. Two goblets, and she'll be—"

"I said, no."

She sighed. "Tomás—"

"*Absolutamente* no! People who deal in drugs do not play nice." He tapped his chest. "Take another look at your own work if you do not believe me."

"But I can help."

He trapped her chin, then her gaze. "*Querida,* you must listen to me. This Shelley, if either she or Señor Callahan is capable of what I suspect, I do not want you involved."

Why did he have to keep using that damned endearment? It didn't mean anything. She didn't mean anything. Her father had been full of endearments, too, but they were empty, just like TJ's. His thumb gently rubbed the hollow of her throat as that smoky gaze of his did its best to convince her he was sincere. After last night, it almost worked, too. Almost.

Dammit, she was not into he-men.

And she was not into *him*.

She tugged her chin from his grasp. "I'm sorry, but this isn't your decision to make. I have a right to be there, and I have a stake in this as well. Maybe even more of one. Especially if that fentanyl came from a naval facility. And let's not forget that note was addressed to me. Oh, I'm taking leave, all right, but I'm spending it in and out of the hospital, getting to know my way around, and who I'm going to be working with."

His frown deepened as he reached for her again.

She took a quick step back and shook her head—firmly. "I've made up my mind, so quit arguing. Besides, you need me and you know it. You work seven to three. If you're seen poking around outside those peak hours—when, incidentally, the theft is likely to occur—it's going to be obvious something's up. I, on the other hand, can come and go as I please."

He dropped his hand and stared at her a moment, then finally nodded. But he didn't look happy about it.

Not one bit.

Too bad. One overbearing man in her life was enough.

"Now, would you like to describe the type of information you're looking for and from whom, just in case?"

Silence reigned again.

Just when she thought TJ might actually give in, the kitchen timer jarred their attention from each other and toward the stove. Her curiosity got the better of her as he grabbed one of the new linen finger towels her mother had bought and used it to insulate his hands as he drew something decadently fragrant and definitely steaming from the oven.

"What's that?"

"Breakfast." He set the covered casserole dish she'd yet to use since she'd bought it down onto the right front burner and glanced over his shoulder as he switched off the heat. "*Cariño,* the refrigerator. Would you pour the juice?"

Juice? In her refrigerator?

Since when?

Come to think of it, she didn't have the ingredients for a poached egg, much less that mouthwatering concoction he'd just plunked down in front of them. Where the devil had he…? But when she opened her mouth to ask, his dark brows rose. The message was clear. Medicine might be her domain, but cooking was his.

Fine with her.

She turned to the refrigerator and opened the door, expecting to find a carton of juice and whatever else he'd used to create that pungent feast—and gasped. There was food in here, all right, all kinds of food. And it was everywhere.

The glass shelves were crammed with plastic tubs, cartons and jugs. Several cartons of brown eggs were stacked next to another carton of what, she had no idea. And the door. Slots that had been empty four hours ago were now full of bottles of every shape, size and color. Sauces, dressings and at least six different liquids with labels she didn't even recognize, let alone know how to pronounce. She reached out, inexplicably drawn toward the meat bin, and slid it open.

Butcher paper?

She turned around and gaped up at TJ.

A slow smile crooked his lips. "I like fresh meat."

Uh-uh. She was not going there.

She stared back at the brimming shelves. "But, how…? Where? When?" She swallowed the sudden, inexplicable lump in her throat as she spied the mini-cartons of gourmet yogurt, mammoth oranges and flavored coffee creams. "*Why?*"

Despite her utter confusion, he figured it out.

Thank goodness.

"Where—you have an all-night store several blocks

away. When is obvious. I could not sleep. How? A cab. And why? To thank you, of course.''

''But all I did was stitch you up. You certainly didn't have to do all this.'' She turned back and opened the vegetable bin. She snagged two pieces, a heavy red orb with a knot at one end and an oddly angular yellow one. As she stood staring at them, she started chuckling at the absurdity of it all.

Her breath caught as TJ stepped up behind her, his arms sliding around her midriff, burning away the chill from the refrigerator. ''What is so amusing?''

''This, me.'' She waved the vegetables. ''Tomás, I don't even know what these things are, let alone how to cook them.''

He chuckled with her as she turned in his arms. He plucked the orb and held it between them. ''This is a pomegranate, a fruit. Peel it and you will find hundreds of red juicy seeds, ripe for eating and for sharing.'' He returned it to the bin and closed the refrigerator door.

She was still holding the other. ''And this?'' By the time she realized he wasn't going for the second piece, he'd braced his hands on her hips and was lifting her off her feet. ''Tomás!''

His grin spread as he settled her onto the counter beside the fridge. ''*Sí*, I remember. No lifting. *Querida*, despite what you think, you weigh—'' he snapped his fingers ''—*nada*.'' He plucked the second piece from her hands. ''This one is a star fruit. It, too, is juicy, but the flavor is subtle.''

He retrieved a knife from the wooden block behind her before she could protest. A few moments at the sink to wash the fruit and he was back, slicing twice to create a star. He trimmed the skin from the sides and brought it to her lips.

''Taste.''

She dug her fingers beneath the edge of the counter as he coaxed the slice between her lips.

He was right. Subtle. Cool and juicy.

Similar in taste and texture to green grapes, but not quite. She smiled. "It's delicious."

"Mmm." It was more breath than agreement. He was staring at her mouth.

The juice.

"Sorry." She swept her fingertips across her lips, only to find them snared by his. His pupils flared as he brought her fingers to his mouth and gently sucked the juice from the tips one by one. Not cool anymore, not subtle. Dark. Hot.

Wet.

His gaze went black. "*Querida,* you know what I want."

She knew.

Oh, God, she knew.

She wanted it, too.

But this was wrong. She had a job. He had a case. They were going to have to work near each other, at least for a while—what was she thinking? Even if they weren't working near each other, this could go absolutely nowhere. TJ Vásquez—no, Tijuana Jones—was not the man for her.

He was not the man for any one woman.

"Tomás, I don't think—"

"Shhh." He shook his head slowly, firmly. A moment later his lips were hovering inches from hers as he stared deep into her eyes. "Woman, you think far too much." His mouth drew closer, until she was drawing her very breath from his.

She wasn't thinking now. She was feeling.

She was dimly aware of the knife and the remains of the fruit dropping to the counter, then his fingers sliding beneath her chin. "Besides, you must give thanks."

"But I thought—"

He tsked. "Not the food, the taste. Surely, the gift of new experience is reason enough?"

She closed her eyes against that smoky gaze, trying desperately to hold on to reason. She was so out of her depth with this man it wasn't funny. If he knew just how many new experiences he'd given her lately, she'd be indebted to him for life.

He stroked his thumb across her lips, forcing her to open her eyes, if only to see what was coming next. "Come, now. One kiss. And then we shall call this even, *sí?*"

"But we did kiss. Last night—"

Another tsk, another soft shake of his head. "Last night, I kissed you. This morning, you must kiss me."

But she couldn't.

For one thing, she didn't know how. Exactly. Hell, it wasn't like that part was in the damned medical books. God knew, she'd looked once or twice. What if she refused?

What if she didn't?

Would he be able to tell?

Dammit, just kiss the man. It was probably safer to experiment with him, anyway. With that many notches in his headboard, at least he ought to know how to do it. Besides, it wasn't like he'd be sticking around. That settled it. She'd do it.

Except she still didn't know how.

So make him kiss you.

Her fingers still curled and locked beneath the edge of the counter, she inched forward. That was all it took, and she was there. But how to start?

Do what he did.

Why not?

She reached out and traced the tip of her tongue across his bottom lip, tentatively at first, then with more confidence.

No real taste, but soft, yet firm. Warm.

Smooth.

He tensed. So she did it again, hesitating as she reached the corner of his mouth.

Now what? Did she just keep doing this?

A moment later she had her answer as he groaned and took over. His hands lashed up to frame her face, burning away her uncertainty as he plowed his fingers into her hair, tipping her head as he delved deeply into her mouth. It was heavenly. His unique scent never failed to torment her whenever he got too close, but his taste. Oh, his taste.

The leather, fresh air, her vanilla coffee he must have helped himself to, it was all here. But most of all, she could taste passion. His passion—for her. She'd caught it in his eyes now and then as they'd danced carefully around each other while helping to plan Jade and Reese's wedding, had even tasted the tip of it last night when he'd kissed her on her bed. Right now, that passion was back. Even with her fingers still locked beneath the edge of the counter, she could feel that passion. His body was taut with the strain.

Trembling.

She didn't want it reined in anymore. Didn't want him reined in.

TJ was right. The time for thinking had passed.

For once she just wanted to feel.

So how did she tell him? Should she let go of the moan that was building as his lips scorched a path down the length of her throat, nipped the curve at the base, then seared right back up to plunder her mouth again? Would that let him know? And her hands. What was she supposed to do with her hands?

Once again, confusion clouded her need as she dug her nails beneath the counter. Soon he incinerated that as well. He broke the fiery kiss, but not his touch. His fingers were still tunneled into her hair, his body hovering inches from hers, quaking now. "*Cariño*, please…*touch me.*"

She responded to his raw need without thinking. Her fingers came up before she could stop them, gliding across his chest, fitting themselves into the naked ridges and deep crevice she'd tried so hard to ignore last night. She reached his nipples, whirled the pads of her fingers around them, scraped her short nails over them.

He groaned.

The sultry sound swirled into her ears, invading her

mind, seducing her into giving in to one of her darkest
desires, a desire that had invaded her dreams since the day
she'd met this man—she slid her hands down farther. His
groan deepened, roughened, rumbling into a throbbing
growl as she reached the taut muscles of his stomach. Before she could stop them, her fingers had threaded themselves into the trail of black silk that began beneath his
navel. She gave in again, flirting her way down to the waist
of his jeans, where she fought the urge to follow the wisps
even lower.

A moment later she was shuddering along with him.

His hands had fallen from her hair to span her waist. She
gasped as his thumbs found her exposed belly button, worrying in and out with maddening repetition. He tore his
mouth from hers only to drag it down her jaw. She shivered
as his stubble rasped the flesh of her neck as his lips
scorched down her throat. He reached the base again and
this time she arched into his mouth, moaning as he nipped
the hollow.

"Tomás." Her voice was so low, so full of shameful
pleading, she wasn't sure it was hers. "I want..."

She didn't know what she wanted.

But he did.

His ragged breath seared into her ear. "*Sí, querida,* I
want it, too. *Dios mío*, I want it, too."

His hands began kneading a relentless, erotic path back
up her waist. His fingers stopped, hesitating at the hem of
her cropped shirt for a single blinding moment, and then
they were delving beneath. She shuddered as he caressed
her ribs, letting loose a sigh that poured straight from her
core as he finally cupped her breasts and squeezed firmly.

"Oh, yes." *More.*

He gave it.

Moments later his mouth was there, closing over one
aching nipple, then the other. Like a man offered water
after a lifetime of drought, he drank from her—of her—
every drop he could find. Within moments her entire world

had drawn down to TJ's greedy mouth, his lips, his teeth, and his tongue. She gave herself up to the scorching, licking and pulling sensations. Gasping when he bit down gently, moaning when he soothed.

She was dying.

From pleasure, from pain, she didn't know which. All she knew was that she needed relief. She needed him. Five more seconds of this torture, and she swore she'd be giving in to temptation for the first time in her life. She lasted one.

Before she could stop them, her legs came up and locked themselves about his waist, and then she began to beg. Softly at first, then insistently. Soon she was rubbing herself against him shamelessly. He tore his mouth from her breasts, grinding out her name along with half-a-dozen words she didn't understand as both of them grabbed at the stud on his jeans. He wrenched it free, groaning as she freed the zip. But the moment her hand slid deep into his heat, she heard a loud knock on the door to her apartment—and then it opened.

"Honey, are you home?"

They froze.

He cursed and she gasped.

"Oh, my God. That's my mother."

Chapter 6

Her mother?

Despite the cloud of passion fogging his brain, TJ managed to yank Karin's sweatshirt down and zip his jeans in two seconds flat. He wasted another three cursing himself for not throwing the chain on the door when he had returned with the groceries that morning, then spent the remaining moment of his reprieve willing his ragged breath and thundering heart to slow and even out. By some miracle, they complied.

By the time the apartment door slammed shut, he had lifted Karin from the counter and was setting her on her feet. This time she did not scold. She simply stood there. Silent. Shock, no doubt. And something else. Fear? Shame?

Please to God, anything but the latter. Unfortunately he did not have time to be certain.

"Honey, I know it's early. I wanted to catch you before you left for the ship so we could— Oh!''

Feeling more boy than man than he had in years, TJ retrieved the dish towel he had used to take the *chiles rel-*

lenos from the oven and carefully tucked it into the waist of his jeans, praying it would conceal the brunt of his remaining passion as he turned. A face, perhaps two decades older but equally as stunning and as equally stunned as the one he had just been kissing, greeted him.

He stepped forward, his hand outstretched. "*Buenos días,* Señora Scott. It is truly an honor to meet you."

She allowed him to take her hand in his, gasping softly as he brushed his lips over her smooth skin, fingering the strand of pearls at the collar of her black dress with her other. "Th-thank you, Mr....?"

"Vásquez. Tomás Juan Vásquez. I met your daughter through—"

"—the hospital."

TJ froze.

He turned back to Karin, but she was already at his side, her face still flushed, her lips still swollen as she reached down to scoop up the squares of fabric that had fluttered from her mother's hands to settle about the woman's low heels.

"Mom, I checked into the hospital yesterday. You remember my telling you."

Eyes as startling blue as Karin's blinked twice before staring up at him. Her gaze focused, then narrowed as it skimmed down his bare chest to stare at his equally bare feet. Given the hour and his state of undress, it was obvious he had spent the night. He cursed himself again, this time for removing the pillow and blanket from the couch.

"You met *yesterday?*"

He flushed.

It mattered not that the lie and the misconception stemming from it were not his. The guilt was. At the very least he had been fantasizing about doing precisely what he had almost been caught doing since the moment he had met Karin.

Still, he would not let her mother think ill of her. "No, señora. We met well before your daughter's ship sailed."

''Oh.'' The shock faded somewhat, and a dimpled smile twin to Karin's came forth. ''In that case, it's nice to meet you, too. I gather you're a civilian physician, though.'' Her smile grew as she mistook his surprise once again, this time winking at him. ''Your hair. The length does give it away.''

Physician?

His heart began to throb painfully as he noted Karin's reluctance to correct this new misconception. How had his morning gone from scaling the heights of heaven only to plummet to the depths of hell so quickly? He shoved his hair past his shoulders as he swallowed a growl.

A gasp filled the kitchen.

Her mother's.

Carajó—the stitches.

Once again Karin stepped forward, interceding. Once again she was less than truthful. ''Tomás had an accident, Mom. That's why he's here. I was, um, stitching him up.''

This partial fib appeared to go down more smoothly than the rest as her mother smiled. He should have been thankful.

Instead, he was filled with dread.

''I see. Well, Dr. Vásquez—''

''Tomás.''

''You don't mind?''

For a man whose very life often depended on his ability to lie, he was stunned at the depth of his need to bring them to a complete and utter halt. Here.

Now.

Sí, he was certain. ''I would be honored, señora.''

She returned his genuine warmth with more than a hint of maternal speculation. ''Well, then, Tomás, I'm glad everything's okay.'' Her smile deepened, now most definitely teasing. ''I suppose even a doctor can't sew himself up. You'll have to tell us all about it when Karin brings you to dinner. How about tonight?''

''*Tonight?*''

He suppressed yet another wince at Karin's tone. At

least, he prayed he had been able to conceal it. Unfortunately he was not able to staunch the ache that had sliced through him, as well. How much more proof did he need that what he had seen in Karin's eyes before they greeted her mother was fear—and shame? A shame that had nothing to do with his reputation.

It was of him.

He shook his head, refusing the invitation before Karin forced him into yet another lie. "Unfortunately I must work this evening. Perhaps another time?"

There would be no other time.

Karin would make sure of it.

"Of course. Just let me know when. Now if you two don't mind, I'll leave the swatches in the living room and let you get back to your...breakfast." She collected the squares of fabric from her daughter's pale hands and carried them across the room to splay them over the arm of the sofa, each sample but a variation on the virgin fabric beneath.

"They look great, Mom."

No, they did not. They looked bland. Washed-out. As cold and as lifeless as the rest of this wintry room. And as he studied Karin studying them, he swore she knew this.

Why then, did she pretend she did not?

"Well, honey, I'd best be off." The woman skimmed her hand down her shoulder-length hair. "I've got a breakfast meeting myself this morning."

Though he sincerely doubted she had such a meeting, he welcomed the excuse, nonetheless. Anything to get Karin alone again. He must find out what was wrong. From the moment they had heard her mother's voice, she had been pulling away from him, growing colder and more remote.

As cold as this damned room they were standing in.

He watched as she followed her mother obediently to the door. She smiled warmly enough as the woman reached out to hug her, but as her mother bent to whisper something into her ear, her hands clenched, and she stiffened slightly.

So slight was the motion, he did not think her mother noticed.

But he did.

Her mother turned to smile and nod at him one last time, and then she was gone. Awkward silence filled the apartment, nearly stifling him with its intensity. It was made even more so when Karin refused to meet his gaze.

It was not his imagination.

Something had happened. And he would swear it had something to do with getting caught by her mother. But why? He was a grown man, she a grown woman, both unattached. Unless she was embarrassed over being caught *en flagrante* with him because of his heritage. If this was the case, he would know.

This very moment.

He joined her at the door. *"¿Cariño?"*

Still, she would not look.

He tipped her chin. "What did your mother say to you?"

"N-nothing. Why do you ask?"

She was lying.

Pain sliced through him again as he studied the pink washing the tips of her ears. She did not even seem to realize she had been caught so deep was her concentration on…what?

For better or worse, he must know.

He took a deep breath. "Do I shame you?"

"What?" At least she was looking at him now. "No. How can you even say that? No, how can you even think it? Tomás, I am not ashamed of you. It's just—" She reached out, only to jerk her hand back inches before it reached his face. She sighed. "You wouldn't understand. My father…well, he's not really my father. He's my stepfather. Westin's the head of cardiology at La Jolla General. If my mother…if Westin finds out— Hell, I'm doomed."

No, she was not the one condemned. It was he.

Because it was shame.

She could call it what she liked. He knew it by many names. It mattered not. They all felt the same.

His half sister had not been the first, nor the last.

Trish.

Some sister. Not that she knew. She had been too busy staring down her pert wealthy nose to consider he might not be the dirty little lawn boy there to work the yard.

And his father?

The man had no such excuse, no ignorance on which to rely. His father knew. And still he did nothing. Felt nothing.

TJ studied Karin as she skirted around him and headed into the kitchen. Once there, she busied herself with scooping the remains of the star fruit into the sink. Like her eyes, her jerky movements held far more truth than her words. He would have laughed had they not cut so deeply. All these years, and the Virgin Mother had finally decided on his penance. He had finally found the woman with whom he wished to break his fast, and now this.

He could hear the very saints themselves jeering as she turned on the disposal, grinding his hopes and his pride along with the rinds and washing them down the drain.

What had he been thinking?

What made him think she would welcome him into her life?

It was clear she hated this barren apartment, and yet she seemed determined to call it home. Why he even cared, he knew not. He had hoped they could meet somewhere in the middle. That perhaps he could fill other places in her life. But she was not an empty refrigerator. And he would be damned if he would play the stockboy. He could not.

Not even for her.

He had to get out of here. Gather his thoughts.

He glanced at the clock behind the stove, grateful the time had passed so quickly. It gave him an excuse. He grabbed it, rounding the high counter to stack his files and notes together and return them to his bag, zipping it as quickly as he dared. Her head came up as he retrieved his boots from beneath one of the stools and shoved his bare feet into them.

"You're leaving?"

"*Sí.* The hospital, I must not be late."

"Oh." She stood there staring at him, that damnable mix of confusion and hurt darkening her eyes as he grabbed the T-shirt he had borrowed and held it up.

"Do you mind?"

"No. Please…keep it."

He would not.

It would not matter how many times he scrubbed this scrap of cloth, he would never succeed in purging her scent from it. His lungs did not need the reminder. For each time he closed his eyes, they filled with her subtle perfume. He shoved the edge of the shirt into his jeans with more force than necessary and cuffed his helmet, jacket and bag from the counter.

"Tomás?"

He stopped a foot shy of the front door. Coward that he was, he refused to turn around. *"¿Sí?"*

"What happened this morning. Before my mother…"

He closed his eyes as she trailed off. When she failed to begin again, he forced himself to open his eyes and turn. She was still at the sink, but he could see her face clearly.

He wished he could not.

Any thread of hope clinging secretly within his heart snapped as she finally spoke. "Can we…forget it happened?"

He managed a stiff nod.

Relief flooded those blue eyes, drowning him. "Good. I mean, I think it's for the best."

No doubt it was.

But for whom?

Karin pulled the key from the Jag's ignition and took a deep breath as she rubbed her now-throbbing neck. It didn't help. The knot she'd earned from falling asleep on the couch was still nagging her. So was the coffee she'd opted to consume, instead of the once fragrant dish now growing ice-cold on her stove. The brew sloshed through her stomach again. The muted growl and dull cramp that followed underscored her stubbornness and her stupidity. She should have just eaten the damn thing. Or at least grabbed a yogurt. But she couldn't.

Not after the way TJ had left.

What was it about this particular man? How had he succeeded in getting under her skin so thoroughly? Especially now. Here. She stared at the staff entrance to the hospital through the Jag's windshield, coffee sloshing through her again.

Good Lord, she was actually nervous.

This was the one place she'd always been able to hold her own and remain focused. For twenty-seven years she'd managed to keep her hormones in check. It had been easy enough when she was early-admissions premed at La Jolla. Spending her freshman year of college as jailbait had been enough to put a damper on most of her male classmate's interest. The fact that her stepfather guest-taught several senior courses nipped the rest in the bud. Not that she'd cared.

Hell, she'd welcomed the deterrence.

Especially after the fiasco of her sophomore year. By the time med school came around—and Westin Scott wasn't— she'd figured out how to keep the wolves at bay on her own. A saucy comment here, a sarcastic one there, and most men were either put off or put out. Well, most of them.

At any rate the Navy had even allowed her to perfect the technique. By the time she'd gotten to the ship she'd heard every double entendre on the books and made them her own. If there was one universal truth when it came to men and sex, it was that men couldn't handle a woman with more experience.

God, if they'd only known.

If TJ only knew.

Well, he wasn't going to find out. Not today, anyway.

Because she was going to walk right through that glass door and find Shelley Ryder—without running into the man. But she didn't even get that far. Before she could stop it, TJ's face wavered before her mind's eye, and slowly took shape. He was wearing the same expression he'd worn this morning. The one when they'd been discussing the case.

Magdalena.

Despite the man's protests, it was obvious the girl had gotten to him. Not that TJ would admit it. But how could she not? Magdalena was young, Mexican and painfully poor. That was probably it. From what Jade had told her, Reese confessed that his partner had led a particularly dismal childhood. Jade suspected that was why the two men got along so well. Given TJ's reaction, Jade was probably right.

Dammit, there she went again. Softening.

She couldn't afford to.

She could not let TJ Vásquez get to her. Not again.

He reminds me of your father.

Hell, she didn't need her mother to tell her that. She'd spent the past eight months trying to forget it, especially the past lonely six. This morning she managed to do it, too. Thank God her mother had shown up when she had. Who knows what would have happened?

You're a doctor, figure it out.

She rubbed the back of her neck one last time, then tossed her keys into the box of reference books on the passenger seat as she bailed out of the Jag. Moments later she was rounding the hood and hefting the cardboard tote into her arms, slamming the car door with the bottom of her right pump before she headed across the parking lot to the staff entrance. She recognized the hospital corpsman holding the glass door. He worked anesthesiology, as well.

"Thanks, Chief."

He popped a salute as she sailed through. "No problem, ma'am. Need a hand?"

"No, thanks. I've got it."

She shifted the bulky box in her arms as she struck out across the antiseptic tiles and promptly discovered that heels, even low ones, took some getting used to after two years of shipboard khaki uniforms and steel-toed boots. She made it down the first two corridors without incident. But the moment she rounded the third, she plowed into something—or rather, someone—and stumbled.

Her victim caught the opposite side of the box and held on tight as she regained her balance. "Sorry, my fault. I wasn't looking."

"Shelley?"

It had been three years, but there was no mistaking those green eyes and that gorgeous red hair, even bobbed up to her chin.

Talk about luck.

"Karin? Karin Scott?"

"The one and only." She regained her grip on the box and propped the edge onto the stainless-steel handicap railing running the length of the wall as Shelley turned to scan the corridor. "What are you doing on this coast?"

Shelley's gaze snapped back. "What?"

"Coast? As in Pacific? Last I heard you were stationed in D.C.—Bethesda."

"Oh, sorry. Yeah, I transferred. Listen, I've got surgery in a few, and I need to find someone before I head in. Can we talk later?" Shelley's gaze was already back down the hall, scanning.

"Sure thing. I just checked aboard, but I'm probably already in the system." She lifted her hand to rub the back of her neck, but ended up jerking it back down to steady the box of books as it tipped away from the wall. "Shelley, are you okay?"

That got her attention. Sort of.

"I'm fine. Why?"

The hell she was. Shelley's normally clear skin was flushed, and her pupils were huge. There was a slight sheen of perspiration at her temples, and Karin could swear her fingers were trembling. Karin deliberately lost her grip on the edge of the box, checking Shelley's reflexes as her hands shot out.

Yup, definitely shaking.

And Shelley was scanning again.

"Why don't you tell me who you're looking for, and I'll have them paged."

Shelley tore her gaze from the corridor. "*No.* I mean, that's okay. It wasn't that important. Look, why don't I stop by your office tomorrow? We can have lunch. Sorry, I really have to go." Shelley was halfway down the hall before Karin could get the box back in her arms, and then she stopped suddenly. "It's great seeing you again." She turned the corner and disappeared.

"Sure." Karin stood staring down the empty hall, stunned.

Who the hell was that?

Whoever that flighty woman was, it was not Shelley Ryder. Shifting the box in her arms again, she turned back toward her office, determined to track down Shelley's home number and go through her husband, if that's what it took to find out what was going on. Because something was.

She was sure of it.

Two turns later she was close enough to her office to anticipate the coming relief. The heck with Shelley's hands. Her own arms were beginning to shake from the bulk and weight of the box. One more turn and two steps... She gasped as someone yanked her into an open room, only to snap the door behind her. No, not a room, a storage closet.

A dark storage closet.

"What the—" Her heart slammed into her throat as a hand clapped over her mouth. She'd know that scent anywhere.

Leather.

TJ.

By the time he'd flicked on the overhead bulb and plucked the box from her arms, irritation had thoroughly replaced her panic. "Would you care to explain yourself?"

He blinked down at her, still holding the box.

"How many times have I told you not to lift anything?"

His confusion cleared, replaced by a frown. "Too many."

"Well, obviously not enough. Now put that damn thing down before I rip those stitches out of your chest myself—without an anesthetic."

The moment the box hit the floor, she wished it hadn't because silence assumed its place. Silence even more awkward than when he'd left this morning. God, why had she asked him to forget that kiss? As if they could. It was hanging between them. Taut. Brittle.

Break it.

How?

"Your, ah, wound. Does it feel okay? Do you need a prescription for pain?"

"There is no pain."

She doubted that, but she nodded.

Silence locked back in.

She cleared her throat and tried again. "What about infection? Any redness? Streaks?"

As if he'd cop to those, either.

He shook his head.

"You don't mind if I check, do you?" God, now she was really reaching. It hadn't even been twelve hours. She'd be lucky if the swelling surrounding the laceration had gone down.

Maybe he wouldn't know.

Evidently not, because he finally shrugged. But he didn't help.

With no choice left but to follow through, she unzipped the top to his blue coveralls, taking care to stop the tab well above his waist—just in case—then peeled the dark fabric away from his chest. "Could you lean a bit closer? You're casting a shadow on yourself."

He took a step. "Enough?"

Too much.

A set of extremely healthy pectorals filled her view. It took several deep breaths and a stern lecture to her hormones before she was able to focus her attention on the stitches and not the skin surrounding them. "Fine." She finished the exam in record time, stepping back to zip him up. "You look great."

They. *They* looked great.

She opened her mouth to correct herself, but it was too late. His lips had already quirked.

"Gracias."

Damn him. He'd obviously decided not to make this easy on her. Okay, so she deserved it after practically kicking him out of her apartment this morning.

Still.

Another ten seconds of silence and she'd had enough.

She folded her arms across her chest and glared into his dark steady gaze. "Well? I presume there's a reason you dragged me into the linen closet."

She winced as his brows shot up. Bad choice of words.

Words, hell. Bad choice of closets.

She blinked up at the metal shelves lining the walls, for the first time really noticing them. The hospital wasn't storing linen in here; they were storing medical supplies. The only kind of supplies that didn't require a lock and key in this man's Navy. Diaphragms, spermicides, lubricants and prophylactics. The tiny room held them all. She scanned the shelves to the right and left of TJ's shoulders, desperately trying to ignore the taunting labels.

It was futile.

They were everywhere.

His gaze zeroed in on a box somewhere behind her. A split second later, it widened in shock. "Those come in flavors?"

Uh-uh. She was not looking.

She did *not* want to know.

Somehow she managed to toss off a smile as she throttled the urge to turn. ''Nineteen, by my last count. Pretty soon we'll be giving your favorite ice-cream parlor a run for its money.''

His answering smile was very slow and very dangerous.

She ignored it. She wasn't going there, either.

Unfortunately, if she didn't make him get to the point, and quickly, she'd never get out of here. At least not with what was left of her sanity still intact. ''Well? You do have a reason, don't you?''

His smile faded. ''I do. Dr. Ryder. I must ask you not to speak to her. Not yet.''

''It's too late.'' She shrugged off his sudden frown. ''Look, I'm sorry, but I already bumped into her on the way in. Literally. And if you ask me, it's a good thing, too. Something is definitely up. I've never seen Shelley so out of it.''

His frown deepened. ''How so?''

''I'm not really sure. Distracted, upset. And I'll bet you her blood pressure was through the roof. She even offered to stop by my office and pick me up for lunch. Tomorrow.''

''Tomorrow is Saturday.''

''Exactly. Furthermore, Shelley said she was looking for someone. But that doesn't make sense, either, because she also said she was due in surgery soon. If that's the case, she should have been already setting up by then. The Shelley I know would have been. Or at the very least still going over the case, not wandering the halls on her own looking for someone. Why didn't she just page the person?''

''Who was she looking for?''

Karin shrugged. ''She wouldn't say.''

Once again, TJ fell silent. But this silence was different. He was staring at her, but he wasn't really looking at her. More like through her.

''What is it?''

He focused on her. But said nothing.

"Something's wrong. I can see it in your eyes." She took a deep breath and just said it. "Is Shelley using? Is that why she was so out of it? You think she was desperate for a fix?"

He shook his head.

"Then what is it?"

Still, he said nothing.

She grabbed his forearms beneath his rolled sleeves. "Tomás, please. She's a friend, or at least she was."

He stared at her hands, but remained mute.

"Dammit, if you don't tell me, I swear I'll go track Shelley down right now. I'll drag her out of surgery, if I have to."

His gaze narrowed. "You would not."

"I *would*. Now spill it."

He finally sighed. "The envelope."

"What envelope? Wait—the one the note came in?"

"*Sí.* The lab report, I received it this morning. When I saw you in the hallway with your box, I thought to stop you before you involved anyone else."

"Involved anyone else? What do... Oh, God—prints. You found prints on the envelope, didn't you?"

TJ nodded slowly. But there was more. She could see that in his eyes, as well. He knew who those prints belonged to and it wasn't Shelley Ryder.

"Doug Callahan."

Another nod, this one even more reluctant.

"Dammit, I knew it. I knew that bastard was trying to set me up. I'm going to kill that son of a—"

"Enough!" TJ seized her shoulders, shaking her firmly. "You will not speak to him and I will have your word on this, do you understand? You will not even visit his office. *Cariño,* I want your promise that you will avoid this man, and then I want you to go home."

"Then tell me the rest."

"I do not—"

"*Don't.* Don't you dare lie to me."

Because that was exactly what he was doing. It might be a lie of omission, but it was a lie just the same. She might not be able to see though his phony endearments, but she could see right through his worry. He was holding something back.

Something big.

"I mean it. If you want me to stay away from that sniveling excuse for a human being, you'd better give me a damn good reason. And you'd better give it to me now."

Again, that blasted stony silence.

This one lasted a full minute.

It didn't matter. They could stand here until midnight for all she cared. She was going to get to the bottom of this. Then again, maybe that wouldn't be necessary. She studied TJ's face. His gaze was fixed again, this time somewhere over her shoulder.

To her surprise, it finally shifted back to her and then he sighed.

Deeply.

"It concerns Magdalena. The overdose. It was not accidental."

What? She couldn't help it, she gasped. "Are you telling me the girl was murdered?"

To her horror, he nodded solemnly. "*Sí*, I am."

Chapter 7

TJ stared down at the shock in Karin's eyes—at the horror—and waited for his revelation to settle in. He should not have told her, for it would only strengthen her determination to remain in San Diego. But how could he not? He simply could not risk her confronting Señor Callahan. *Dios mío,* he could not even stay angry with this woman. He should be *furioso* with her after this morning. But of course he was not.

Whenever he got this close to Karin Scott, she got to him. Alas, it was happening even now as he stared into those deep, caring eyes. Though he readily admitted these lovely eyes had prompted his initial attraction, they soon paled, along with the rest of her physical charms, beneath her sharp mind and ready wit. That was when he knew he was ready to move forward with her.

But she was not.

So once again he would wait.

He took a deep breath and tried to clear his lungs. It did not help, indeed, only made it worse. The whisper of vanilla filling his lungs swirled through the rest of him. *Dios mío,* he must put this craving behind him. At least until he had solved this case. Perhaps then, they could begin anew.

Slowly this time. Surely.

Sí.

He touched her cheek, rousing her from her shock. But the horror had yet to fade from her gaze.

"You're sure it's murder?"

He breathed deeply and nodded. "As sure as I can be. The autopsy report came back this morning, as well. There were but two puncture wounds on the body and both were recent. One on the underside of her forearm, the antecubital vein, as you would expect. But the other, the other was in muscle. Her right deltoid."

"No way. Even a new user wouldn't try to vaccinate herself. That one was used to subdue her, wasn't it?"

"I believe so."

"Was there any other evidence to support a struggle? Ecchymosis?"

He nodded. "Slight. Her skin is dark, so the bruising did not show during the preliminary autopsy, but *sí,* there is enough to suggest struggle."

"Toxicology?"

He shook his head. "Other than the fentanyl, she was clean, her tissues included."

She closed her eyes a moment, then reopened them. "I'm with you. It definitely sounds like murder." A pause, then a deep breath. "You think Doug had something to do with it, don't you? That's why you don't want me to see him."

He grasped her shoulders again, this time gently. "No. As of now I know nothing but what I have already told you. Señor Callahan's involvement may be as simple as knowing who is behind the theft of the fentanyl. As of this morning, his prints have only been located on the envelope, not the note. I have a latent-print specialist examining the sheet of paper, but this will take time. Too many of your prints overlap the others."

Pink washed her ears. "Sorry."

"Do not be. You could not have known."

"But why would Doug send a note to me?"

"Perhaps because you are honest. He has firsthand knowledge of this, no? And there is the problem of his own credibility. It has been called into question once already. He may not have wished to risk being suspect again."

"So he throws it in my lap. Great." She closed her eyes, rubbing her shoulders as she sighed, only to wince as she arched her neck. She was hurting. Sore from sleeping on the sofa.

He knew he should have moved her back to her bed sooner. But he had waited until he could trust himself to lift her without letting his hands wander where they would. Where they wanted to wander now. He cupped her shoulders, determined to allow himself this much and no more.

Her eyes flew open.

He ignored the second, darker tide of pink washing her ears as he rubbed the knot of tension he found at the base of her neck. "Turn around, *Cariño.*"

She must hurt indeed, because she did.

"Thanks. I think I pulled a muscle last night on—"

"I know." Hoarse, deep. What had happened to his voice? He swallowed firmly as he slipped his thumbs into the collar of her shirt and began working the muscles.

His groin tightened as her soft groan filled the tiny room.

What was he doing?

Massaging, ha.

Again, without even planning to, he was trying to seduce her. He could feel his fingers wresting control from his resolve even as they slipped about the column of her slender neck to rub the hollow at the base of her throat. And then they slid lower, most definitely caressing now.

Soft. Warm.

He inhaled her scent slowly, deeply, savoring the faint vanilla as it filled his lungs. For several minutes he was content to let his fingers speak for his heart. But then it was not enough. Before he realized his intent, he had leaned down and pressed his lips into the curve of her neck.

Another sigh.

Just like that, he was ready. His groin hardened to the point of pain as she melted against his chest, the curve of her bottom nestling into his thighs. No longer content, his fingers now ached to leave her neck, to slide over her breasts and hips and tug that white skirt out of the way, to strip the silk from her shapely legs. Soon his entire body was rigid, aching. What he would have given for her next breath to be swirling into his lungs, along with her dizzying scent.

And then it was.

He could not have said for certain if he had turned her or if she had turned into him. Once more he did not care. He simply followed the hunger burning within his soul and inhaled her. Deeply.

His craving for her filled him, consumed him, searing all thought from his brain save one: Karin wanted him. Perhaps not forever, and certainly not enough to take home to her papa—but she wanted him here. Now.

Dios forgive him, he allowed need to conquer his resolve.

He gave his hands free rein then to seek out the curves he had caressed scant hours before. He tugged the tail of her shirt from her skirt and slipped his fingers beneath the cotton T-shirt clinging beneath, pushing both out of the way as he worked the clasp at her back. It snapped free, and he swallowed a groan as her breasts spilled from the lace cups into his waiting hands. He palmed them, swallowing her sigh, as well, as he savored their plump weight, then fingered the stiff tips.

How he wanted to taste.

But not here.

He should stop. They should stop.

Before he tore into the first box he laid his hands on and used whatever method of protection contained within.

Somehow he found the strength to tear his lips from hers and press his face into her neck. Air ripped through his lungs as he struggled for speech. *"Querida..."*

Her lips found his ear. He shuddered as her tongue drew liquid fire along the edge, erasing the very words from his mind. On his life, he could not remember a single one he had intended to speak. Not even *en español.*

Smoke filled his ear, clouding his mind further. "Yes, Tomás, *yes.*"

Sí, this was it. This was what he had intended to say.

No, this was not it.

They must end this. While they still could.

"Dr. Karin Scott, please dial seven-five-three-two."

They stiffened together, then tore apart, her ragged breathing filling the room as she jerked back another step only to slam into the shelving behind her. Seconds passed, each thickening the air to painful intensity as he held his hands and even his breath hostage as she stared at him.

And finally she blinked. "Oh, God, what was I *thinking?*"

His heart shattered.

He swept the fragments aside and allowed the air to bleed from his lungs as she ripped her gaze from his.

He deserved her mistrust.

He had earned it. If he had any hope at all of gaining it again, he must be patient. Only time would prove his intent. He clenched his fingers to keep from assisting as she thrust her T-shirt and shirt back into the waist of her skirt. Her movements slowed as she reached the brass on her belt. There, she carefully aligned the leading edge of the buckle to the placket of her uniform. Too carefully.

She was stalling.

She combed her fingers though her curls as she finished and finally raised her gaze. It stopped just shy of his, then shifted to focus behind his right shoulder. He knew already the request floundering amid that tortured sea of blue.

He forced himself to give it to her.

Again.

"Please accept my apology."

"Th-that's okay. I—"

"No, *Cariño,* it is not. I took advantage of the situation, of you, and I am sorry. It will not happen again."

For a moment he would have sworn she was disappointed.

But then it was gone, and relief assumed its place.

He turned to avoid it, spying the box of medical books she had carried into the hospital and bent to heft it into his arms.

"I'll get that."

She would not.

Perhaps he was willing to put this morning behind him. He might even be willing to force himself to do the same with what had happened between them just now, but this was all. He had seen her struggling with the box before he had decided to pull her into this closet, and he refused to let her do so again. Small consolation though it was, he would take it.

"We should go. You have a page to answer."

"But your stitches—"

The devil take his stitches!

He twisted the knob with more force than necessary and shoved the door open, effectively ending her argument as he stepped into the hall.

Empty.

At least one prayer had been answered in his favor this day.

There was nothing left for Karin to do except follow, and he gave thanks again as she did so. They walked in silence until they reached her office, the cleaning cart still idle outside the door where he had left it to seek her out. She reached for the knob, jerking her hand back as it turned on its own.

Señor Touch-My-Desk greeted them.

TJ forced himself not to stiffen, drawing on nearly a decade of practice to blend into the background, instead.

"Hey, I didn't miss you, after all."

Karin blinked. "Excuse me?"

"Eric Hunter? Officemate extraordinaire for the next 365 days?" His grin dimmed a bit. "You do remember meeting me, don't you?"

TJ used the corner of the box to nudge her from her stupor.

"Of course I remember. I'm just…surprised. Did we set that rain check for today?"

"Nope." The grin was back to full intensity. "But we must be on the same wavelength. Your page? That was me. Chief Randall said he met you on the way in, but you never showed up here. Anyway, step in and I'll lay it out."

"Lay what out?"

He swung the door wide. "Come on in and find out."

TJ hung back, hoping Dr. Hunter would forget his presence. Success flooded him as the man left him at the entrance to the office and left the door still open—only to be staunched by Hunter's undue, though somewhat discreet, interest in Karin's legs as she reached her desk and turned to lean against the edge.

"Okay, Eric, I give up. What's the big secret?"

"No secret—opportunity. I did promise to introduce you around, remember?"

"You did."

"Ever hear of Dr. Manning's infamous blowouts?"

She chuckled. "Who hasn't? But I've also heard they're by strict invite only."

TJ dug his fingers into the edge of the box as triumph spread across Hunter's face. He had worked undercover long enough to recognize that smile for what it truly was— slightly too wide and much too smooth— "Consider your invitation engraved."

Karin shook her head. "No way. I've also heard about

Manning's Rule. No first-year residents allowed—ever. You have to prove yourself worthy.''

This time, the man's gaze swept her curves openly. ''Oh, you're worthy, all right. Besides, I heard the incoming chief of staff is in town house-hunting. Rumor Control has it he'll make an appearance. You're not going to give the weasel a chance to elbow in and schmooze the new chief first, are you?''

The color bled from her face. ''You *know?*''

Hunter nodded and stepped closer to Karin. Again, a bit too much sympathy in his gaze for TJ's comfort. ''You know how it is. Things get around. I wouldn't worry, though. Most everyone knows Callahan for the ass he is. Manning was just in a tight spot. Your word against Doug's and all.'' TJ clenched his jaw as the man dared to tip up her chin, bringing a hint of color back to her cheeks as he oozed his charm down on her. ''I know who I'm siding with.''

''Thanks. I appreciate it.''

''Enough to let me drive?''

TJ coughed. Loudly.

Hunter whirled around, his smile evaporating as he spotted TJ at the door, box still in hand. ''Toss it on the desk, José. Then feel free to take a break. You can finish later.''

TJ schooled his tongue as he stepped into the office and lowered the box to Karin's desk, staring hard into her eyes as he pulled back, using his body to block the other man.

Tell him no.

He knew she had gotten his message, because she shook her head slightly.

He frowned.

''Well? What are you waiting for?''

TJ ignored the man. ''Will this be all, Dr. Scott?''

''Yes. Thank you, José.''

''*De nada.*'' He lifted her hand, brushing his lips across her skin as he fused his gaze to hers, this time pleading.

She held firm.

His heart raging, his mind racing and no choice but to cede, TJ forced himself to straighten and turn back to Hunter. He slowly crossed the room and locked his hand to the handle on the door. Please God, make her change her mind. Make her see he was right. She must not go.

"Hey, José."

He spun back.

"You forgot something." Hunter brandished the feather duster TJ had left on the man's desk earlier. TJ caught the duster as it was tossed to him, Hunter's stare still leveled on him as he spoke. "So, what do you say, Karin? Is it a date?"

"Sounds good to me."

TJ turned and shut the door firmly behind him, closing his eyes, as well, as he sealed the two within.

How?

How was he to keep her safe now?

A moment later he stiffened as vibrations drilled through his sock and into his left ankle. He scanned the corridor swiftly, ensuring it was empty before he dared to draw the beeper from his boot. He stared at the readout and frowned.

Joaquín.

Had his fellow agent uncovered something new? Evidence that would link Doug Callahan directly to Magdalena's death?

Perhaps.

Though he now suspected not.

Perhaps it was this same instinct that told him it was time to move Dr. Eric Hunter to the top of their list. Slipping the beeper back into his boot, he straightened as he assured himself this new suspicion had nothing to do with the desire he had seen burning in Hunter's eyes. Absolutely nothing.

He almost believed it.

He's here.

No, he isn't.

It didn't help. Karin groaned softly. She really had gone round the bend. She still couldn't believe she was standing in the middle of Captain Manning's living room arguing with herself. TJ Vásquez was *not* here.

So why do you feel him?

Because she was insane, that's why.

It didn't even make sense.

There was no way TJ could have infiltrated Dr. Manning's Annual Invite. Invite, hell. She succumbed to the urge to look yet again and scanned the rainbow of shimmering gowns and tailored suits milling and schmoozing about. This was no mere invite. It wasn't even a party. It ranked right up with her mother's Christmas ball. Just as packed, just as pretentious and just as stifling. Frankly she was surprised Manning had opted for civilian attire, instead of the Fleet's more formal and distinctive choker whites.

Then again, perhaps not.

With half his staff civilian, it would have ruined the effect.

Manning and his wife had, however, opted to abuse the time-honored naval tradition of hiring enlisted personnel under the table to cater and clean up the mess. She'd exchanged greetings with a former *Baddager* mess cook not more than five minutes after arriving. Word had obviously spread about the three-foot ship the chief had sculpted from ice for the *Baddager*'s last change-of-command ceremony, because there was an identical one anchored atop the buffet table at the far right of the room. She spotted the chief again as she made her way through the sea of bodies. He was restocking the prawns.

Unfortunately she'd yet to spot the spineless jellyfish she'd come to net. Doug Callahan.

Where was he?

Come to think of it, she hadn't caught so much as a glimpse of Shelley Ryder, either. Then again, she'd be lucky to find her own heels in this crush.

"There you are."

Karin spun around, nearly upending a tray of champagne onto the waiter behind her.

TJ?

No, but the man was Hispanic. He even looked startlingly similar to Tomás, right down to the thick flowing hair. But it wasn't him. The lookalike managed to right the tray of half-dozen flutes and save his tuxedo from a drenching as she stared.

She wished she could douse the fire searing her cheeks as easily. "Sorry."

"Quite all right, señorita. Champagne?"

"No, thank you."

The man drifted away, leaving Eric Hunter behind.

Lovely.

Except for her recent reprieve, she hadn't been able to get two feet between the two of them the entire hour they'd been here. Once again Hunter closed in, trapping her against the French doors leading to the patio beyond. "I thought you'd abandoned me."

No, but she was trying.

She forced a smile. "I had to use the ladies' room, Eric. Next time, I'll be sure to ask permission."

He didn't even have the grace to flush.

She frowned. "Look, it's been a long day. And frankly it's a bit too crowded in here for my taste."

Wrong thing to say.

He was already glancing through the doors behind her, at the patio beyond. "Why didn't you say so? Let's get some air."

And subject herself to his wandering hands in private?

Not a chance.

"Actually I'm probably too hungry to enjoy it." She shrugged, hoping it was sheepish enough. "I didn't stop for dinner on the way home, and except for a carton of six-month-old milk, my fridge is still bare from WestPac."

Liar.

But it worked, because he smiled. "Been there. Tell you

what, I'll grab a plate from the buffet to tide you over. Then we can hit the patio.''

''Thanks.''

She let out a sigh as Eric turned and weaved through the throng. She had to get out of here. She didn't know how many more of those easy smiles and that suffocating attention she could take. She had absolutely nothing to base it on, but something was not quite right about Eric Hunter, and it was more than his recent metamorphosis into stud on the make. Then again, it was probably her. Her sixth sense was definitely off tonight, because she could feel TJ again.

Dammit, he was not here.

She caved in to the temptation, anyway, and slowly scanned the room. Fifty glittering and tuxedoed bodies later she'd located four towering potted palms, ten doctors she knew, six nurses and at least that many wives, but no special agents—least of all one named Tomás Vásquez.

See, I told you he wasn't here.

But Doug Callahan was.

He was on the opposite side of the room, entering a set of French doors identical to the ones behind her. He'd obviously just arrived, because he was still tucking his invitation into the inner breast pocket of his tux. He raked a hand through his hair, combing the waves from his forehead, as he scanned the room.

Who was he looking for?

If it was a date, Karin could only hope the woman wouldn't take as long as she had to see the real man beneath that smooth blond exterior. Not that she'd wanted to see it. There was something about turning twenty-six and facing the realization that you were probably the last remaining virgin on the planet that made you overlook the little things in a man, including a man as obvious as Doug. Even from here she could see his gaze lighting on every woman in sight. The tighter the dress, the longer he lingered. He was paying particular attention to a shapely brunette in red when Eric coughed to her right.

She managed not to jump. "Great, I'm starved." She reached for the plate as she turned, but came up empty.

He smiled. "I was about to grab a few prawns when I had a better idea. Why don't we just cut out and go have dinner somewhere? I know this little restaurant next to the Hotel Del Coronado that serves great seafood."

Wonderful. Now what?

She was not leaving until she'd talked to Doug.

TJ's concern be damned, she had to know why Doug had sent that note—and what else he knew.

"You know what, I need to find a friend before we leave. We ran into each other today, and I think she's supposed to be here tonight." She scanned the room for effect as she turned back toward the entrance, hoping Doug hadn't moved. He hadn't, and his companion had finally joined him.

Shelley?

What the hell was Shelley Ryder doing wrapped around Doug Callahan's body? She was practically crawling into his tux. Where the devil was her husband? And what exactly did Doug's arm around her waist mean?

TJ. She had to call him.

If she got out of here now, she might be able to catch him at his apartment. If he wasn't out on a date tonight, too.

"Who?"

She was dimly aware of fingers snagging her chin, tugging her face around. She blinked up into Eric's gaze. "Wh-what?"

"Who are you looking for?"

She shook her head. "Uh…no one. Come to think of it, I don't think she's going to show." She found a smile and slid it firmly into place. "Did you mention dinner?"

He grinned. "I did. Let's just find Manning, do the face time, and then we can cut out."

"Sounds good. I'll grab my wrap while you locate—"

"Damn! What's *he* doing here?"

Her gaze snapped to Doug and Shelley's cozy cocoon before she could stop it. "I thought you said Dr. Manning invited him."

When Eric failed to respond, she glanced up at his face. But he wasn't looking at Doug or Shelley. He was staring at someone several feet to the right. She followed the fury in his gaze and blanched.

Oh, this time it was him, all right.

TJ might be using his own heart-stoppingly tailored tux and blasted tray of champagne to blend in with the rest of the waiters, but that was where the similarities ended. While the other men sported the distinctive clip-and-taper of a Navy cut, TJ had drawn his thick hair in a ponytail at his nape, making his stark brows and exotic cheeks stand out even more.

And his eyes.

God, even from thirty feet away she could see them clearly, feel his gaze. Feel him. No wonder her skin had been on fire from the second she'd stepped into the room.

At least she wasn't nuts.

"He's watching you."

She swung her gaze back to Eric's—and prayed. Please, God, don't let her blow this. "Doug?"

His frown deepened as he shook his head. "Not Callahan, the janitor. Who the hell put his name on the work list?"

"Who cares?"

"I do."

She managed a light laugh. "Why?"

"Because the man's got it bad for you. Karin, get a clue. You said yourself the man just happened to be around when you needed your things carried in today. Happened, like hell. He was looking for you, for an excuse. Why else was that cart sitting outside our door for damn near twenty minutes?"

This time her chuckle was real. It would have sounded a heck of a lot ruder, too, if she wasn't so worried about TJ's cover. "Eric, you said yourself the man's a janitor. I imagine the cart was there because he took a break from cleaning, not lurking."

"Wanna bet?"

Karin sucked in her breath, and it wasn't because of the woman in the bronze sheath who'd elbowed her as she and her date made their way to the French doors beyond.

"Eric."

His lips grazed her ear as he bent low. "Relax. I'm just proving my point."

No. What he was doing was touching her.

Intimately.

His fingers were gliding down the back of her neck, slipping beneath the two-inch shoulder straps on her cocktail dress. She inhaled again as his fingers left the straps and took a leisurely detour down her spine. Served her right for wearing the backless one.

"See?"

Somehow she managed to keep her gaze fused to the laughter lurking in his green eyes and not follow his stare across the room. "I'd rather not."

He chuckled. "I swear to God, the man is bristling. Oh, he's trying to hide it, but it's there. Honey, if looks could kill…"

"I get the picture." She couldn't stop her lips from tightening as his hand ambled lower. "That's enough. You've conducted your little experiment. Now stop."

"Ah, not before we verify the results, Doctor."

This time she didn't gasp.

She burned.

"If you don't get your hand off my ass this instant, *Doctor,* I'm going to remove it for you. Surgically."

His fingers slid up to toy with the strap at her shoulder.

"Thank you. Now if you don't mind, I'd like you to remove your hand altogether."

It disappeared, along with his smile.

"Sorry, Karin."

He didn't look sorry.

And she was well past amusement. She forced a smile, anyway. "No problem. I just don't happen to be into public displays of affection." Not to mention phony endearments.

Except from TJ.

Eric's easy grin slid back into place as he leaned close. "I'll make sure to try it again when we get someplace private. In fact, why don't we skip the restaurant altogether? I hear the Hotel Del has an excellent view of the Pacific from their suites—as well as room service."

"So I've heard." She stitched up her lips. "I've also heard you've been to the Del before—with the entire nursing staff."

Instead of collapsing, his grin swelled, nearly matching his distended ego. "You've been checking up on me, honey. I'll take that as a good sign." He closed in, his breath filling her ear. "But I've only had half, and always one at a time."

What a jerk.

She made a mental note to see if she could get the Navy to up the date for his annual HIV test.

"Perdóneme."

They stiffened together—and turned together.

TJ extended the tray toward her and smiled.

Eric scowled. "No, thanks, we're leaving. Why don't you try Captain Jacob's daughter? I hear she's got it big for—"

"Dr. Hunter, Dr. Scott, glad you could make it."

She and Eric turned again, and this time TJ joined them.

Karin nodded. "Dr. Manning. I appreciate the invitation."

"My pleasure." Manning clipped a flute from TJ's tray. "Glad to hear you're settling in to your new office. Next year you'll have to drag Westin along."

She nearly groaned out loud. She'd suspected her step-

father and his position at La Jolla was Manning's major
source of faith in her side of last year's debacle with Doug.
The gleam in his sharp brown eyes confirmed it. Too bad—
she wasn't giving up the professional distance she'd managed to place between her and her stepfather that easily.

"I'll be sure to mention it, sir."

"Excellent. And perhaps you'll forgive me for stealing
your escort for a moment? There's a case I need to fill him
in on."

Eric, she gave up freely, a genuine smile along with him.
"Go right ahead. I'll just mingle."

They left.

"Have you ignored my wishes and spoken to him?"

She refused to look at TJ. But she didn't ignore the question. "No. But I did see something. He and Shelley—"

"I know."

"What?" She was staring at the pearl strands of an older
woman's choker six feet away, desperately trying not to
feel like an informant in a cheap spy movie. "You know?"

"*Sí.*" A sigh. Dulled, but it still cut. "*Cariño,* I told you
I did not need you here. At the time of your invitation and
on your answering machine."

She winced. That would be the message she'd hung up
on.

"You did not listen to it, did you?"

This time, she did ignore the question.

"*Querida,* what am I to do with you?"

She welded her gaze to the gold clasp securing the
woman's pearls to the base of her neck. "Me? What about
Doug? He's the one you need to be worrying about and
skulking around."

His soft chuckle washed over her. "Señor Callahan no
longer requires my skulk. He is leaving."

"But he just got here."

"No, do not turn. And, yes, Dr. Ryder appears to be
leaving with him."

"No way." Any second now, the owner of that pearl

choker was going to turn and have her arrested for plotting a jewel heist. "Shouldn't you be following them or something?"

"Or something." Another soft chuckle. "Someone already is."

"Oh."

"Now turn and face me, so I may feed you and Señor Hunter's paranoia at the same time."

"You *know?*"

This time there was no chuckle, but she swore she saw him frown. "I know." And when she turned, she could see it.

Despite it, she sucked in her breath.

Damn, he looked good.

TJ flicked his smoldering gaze across the room. "You dislike this Dr. Manning, no?"

Apparently nothing had gotten by him tonight. She nodded. "Who doesn't?"

"Your *date.*"

The emphasis left no doubt as to TJ's feelings toward that man, as well. She shrugged. "I'd be surprised if Manning doesn't turn Eric's stomach, too."

"I would."

She frowned. "You don't understand. We have to get along with Manning. Not only is he our boss, we can't get certified without his approval."

"So you subject yourself to his whims?" TJ stared at her intently. Looking for what, she had no idea.

But then she did.

Dammit, he knew why she was here.

Still, she felt the heat searing her ears moments before his gaze settled on them. "I'm sorry about that. Eric was trying to prove a point. And in light of your real job, I thought it was best to play along."

"You played well...but you did not like it."

It wasn't a question.

Eric was right. TJ had been watching. Intently.

Just as he was now.

She shook her head. "No, I didn't."

He simply nodded.

Those eyes.

He was kissing her again. Right here in the middle of a hundred murmuring mingling people. It didn't even matter that he was doing it for Eric and God knew who else's benefit. All that mattered was that TJ was kissing her. Slowly. His gaze slid down her cheeks, grazed the lobe of her ear, then smoldered a path down her throat. It stopped at the hollow, lingered, then slipped to the side, caressing her pulse, flaring as the throbbing increased. And then it slid lower.

She couldn't breathe.

For the life of her, she couldn't remember how.

A room full of doctors, and she was going to suffocate— or beg for mouth-to-mouth. His. Why wouldn't he turn away? He had to look somewhere else. Anywhere.

His gaze seared back to hers. "Champagne?"

Why? She was already drunk.

On those eyes.

She didn't see the flute until he'd pressed it into her fingers, and then all she could do was feel. Cold, smooth.

But she couldn't quite seem to grasp it.

"Close your hand, *querida.*"

She could hear the smile in his voice, and then she saw it. The curve spread across his lips, burning straight through her, reigniting the desire he'd fanned twice today already. She wanted him. Right now.

Right here.

"Please." The whisper bled out before she could stop it. She swallowed her pride and begged softly, "Please don't do this, Tomás. Not here. I can't—"

He stiffened.

His name. Oh, God, she'd used his name. But surely no one had noticed? It didn't matter. The spell was broken.

He stepped back into the crush, looked ready to voice the apology already forming in his eyes, but blanched, instead.

"Madre de Dios."

"What?"

His hand shot up, closing over the one she was using to hold the flute. "Do not turn, *Cariño*. Not now. Please." A second later his hand was gone. And he was breathing again, but the color still hadn't returned to his cheeks.

"What's wrong?"

His gaze fused to hers. The apology long gone, shattered, horror erected in its place.

"What is it?"

He shook his head slowly. "Not what—who. To your left. A man. Older, about six foot. Perhaps fifteen feet away and standing next to your escort. You know him?"

She turned slowly, seeking out the man as smoothly as she could manage, nodding when she found him. Black hair with heavy silvering at the temples and sprinkled generously throughout, early sixties. Still well muscled and striking. Though he was wearing a tuxedo, his command photo had just gone up on the quarterdeck to the hospital that afternoon. "That's Admiral Banks. He's the new chief of staff. Why?"

She turned back to TJ, suppressing the urge to check his pulse and his brow. He was so very pale.

She felt more than heard his swallow.

"Cariño, that man is my father."

Chapter 8

"Your father?"

TJ nodded, understanding the shock and confusion exploding within Karin's deep blue eyes—for the blast was still rocking through him, as well.

"Sí." It was he.

TJ had stared at the man's photograph often enough these past eight years—and of course, her assigning him the correct name proved it.

"But...I don't understand."

Neither did he. He should have been warned.

Alas, he would have been, had he bothered to check in. Now that he thought about it, he had not placed a call to Manuel in Washington since he had met Karin. He had thought himself beyond the need to watch this man. To wonder.

To know.

"Does your—he—know you're here underc—"

TJ shook his head. "No, and perhaps I should warn you. He does not know me at all."

"What? How can he not—"

"Karin!"

She tore her gaze from his. "Oh, no. Eric."

TJ tightened his fingers about the tray of champagne as Hunter waved her to his side like a pet. "You must go."

Her twin seas of blue swept back, still churning, still uncertain. "I...okay. I'll go get my face time. You get the hell out of here. Tell them you're ill. Stomach upset. I'll verify it if I need to. I'll call you when I get home, all right?"

Sí. His work here was done. He had already passed his mark off to Joaquín. It was best not to risk compromising his cover by remaining. He nodded and was about to do what Karin suggested when Hunter waved his hand again, this time with even less finesse. The snap of fingers that followed ricocheted down his spine for more reason than he would care to admit.

This command was most definitely his.

He drew a deep breath as he shifted the tray to his left hand, furious at the sudden quake in his right that caused the remaining trio of flutes to spark and chime against one another. Doubt, heavy with dread, ripened inside him, harvesting the sweat from his glands and drawing it down his back in cold rivulets. It pooled at his waist, soaking the shirt beneath his tuxedo.

Dios forgive him, he could not do this.

Enough. *Move.*

Karin had already reached the men and turned back.

Somehow he found the clarity of thought to put one foot before the next as he focused on her, following her steady soothing gaze as obediently as a lamb to the slaughter. A third of the way, he received a brief reprieve in the form of a silver-coiffed woman who stopped him to take one of the flutes from his tray, and then he was forced to continue.

Karin.

His *Cariño.*

He focused on her and only her until all he could see

was her deep-blue gaze, her soft smile. If the Virgin Mother smiled upon him as sweetly, he might just lose the remaining flutes before he reached the man who had fathered him so carelessly. Though he was not proud of his desire to run, it was wiser than staying here and damaging his cover—and his case—beyond repair.

In the end the Virgin did not smile.

He reached Karin's side with two flutes intact, then immediately lost one to Dr. Manning. No choice but to turn and face his father, TJ steeled his nerves and his grip and did so, for the first time looking into deep-set eyes nearly as blue as Karin's. But these eyes were different. These eyes held absolutely…nothing.

No smile, no warmth, no joy.

Not one shred of recognition.

He might well resemble the potted palm towering beside him for all the notice he received from his so-called father. The pain cut to the bone as he stared, for this man was most definitely his relation. The near-matching height, the thick hair—though now more silver than black—the straight brows, the same long full dark lashes. *Sí*, the similarities he had long denied in photographs were all here in person, though thankfully not obvious enough to overcome the obscuring hurdle of race.

At least not with these men.

With *him*.

Cease. This was good. No, this was better than good. This was precisely what he needed.

Why, then, did he feel so damnably empty?

His father clipped the final flute of champagne from the tray and turned to Eric Hunter. Just like that.

Not so much as a nod.

"Thank you, José."

Karin.

She was trying to tell him something. But what?

Leave. Go. Get out of here.

Sí, that was it.

He did not know how he managed to obey, but he did. Perhaps it was the thread of something he could not quite place in her eyes just before he turned, he would never be sure. All he knew for certain was that it—she—gave him the strength to turn and leave his father behind.

As quickly and cleanly as the man had left him.

Karin wrenched open the door to her apartment and practically dove inside. She would have slammed the door, but fear held her back. Fear that Eric Hunter, or rather Eric-the-Hunter, would hear the thud echoing all the way down at the elevator where she'd managed to finally escape his clutches. She settled for throwing both bolts just to hear them clunk, then slid the chain for good measure before slumping against the door.

"That man is a pig."

"*Sí.*"

She jerked away from the door and stared into the darkness. "Tomás?"

His chuckle filled the dark—at least, she thought it was his. She'd never heard quite that note in his laugh, and it was nowhere near amusement. It was bitter. Angry.

Hurt.

She crossed the short entryway, blinking rapidly as she entered the main room, wishing her eyes would hurry up and adjust to the dark.

There, between the windows. Sitting on the carpet with his back to the wall.

She dumped her purse on the breakfast bar, slipped out of her heels and crossed the remainder of the room. It was him all right. The moon wasn't full, but there was enough light streaming through the sheers for her to be certain. TJ had changed from his tux to his familiar black T-shirt, boots and jeans. She wasn't sure if it was his clothes or the fact that his hair was loose, partially obscuring his hardened features, but the civilized air that had always managed to cling to him despite his looks had thoroughly evaporated.

This man was one hundred percent dangerous.

And it didn't have a thing to do with the darkness.

She knelt beside his extended leg and laid her hand on his bent knee. "Tomás, are you okay?"

Another laugh, this one shorter, even more curt. "Not Tomás. TJ, Tijuana Jones. Call me *bastardo* for all I care. Just do not call me Tomás." He spat the name, then tipped his head back against the wall, staring blindly into the vaulted ceiling.

His father.

TJ was taking this worse than she'd feared.

Dammit, she should have forced Eric to take her home sooner. Except she hadn't wanted to leave so soon after verifying TJ's sudden illness to the man-in-charge. Lord knew, she'd had enough on her hands dealing with Eric's rising ardor without arousing his suspicions, as well.

"Do you want to talk about it?"

"I do not."

Okay.

Not that she blamed him. She had a bit of experience in the lousy-father department herself. But at least she hadn't had to face him, not since the divorce, anyway. A distraction. That was what she needed. Something to focus his mind on while she figured out a way to get him to discuss what was really on it.

She was working on something when he sighed.

"My apologies, *querida*. I had no right to pick the lock to your apartment and violate your space. I will leave."

"No." She tightened her grip on his knee and held him there. If he left, he'd get back on that damned bike of his. She hadn't seen it parked on her way in, but it had to be around.

What if he totaled it?

What if the next time she saw him, it was to identify his body? Even before the image formed in her mind, she knew there was no way she was letting him back on that thing.

Not in this mood. No matter what.

She took a deep breath. "You haven't said what happened with Doug and Shelley."

He covered her hand with his and sighed. "It will not work. I should not have come. I will leave you to your space and go to find mine."

"Tomás—"

His hand flinched.

And she realized why. It was the connection. She hadn't realized it when she walked in, but now that she thought about it, it was as clear as a liter of IV fluid. Admiral *Thomas* Banks. Whether or not the man knew he had a namesake was irrelevant. His son knew.

She also knew it was the first hurdle.

Her hand still on his knee, she scooted around until she was sitting beside him, her back joining his at the wall. Once settled, she turned her hand in his until their fingers were linked, sucking in her breath at how hard his grip had become.

It strengthened her own resolve. He was not leaving.

She squeezed his hand just as firmly. "Tomás, I understand what you're feeling."

That curt laugh again. "You do not."

"Yes, I do."

"*Cariño,* I mean no disrespect, but you cannot."

She took a deep breath, but he cut her off before she could suck up her own pride and start in again.

"How can you, who lives in this…" He jerked his chin to the couch, then the entertainment unit across the room. "How can you drive the car you do, wear that watch you do, have the parents you have and dare to tell me you know how I feel? You do not. When I was eight years old, I had yet to see my first running faucet. I was nine before I knew it could contain water as hot as the cold. I was…" He broke off with a growl and fell silent.

She waited.

This wasn't about the money. He might want it to be, but she was smarter than that. His pain went deeper than that. But when he refused to say anything, she knew she was going to have to prod. If TJ wasn't ready to face his father, he might start somewhere else. "Tell me about your mother. What was she like?"

"I do not remember."

Yes, he did.

She knew because he closed his eyes and brought his free hand up to cover them. The memories were there, all right. No doubt images, too. But how awful must they be for him to want to forget them, and yet be unable to?

She brought her free hand to his face, as well, smoothed the dark strands of hair from his face, stroked the side of his taut jaw. "Please, Tomás, just start at the beginning. Did your mother love your father? Was she devastated?"

His jaw locked beneath her fingers, but then it eased. He shook his head and sighed. Deeply. "No. The answer to both your questions is a most definite no. *Mi madre no amó a mi padre.* I do not think she even liked him. I know she did not like herself...or me."

She couldn't help it, she inhaled sharply.

His grip grew so tight she nearly lost the circulation in her hand. "I see you are shocked. Perhaps even horrified, no? You think to help me, do you? You think to wash this wound as you washed my other and stitch me whole again? You think to bleach my soul as white as you have bleached this room? You cannot. *Cariño,* I cannot be cleaned because I have never *been* clean." He released her hand and vaulted to his feet before she could work the blood back in.

"Tomás, don't go. Please."

He whirled around, glaring down at her.

Her eyes had finally adjusted to the silvery moonlight, and she could make out his features clearly enough. Certainly the agony—and definitely the rage. Then he was moving, pacing.

Any moment he would bolt.

"You are repulsed by my reputation, *sí?*"

"I don't think—"

"Answer me!"

She flinched, and considered denying it. But what would be the point? She swallowed softly. "Yes."

"Finally, the truth. I thank you. And now, I will give you the truth in return. I will give you the answer to the one question you did not ask me that day in the courtyard of my home, but wanted to ask."

"I don't—" But she did, and he knew it.

"*Sí.* Now ask."

Oh, God, she couldn't. She couldn't just say it.

But he was right, she wanted to know. Hell, lately, she'd needed to. Ever since he'd kissed her in her bedroom, the question had been burning inside her brain and on her tongue. Torturing her. But, dammit, she couldn't just ask.

What if the answer was worse than she feared?

"Please, Tomás, don't do this."

"Ask me."

She took a deep breath and stared at her fingers, now clamped together in her lap. "How m-many?"

"I do not know."

She closed her eyes and bowed her head as the truth in his whisper burned through her. Within seconds the fire in her heart had ignited her lungs. Each breath seared in deep, then out. She tried to prevent it from spreading, but why? What would be the point in even trying to douse it? How could she ever heal from this? He really was her father all over again.

Only worse.

The silence between them thickened.

But he didn't leave. So finally she opened her eyes.

He spread his hands wide and shrugged. "So you see? You were right to run from me. And I had no right to chase after you. The shame is mine, and mine alone. When this case is done, I swear to you, I shall right it. I shall depart from your life, and on my honor, I shall not return."

Shame?

She blinked. Was it possible? Maybe he wasn't like her philandering father, after all. Not exactly, anyway. And if the self-loathing she'd just heard in his voice was real, he might not be like her father in the way that really counted. Still, it was a fairly slim *maybe*. And even if that *maybe* existed, she would have to know the rest.

"Why?"

He stiffened.

Before he could use his anger to force her to become as disgusted with him as he was with himself—and that was what he was trying to do—she qualified it. "Not why you can't remember, not even why so many women. Why did you do it? Especially when you really didn't want to."

His laugh was short, ugly. "Oh, but I did, *Cariño*. And I enjoyed it. I enjoyed them. Every one of them."

"No, you didn't." She came to her feet slowly, advancing on him just as slowly, until she'd trapped him between the coffee table and the end of the couch.

And she had trapped him.

The moon might not be full, but this close there was more than enough light for her to see what was really burning in those dark-brown eyes. Just as he hadn't been able to hide his desire from her these past two days, he could no longer hide his fear. Nor the tears.

She reached up and gently stroked one side of his face, then the other, smoothing away the glistening paths his silent tears had made, drying them. "Tomás, if you enjoyed it, you would have remembered them."

His eyes closed as he sank to the couch and bowed his head. "*Sí*. You speak the truth."

She knelt before him, encouraged when he allowed her to take his hands in hers. "Then tell me why."

He inhaled deeply and then exhaled just as deeply. "Because I had been abandoned…again." He raised his head and stared at her, the ghost of a smile twisting at the edges of his lips. "No, I did not come to this realization on my own."

"Reese."

He nodded. "Reese."

Reese had told her eight months before to ask TJ what had driven him all those years ago. Reese had even warned her she'd probably have to pin the man to the wall to get it out of him. But he'd also told her TJ was worth it.

He was right.

"What happened?"

"My friend laid my Glock on the table and invited me to blow my brains out."

"What?"

TJ actually laughed.

The first real sound free of pain since she'd walked in. Still. "Tell me you're kidding."

"I am not."

"I take it this charming advice had something to do with Reese Garrick's psychoanalysis?"

"It did."

She squeezed his hands. "And I'm waiting."

"My father had died."

His what? "But I just met—"

He shook his head. "Not Thomas Banks. I have heard an accident of birth does not a father make. In my life this was most true. Thomas Banks may have unwittingly left his seed in my mother, but he was not my father. Just as she who bore me was not my mother. Neither wanted me. But Thomas had decided to abort me. My mother did not argue. She was a maid in his employ when he was stationed at your own hospital thirty-two years ago."

"But you're here."

He nodded. "It would seem so, no? My mother squandered the money he gave her for the abortion, and since there were no free clinics, she went home." He shrugged. "But my grandfather threw her out, as well, because my sire was a gringo."

Running water.

"You were raised on the streets."

"I was."

Magdalena. Prostitution.

Did she dare? Could she even ask it?

"Wh-what happened to your mother?"

"Legally dead when I was eight. Spiritually?" He sighed. "Years before. I survived perhaps a year alone before I picked the wrong pocket. The wallet was empty, but for the badge."

"Your father."

He smiled. "In the end, it was my largest theft, for somehow with it, I managed to steal a life. Mine. Antonio was a DEA agent working a case south of the border with *la policía mexicana*. When he returned north, he brought me with him."

Thank you, Antonio, wherever you are.

A second later her heart clenched, because she knew exactly where Antonio was. *I had been abandoned again.*

TJ nodded. "*Sí*, he is dead. He was killed in the line of duty five days after I completed my probationary period with the DEA."

Tijuana Jones.

"That's when it happened, isn't it? When you gained your...reputation?"

TJ fell silent, unable to continue as he smoothed his fingers over Karin's hands. What he would have given to be able to smooth the pain from her whisper, also. Why he did not hear disgust, he did not know. But he was grateful.

He had hoped to hurt her earlier.

Perhaps because he was hurting.

But again she seemed to take the hurt and soothe it from him. He had told himself when he found his hands picking the lock on the door to her apartment that he was here for the case. To see if she had learned anything that would help him solve Magdalena's murder and explain the other two deaths.

He was not.

He was here for this.

He was here for these soft hands linked to his. For these gentle fingers she had used to smooth away his salt and his shame. He was here for these clear blue eyes shining softly in the moonlight. *Sí*, he was here for absolution. *Dios* knew, he did not deserve it. But how he wanted it. From this woman most of all.

Tijuana Jones. He had welcomed the name. At first, when it was whispered in envy, then more when it turned to a curse. While he had never risked the lives of his fellow agents, he had risked his. Unconscionably. For nearly two years.

Until Reese.

A year younger in time, but a hundred older in life, his friend had already come to terms with his own father—and one night he had had enough and had forced him to do the same. *Sí*, Reese had shown up at his house, laid his pistol on the table and dared him to take his life. But then he had walked to the door and turned. From there, his friend had said his piece. If Reese was wrong, and dying was not what he truly wanted, perhaps he should strive to do the opposite.

On that day his friend had also dared him to live.

He squeezed her hands to find the strength to continue. "That motorcycle you detest so much—"

Karin shook her head. "I don't—"

He cupped her cheek. "We are being honest, no?"

A pause.

And then, "Yes."

He smiled as he brushed the curls from her ear, marveling when she did not flinch. "That motorcycle you detest came from him. My father, my mentor—whatever name the world chooses to assign him. Three days before he died, he had made the gift, though it needed much, much work."

His confession found reward in her soft smile. "You put the gun away and decided to live."

"I did. It was difficult at first." But Reese had helped him through. "No women, no alcohol and only as much risk as the job required—not one bit more. I started with the bike. It was a year before I was satisfied.''

''How long did learning to cook take?''

He laughed softly and nodded. ''The bulk of it? Perhaps two years. Though I have continued to learn these last three, as well.''

''And the…the…''

He skimmed his thumb across her bottom lip. ''The women?''

She nodded, but could not quite meet his eyes.

''None.''

She did then. ''In six years?''

TJ chuckled. ''It has not been so difficult.'' At least not until these past eight months. Since he had met her.

At three years, he had decided. The next woman would be one for whom he cared. She would hold more than physical desire. It had taken three years to find this woman kneeling before him.

Simply ask. Better to know, *sí?* than to spend another eight months wondering, hoping. Craving.

He stroked her cheek, savoring the silk beneath his fingers. ''*Querida,* do you think… Could you possibly…''

Ay, he could not ask. He should not. He did not deserve—

''Will I have sex with you?''

His fingers froze. Indeed, his heart froze.

To put it so.

But he swallowed. *''Sí.''*

Her gaze withdrew and found the wall behind him. There, it lingered. ''I honestly don't know. I want…I mean, what I'm trying to say is…there's something you should…'' She ground out a sigh and closed her eyes.

A thousand suns rose and then set as he waited.

He was about to stand, to move away, to try to spare both of them this humiliation, when she opened her eyes and stared straight into his.

''Tomás, I'm a virgin.''

He blinked.

Surely he had not—

"You heard right."

His hand fell to his lap, deadened from the shock still exploding within. "But…you are a doctor. You have lived twenty-seven years. And you…you…"

"Are a virgin."

Somehow he managed to swallow his astonishment and quickly set about searching for the voice he had somehow lost. When he finally found it, it was hoarse with barely enough strength to use. "How?"

She laughed. But it was not humor that drove the sound. She shrugged. "The how's kind of obvious, don't you think? Especially in light of your own recent past. I simply didn't."

"Why?"

Abruptly she stood. A moment later she was moving.

TJ caught the silken expanse of her back in the moonlight as she retreated across the apartment. He suspected her soul now felt as naked as that soft flesh. He was certain when she reached the breakfast counter and fingered the light switch on the wall beside it.

In the end she did not flick it on.

She turned around, instead.

He could no longer see her face. She was too far away, the room too dim. Perhaps it was for the best. For if he could not see hers, then she would not be able to see his—and that was perhaps what she needed. He waited, determined to give her the same gift she had given him, in whatever form she wished to receive it.

"You told me I didn't know how you felt. You were wrong. While it's true I didn't want for food or toys when I was young, I did yearn for a father. At least one who loved me for me, and not what he could take from me. My innocence."

He sucked in his breath and vaulted to his feet.

"No! It's not that." She stretched out her hand, and only when she used it to bid him to sit was he able to sink down to the couch again. "I'm sorry if I gave you the wrong impression. My father never touched me, but he took my innocence all the same. I was six the first time I caught on. We were at the zoo. A father-daughter date, my parents used to call it. Except most dates involved two people, and there always seemed to be three on mine. The beach, the zoo, the park, it didn't matter. Sometimes it was the same woman, sometimes not. Sometimes he actually dropped me off with another friend of his to play. Those were the easiest and the hardest. But the result was always the same. *Don't tell Mommy*. It was our secret. No one else must ever know."

Madre de Dios, he would kill this man anyway.

She fell silent again, and this time he was driven to break it.

"How long did your father use you as his cover, *querida?*" He did not need to see her bitter smile to know it was there.

He could feel it.

"His cover. That's an interesting way to put it. But I suppose it fits." He did see the shrug. Again, not so careless as she would have him believe. "They divorced when I was ten."

"And you never told."

"Nope."

"Why?"

"What would be the point? What would it solve? Hell, I was relieved to see him go. Besides, as soon as they divorced I was more hindrance than help, anyway. Maybe he just didn't know how to talk to me without his eyes on someone else. At any rate, the dates stopped, he moved away, and I never looked back."

Ah, but she did. He would wager she looked back often.

And since she had met him—because of him—he now saw, she was forced to look even more so.

She would never trust him.

How could she? Why should she?

He had cast his lot years before they had even met. No amount of waiting would change this. A woman who waited twenty-seven years for her white knight did not trade that dream for a devil with a soul as black as sin itself.

He could not even ask.

He stood—and tried to ignore the knife to his heart as she stepped back. "I should be off."

"Wh-where are you going?"

Perhaps because they had been so brutally frank this night, he felt compelled to speak the truth again. Where would he go? He shrugged. "I do not know."

"Don't. I mean, I really don't feel like being alone tonight. You could take the couch again…or the bed."

He closed his eyes as the knife stabbed deeper. "I would prefer—"

"Please."

He drew down on his breath as it stabbed the whole way through. Why she wanted him here, he did not know. But she did truly seem to desire—perhaps even need—a companion. "I will stay. On the couch."

She nodded quickly and turned to her room. He waited until she returned with the blanket and pillow he had used before. She crossed the room, her hands not quite steady as she held them out. He reached for the bedding, cursing himself as their fingers brushed.

He truly was a bastard, for the desire still raged.

"Do you need anything else? Coffee or—"

"Querida?"

"Yes?"

"Go to bed."

Before sanity returned and he changed his mind.

"Okay." A stiff nod. "Good night, then."

Though the night promised to be anything but, he nodded. *"Buenas noches, Cariño."* He stacked the blanket and the pillow on the couch, waiting until she returned to her room, flinching as the door closed softly, but firmly. Then he lowered himself to the cushions of the couch in order to remove first one boot, then the other, dumping both onto the floor.

There he sat.

For how long, he knew not.

Once again, alone in the dark, his hopes and his dreams lying shattered about his feet, wondering how he would ever find the strength to rise again.

Chapter 9

He was gone.

Karin knew it when she opened her eyes and stared at the ceiling fan suspended above her bed. The blades were slowly sweeping the air, sending a soft breeze down to her bare midriff. Why she'd worn the damn outfit, she didn't know.

Or maybe she did.

Either way, it didn't matter. Her watch read eight forty-five.

TJ was gone.

Hell, he'd probably slipped out as soon as he was sure she'd fallen asleep. That couldn't have been much after two in the morning, because at one-thirty she was still awake, lingering in Neverland when he'd quietly opened the door to her room. He hadn't crossed the threshold. Just stood there, staring.

Watching.

For how long, she wasn't certain.

Eventually she'd heard his sigh, soft and deep, and then

he'd closed the door and left her alone again. Except, for the first time in her life, she wasn't sure she wanted to be alone.

Dammit, it wasn't fair.

Fair, hell. It didn't make sense.

She hadn't even slept with the man.

So why was she lying here wondering when he was going to walk out of her life just the same?

Karin sighed and pulled the twist of covers binding her waist and legs and tossed it over the brass spindles at the foot of the bed as she rose. It was time to face the day— even if she didn't have a built-in excuse to see him. On leave or not, she couldn't show up at the hospital on a Saturday morning without being on call. Not with having just checked in. Besides, TJ wouldn't be around today, anyway, because he wasn't working.

She raked her fingers through the tangles on her head and shoved open the door to her room—and promptly froze.

TJ.

No, Tomás. He wasn't TJ anymore. He knew it, too. Tijuana Jones was his penance. His reminder.

And still, his escape.

He was standing with his gorgeous back to her, bared to the waist on the far side of the kitchen, between the refrigerator and the stove. Chopping something on the cutting board from the sound of it. Intently.

She smiled.

Cooking. It probably worked better than a cold shower. Mainly because it required concentration—at least it did from her. No doubt she'd be taking it up herself soon enough.

But in the meantime, "Morning."

He turned around, that toe-curling sexy smile of his already spreading across his lips.

A good sign.

"*Buenos días, Cariño*. I hope you are hungry."

"Starved."

"Then perhaps you will retrieve the cream?"

That was when she noticed the coffeepot was on. The first drops splashed into the glass vat as she rounded the counter. But as she opened the fridge, the intimacy of the moment hit her. Especially when Tomás closed up behind, reaching into the door to snag a bottle of hot sauce. His arm burned her waist as he pulled it back.

"Perdóneme."

"It's okay." All right—where the hell was her voice this morning? And who'd wedged that stupid frog into its place?

Against her will, her gaze slid over his chest. She told herself she was merely checking his stitches. The excuse would have worked, too, if she hadn't assessed them in three seconds flat and then moved on to the rest of those wonderfully sculpted muscles as he set the hot sauce on the counter. She dug her fingernails into her palms as her gaze reached the waist of those dark jeans, relieved when he turned to resume his chopping.

She couldn't do this.

She couldn't stand this close to that naked body and just eat. What was it about this man? Flesh and bone. That's all Tomás Vásquez was, dammit. A body. A blasted collection of cells forming muscle, bone and skin. But, Lordy, what a collection it was. And this particular combination had been honed to perfection.

Every single dusky inch.

She stared at his biceps, transfixed as he scraped the onions, peppers and whatever else was on that chopping board into the waiting skillet. A cloud of steam seared the air as they hit the cast iron, causing her to jump.

"Querida?"

Her gaze flew to his as she moistened her suddenly parched lips. "Yes?"

It was his turn to stare. "The cream." Somehow the frog had leapt from her throat to his. His hand came up and she swore he was about to reach for her, when something singed her nose.

Smoke.

The skillet.

TJ swung back to the stove, and she took advantage of the distraction, practically diving into the overflowing refrigerator. She came up with a carton of cream—who cared which one—and abandoned the kitchen altogether, anchoring herself firmly to the other side of the counter.

Folders.

They were stacked on the counter next to his canvas bag. A spiral notebook lay beside them, the top page filled with bold even scrawl. She couldn't read a word of it. Evidently TJ still thought in his native tongue. "How's it going?"

He glanced over his shoulder, obviously confused.

"The case?"

"Ah." He shook his head. "Not so good. A moment, *por favor.*" He turned back to the stove and scraped the vegetables onto an empty plate, then poured the bowl of beaten eggs into the skillet. A couple more scrapes of the spatula and they were finished and resting beside the vegetables. He laid them on the counter in front of her, along with a stack of tortillas.

The coffeepot followed.

Karin poured the coffee into the waiting buttery mugs she'd picked up in Hong Kong the month before, leaving TJ's black as she added cream and sugar to hers. Had she known her mom was pulling a Jack Frost on her digs while she was gone, she would have opted for the fire-engine-red set—probably the matching plates, too.

Oh, well.

She glanced up to find a stuffed tortilla inches from her lips.

"Eat."

She took it, biting in as TJ retrieved his notes.

"I called the lab this morning. Señor Callahan's prints are not on the note."

"What?" He patted her back as she choked on the bite, then grabbed the glass of orange juice he held up, swallowing half in one gulp. "But his prints were on the envelope."

"They were. However, the results have been verified several times. There are only three different sets of prints on the note—yours, mine and a still-unidentified set. This last set was found on the envelope, as well."

"Meaning someone other than Doug wrote it."

TJ nodded. "It would seem so. It does not follow that the man would take care with the note, but not the envelope."

She swallowed her second bite. "But Doug still knows who's stealing the drugs, right?"

"Perhaps. But there may be another explanation. With your consent, I may be able to eliminate this other theory."

Her mouth full, she nodded.

"I would like to test the rest of the documents that were in your box."

She choked again.

He clapped her back again, frowning as he held up the remaining juice. "Perhaps we should wait until you have eaten."

"That's okay. I just lost my appetite." She set the remaining half of the tortilla back on her plate, suppressing a shiver as the implication of his request hit her. "You think Doug's prints were on the envelope because he was rifling through my box, don't you?"

"It is possible, but I do not know. I will not unless you give me leave to remove the contents from your office."

"Fine, take them. I'll go get them as soon as we're done."

He shook his head firmly.

"Tomás—"

"No. I have made arrangements already. I am to attend a one-hour training session on infection control before the coming week is out. Naturally I signed up for later this morning."

When the offices were deserted.

He was good. "I'm impressed." Her breath caught as he returned her smile with an even broader one.

"*Gracias.*" He nudged her coffee mug closer to her hands and filled a tortilla for himself. "But there is more. I was called on to perform an unusual cleaning service at the hospital yesterday afternoon—in the pharmacy."

She sucked in her breath and somehow managed to wait until he finished his bite. "Are you saying you finally met Doug?"

"Unfortunately, no. I met his assistant. A chief by the name of Howard Tassinger—who is also the man who suggested I fill in for him at the party." A faint frown settled about his mouth. "This much I left on your machine."

The message she'd erased upon hearing TJ's voice. Dammit, she wasn't going to do it. She was not going to blush.

She did.

She covered with a sip of coffee. "What did Chief Tassinger spill?"

"According to Tassinger, nothing. Señor Callahan, on the other hand, dropped a lot of fentanyl."

She was lucky she didn't drop her cup. "An entire lot?"

"*Sí.* But it was not fentanyl."

The mug hit the counter. "You tested it?"

He nodded. "Water."

"And the broken ampules?"

"They were clearly marked as fentanyl. Also, the lot numbers match records we have already obtained."

That son of a— "He'd already swapped the drugs." But why would Doug let someone else clean up the mess? Of course. "A witness. Doug needed a witness so he could write off the loss."

TJ nodded.

Except that still didn't make sense. Not in light of what she'd seen last night. But again, she knew. "Shelley."

"Perhaps."

She shook her head. "There's no perhaps about it.

They've got to be in on it together. Why else was she so damned chummy with the guy? According to Eric, she's still married to Chuck.''

He stiffened and set his mug down. Carefully. "You questioned Dr. Hunter about this?''

Oh, boy. Those eyes.

They were smoldering again, but this time they weren't kissing. More like upset. No, they were more than upset. They were downright pissed. She tried not to flinch beneath them.

It was no use.

She could feel herself squirming. And she was certain those dark razor eyes caught every subtle twitch. God pity the man Special Agent Vásquez was sent in to interrogate.

Who was she kidding? God pity her.

And *he* was still waiting.

She strangled a gulp. "I wouldn't say I questioned him...exactly.''

"What exactly did you say?''

"I was trying to help.''

"What?''

"All I did was tell Eric I'd run into Shelley that morning.''

"And?''

"Wh-what makes you think there was more?''

His steady gaze didn't even flicker.

She finally cracked. "Okay, I also wondered if Shelley had been looking for Doug, if they were seeing each other on the side. I might have even wondered if Doug was swapping sex for substances.''

"You *discussed* this with Dr. Hunter?''

"Why not? The man's a pharmacist and a proven sleaze. Hell, you saw them. He and Shelley were practically going at it in the middle of Manning's house and then they left. Don't you think it would have been stranger if I hadn't said anything?''

He didn't say a word. Not one single word.

She almost wished he would.

Nothing. Just this interminable silence.

And then, "You realize you may have compromised my cover?"

Now she did.

She slid her gaze down to the counter, staring at the half-eaten tortilla on her plate, the barely touched one on his, not knowing what to say. As if there was anything she *could* say.

"*Querida?*"

He was still using endearments. That meant he wasn't livid, didn't it?

She forced herself to meet his gaze. "Yes?"

"You will not return to the hospital until your leave has expired, is this clear?"

"Yes."

"You will not open the door to anyone when I leave, and while you are waiting to hear from me, you will pack a suitcase and prepare to visit your mother. Is this clear?"

"But—"

"Is this clear?"

"Y-yes." The frog was back.

"Finally you will not use your phone. If someone calls, you will let your machine pick up. You will not speak to anyone from the hospital. Is this also clear?"

"Yes."

He nodded curtly and rounded the counter. She held her breath as he reached into his bag and retrieved his folded black T-shirt and matching leather wallet. He pulled the shirt over his head and tucked it into the waist of his jeans. That done, he raked his hands though his hair and picked up his notebook. He closed it and stacked it atop the manila folders.

Was that it?

Would he say nothing else? Was he just going to leave? True, it was what she deserved. But when he reached into his bag and pulled out the next item, panic slammed into her.

His gun.

"Tomás?"

He didn't even glance up. He just leaned over to slide the deadly looking thing into his right boot. He tugged the hem of his jeans down over the leather, then reached back to the counter. The wallet, no doubt containing his DEA credentials, followed his gun, this time into his left boot. He tugged that leg down and stood.

And stared.

She swallowed. "I'm sorry."

Another nod. He picked up his leather jacket and shrugged into it before reaching for his helmet and bag. Her hand shot out before she could stop it, locking on to his forearm, refusing to let go.

Again he simply stared.

"I swear, I was just trying to help."

He finally sighed—heavily. "I know." Her chest tightened as his hand came up to cup her cheek, his thumb smoothing away the tears burning at the corners of her eyes before they could fall. "The class is but an hour. I will obtain the papers beforehand and return here by one. We will talk, *sí?* And after, I will see you to your mother's."

Her throat was so thick all she could do was nod.

Good God, what had she done? What if she had blown his cover? What if Eric said something to Doug or Shelley? Or worse, what if Eric was also involved? That *gun.* What if Tomás—

She closed her eyes.

She couldn't even think it. She wouldn't.

Before she could open her eyes, he tipped up her chin. His lips brushed lightly over hers, then settled against her forehead. "I shall be fine, *querida.* I have done this many, many times. Promise me you will not worry."

She managed a jerky nod, holding her eyes shut as

tightly as she held the lie. His warm breath fanned her face as he leaned down to kiss her one last time.

Slowly, gently.

And then he was gone.

He should be angry with her.

TJ brought his motorcycle to a halt in the hospital parking lot and twisted the key from the ignition, tucking the ring into the pocket of his leather jacket, then lifting the bike to kick the stand into place. *Sí,* he should be angry.

But he was not.

He had been. Indeed he had been more than angry. But then he had looked into those beautiful blue eyes and seen the pain. He pulled off his helmet and swung his leg from the bike, sighing as he retrieved his bag and headed for the service entrance at the rear of the hospital. Once he was through the door, he made his way quickly to Karin's office.

That pain.

He knew it well. He had felt that same searing ache he had seen in her eyes as he watched her ship slowly depart six months before, not knowing whether she would return or not.

At least not the way she had left.

Free.

Though he had dreaded the separation, he had not feared it. He had feared something far worse than empty days. What if she took a lover while she was away? A sailor, a pilot, another doctor, it mattered not which. What had driven him insane was not so much that she might give this phantom man her body, but her heart.

She still might never gift it to him.

After last night he knew this with painful clarity.

But that expression, that stark fear in her eyes, those unshed tears. For a brief moment she had allowed him a glimpse into her soul—and had given him far more hope than he had ever had before. He would wait. He would give her the time she needed to know he was not her father. And in the meantime he would solve this case. For while his anger over her slip had faded, the possible complications had not.

If they came to pass, he would deal with them. Adapt.

It was what he was good at.

And if his theory proved correct and Señor Callahan had merely handled the envelope while rifling through her things, her blunder was perhaps for the best. For it would keep her out of harm's way until he had solved this case. In all his years with the DEA—not even as a boy on the streets of Querétaro—had he known such roiling fury or icy terror as when he had seen Eric Hunter's hands on his beloved. Señor Callahan might well be guilty, this Dr. Ryder, as well. But until he was absolutely certain, he would take no chances.

With anyone.

TJ reached the door to Karin's office and discreetly tried the knob. Locked.

Excellent.

Glancing down the hallway one last time, he pulled the spare key from the pocket of his jeans and slid it into the beckoning slot.

The lock popped open.

He tucked the key away and slipped through the door, closing it gently and relocking it behind him. He glanced at his watch as he unzipped his canvas sack and withdrew the evidence collection bags from within. Then he made his way to Karin's desk, snapping on his gloves and setting about retrieving and cataloging the papers he needed. Fortunately most were in her bottom drawer. Still, Joaquín would be ready for the handoff inside the restroom down the hall in less than eight minutes.

It would be unwise to force his fellow agent to loiter.

He worked quickly and methodically, finishing the task with minutes to spare. He zipped the bag, then turned to stare at Eric Hunter's desk. He had been through it the first night, but the opportunity to double-check the contents for telling changes was too good to pass up. The decision made, he set the canvas bag next to the crystal paperweight and rolled the chair away from the desk. Moments later he had picked the lock to the main drawer.

Nada.

Nothing unusual in the least but for the largest collection of paperclips TJ had ever seen crammed into a single tray. That the clips were gold-toned, the pens the same, told him much about the owner, however. Eric Hunter was as pretentious as his belongings. Though from what TJ had uncovered about the doctor's past, the man had come by his snobbery honestly.

Like Karin, Hunter came from money.

But unlike her, the men in Hunter's family had formed the tradition of serving their country before they set about increasing the family coffers in the civilian world. Scandal had rarely touched the family, making it unlikely Eric would be the first.

There were always exceptions.

Finished with the two left drawers, TJ moved on to the bottom one on his right. He had already removed the manila envelope that had not been there before when his spine stiffened instinctively.

The door—a key fitting into the lock.

Hunter.

A split second later the knob began to turn.

TJ shoved the envelope back into the desk.

Too late. The drawer was closing as the door opened. But it was not Hunter. It was much much worse.

It was his father.

"Just what the hell are you doing in here, mister?"

Think—and quickly.

No hablo inglés. It worked most times. "The lady doctor, she ask I clean the desk for her."

"Her nameplate is on the *other* one."

TJ forced his gaze across the room and made a show of

squinting at the silver plate crowning Karin's desk. He would guess another gift forced upon her by her mother. *"Perdóneme,* señor.'' He pushed forth a sheepish shrug. The flush heating his neck needed no coercion. ''I read little *inglés.''*

Even with a simple blue polo shirt and jeans in place of his admiral's uniform, it was obvious his sire was used to command. His barrel chest, squared shoulders and iron jaw made for a posture so rigid it would put a marine corporal to shame. TJ was actually tempted to shed the subservient slouch of José Rodriguez and see what that additional inch of height he had noted on paper gave him in person.

But he did not.

"Follow me." He did not wait for argument, but turned and marched stiffly from the room.

What in God's name was he to do?

A hospital janitor did not disobey the chief of staff.

Though it chafed severely, TJ followed.

The bag. He must rid himself of the evidence.

He stopped at the restroom door. "Señor?"

"What?"

"Un momento, por favor. I must…ah…''

"Go. But if your ass isn't back front and center in two minutes flat, you'll be headed for the unemployment line."

At this moment he would be hard-pressed to single out the bastard between the two of them.

Joaquín had better be waiting.

He was. His fellow agent cocked his dark brows at the door even as they swiftly traded identical bags. A rapid hand sign followed. *Did he need assistance?*

TJ shook his head.

Another sign. *The man in charge?*

TJ nodded.

You sure you need no help?

TJ shook his head again, firmly.

He waited through Joaquín's shrug and several silent beats, then flushed the urinal closest to them and tucked his helmet beneath his arm to wash his hands for good measure. A deep breath, and a moment later, he was facing his father for the third time in two days.

Dios, but this did not grow easier.

Thunder still marring the graying brows, the man executed an abrupt about-face and led the way through the deserted antiseptic maze. Silence appeared to be his sire's preference, for it settled tersely between them and lay untouched until they reached the elevator. Once there, the admiral punched the upward arrow, flicking his stony gaze over his shoulder as the steel doors slid open.

''Get in.''

The walls of the lift closed in along with the doors, magnifying the silence as the elevator lurched into motion.

Carajó, he had had enough.

He blessed the day he had left his half sister sneering down her nose. This man was not worth the time it had taken to track him down. Nor was he worth the agony that had followed, and he certainly was not worth the sweat that had trickled down his back last night—or now. *Sí,* he would find a way to soothe this stranger's ire, and then he would depart from the man's life. Permanently.

The lift came to a halt.

Again he was left tagging behind like an errant schoolboy until, finally, they reached a door marked Chief of Staff.

''Inside.''

The door snapped firmly shut behind them. TJ waited as his sire crossed the plush carpet, leaving him standing in the middle of the room as he lowered himself into the leather chair behind the oak desk with naught but a briefcase upon it. The line of ceremonial cloth flags—American, California, U.S. Navy and the command's—locked to attention behind his sire added to the effect, leaving no doubt as to why he had been brought here.

Intimidación.

It would not work.

TJ knew the revered Admiral Thomas Banks for what he truly was. A man so ruthlessly intent on furthering his career and hoarding his wife's money that he would kill an innocent child to keep that child from sullying it. But now was not the time for retribution. He had his cover to preserve.

"Señor, I meant no trespass. The lady doctor, she gives me the key." He pulled the spare he had made from his cleaning set, knowing Karin would vouch for him. "You see? I was to—"

"I don't give a damn about the key, *Agent Vásquez*."

TJ stiffened, then recovered immediately, shedding José's posture and mannerisms as he drew himself up to his full height. The paper inch pleased him immensely as he stared squarely down into those shrewd blue eyes for the first time. How much did this man know? Who had told him? When?

And did he know the rest?

Impossible.

That someone above him in the agency had decided it was prudent to talk was obvious. It would have been of benefit to have been included in the conversation, but no matter. It was done. Still, he would force this man make the next move as well.

He did not have long to wait.

"Well?"

TJ arched his brows along with those of his sire, taking care to keep the insolence from showing through, but that was all. He did not answer.

"Is Dr. Hunter the man you're investigating?"

He shrugged.

"Dammit, man, you infiltrated my hospital!"

"I understood, Admiral, that the command was not quite yours…yet." *Dios*, forgive him the taunt. But if this man knew he was his son, he must also know the scandal might well destroy his illustrious *preciosa* career, even at this late a date.

In the end the taunt made no difference, for that steel gaze did not waver. "What have you got on the man?"

TJ took his time shifting the canvas bag and helmet to his left hand. "I am afraid I am not at liberty to discuss my case with you, señor. Should you wish a briefing, you may contact—"

"I know who you work for."

But evidently not who he was.

TJ masked the searing bitterness with a slight smile. What had he expected? "Then I will leave you to make the call." With that, he turned and headed for the door. He was a moment, perhaps two, from freedom when—

"Wait."

He would not.

He must leave this room. *Pronto.* Before he said something he should not say. Before he felt something he should not feel. He locked his free hand to the knob and twisted.

"Please, son. Don't."

The knob slipped from his hand—how, he did not know—as did his helmet and bag from his other.

They fell to his feet with a thud.

Son.

¡Idiota! It was but an expression, nothing more. Like boy, *amigo, hombre*—he had heard them all through the years.

It meant nothing.

"You are my son, aren't you?"

TJ reached out, splayed his hands against the door, at once welcoming the solid support beneath his palms and yet hating that he needed it. It was last night over again. This burning in his heart, in his lungs. The thickness in his throat.

Sweating, choking.

Run.

He would not. He turned. "I am not."

The admiral popped the locks on the briefcase and raised the lid. A file hit the desk, thick and worn. The cover deep blue. Almost as blue as Karin's eyes. Somehow he managed to tear his gaze from the papers spilling out and pull it back to steel.

"Open it."

"Why?"

"Open it and see." The admiral's hand came up to rub his neck. Though slight, it was the only betrayal of nervousness TJ could find. It was enough.

"No."

"Why not? Are you afraid of what you'll find?"

He refused to answer.

To this man—and to himself.

"Fine, I'll fill you in. The first pages contain notes I drafted before I gave them to a private detective I hired eight years ago. You see, a young Hispanic man showed up at my door. A rather tall man with shoulder-length hair. He asked for me by name, said he knew me. This in itself was odd, because I'd never met a man fitting that description. My wife and daughter blew it off. I didn't. Would you like to know why?"

Again he refused to answer.

But his heart shouted. Raged.

"I see you already know, but then I suspect you have known for quite some time. Certainly longer than I have. As for the rest of the file, the bulk contains periodic reports from the detective I settled on. Through the years, he brought several possibilities to me, but it wasn't until he located a man by the name of *Tomás Juan* Vásquez seven months ago that I knew he'd found the right one." He paused, obviously waiting for a response.

TJ banded the muzzle about his still-clamoring heart as tightly as he could and again gave none.

The admiral sighed. "You see, I knew he'd found my son because, not only was the age of the man correct, but the woman I'd had the affair with had a father named Juan. Unfortunately I didn't know much else about her. The affair lasted a few weeks and then she left. She showed up a month later and told me she was pregnant. She demanded enough money to take care of it. What could I do? I couldn't force her to have the baby, and I admit, I was scared, too. I gave her the money and never saw her again. Her name was Rosa. Rosa Magdalena Lopez.''

Another pause.

''Do I need to go on?''

''No.'' His voice was hoarse.

It did not matter. Lies.

It was all lies anyway. ''You are not my father.''

''I am. There's a blood test in here that proves it. That sample they took downstairs when you applied for this job? I had a friend run it against mine. You are my son. Tomás, you are the child I've been searching for since the day I thought you might be alive. Good God, if you don't believe me, just look in the damned mirror!''

The band on TJ's heart finally snapped.

He stalked up to the desk and grabbed the file, shoving it under this cursed man's nose. ''I do not care what you think this paltry stack of paper proves. You are not my father. I was raised by a man named Antonio Vásquez. He was the man who wanted me—as I was, and when it was *not* convenient to accept me. He, who did not show up feeding me deceit thirty-one years too late—that man is my father. You, Admiral Banks, are nothing.'' He slammed the file down on the desk, not even caring when the contents spewed over the edge to litter the floor.

And then, he froze.

Antonio.

Madre de Dios, the man lay right there at his feet in five-by-seven close-up color, embracing his own, though much younger, self. He could not help it, he stared. Transfixed by the photo, by the man. Both so close and yet so far away. He would never know that man again, that joy. The photograph had been taken the day he had graduated from the DEA academy. Even in profile he could see the pride shining from Antonio's dark eyes, as well as the silver time had threaded at his temples, the lines it had carved about his eyes and mouth. The wisdom.

How he missed it. How he missed him.

Unable to stop, he reached down to touch this man, even remotely, once again. But before he could, his gaze strayed to the right. To a small square of paper. A copy of a certificate of ownership—a title. To a motorcycle.

His.

He retrieved the paper, trying to focus, to read. To think. It could not be.

But it was.

Indeed, it already had been. For eight years. The evidence was right here in his hands. The cherished bike his mentor had purchased and then given to him in celebration had once belonged to the very man standing before him.

And Antonio had known it.

"He, ah, showed up a couple of months before you. At the time, I didn't think anything of it. I assumed he was there to look at the bike, since I'd put it up for sale. Guess he was really there to look at me."

He should respond. Say something.

But what?

"Son?"

He flinched, instead.

A moment later he succeeded in forcing his gaze from the title, still numb as he watched the admiral sweep the papers he had strewn across the desk into a pile. The man shoved them back into the folder, the knot in his throat working as he held it out.

"Perhaps you'd like to take the file with you? For later?"

Enough.

He did not have time for this.

His case. Three deaths, one most definitely murder. A cover that may well be blown. From Karin's blunder, *sí.* But now his own, as well. What was he doing here in this office?

The chief of staff.

If this did not draw attention, what did?

He must leave. Now.

And pray the devil did not see him descending back down.

TJ ripped his gaze from the battered folder and shook his head curtly. *"No gracias.* You may keep your file." The lies as well. "Also, I would appreciate it if you would keep your distance, as I have a cover to maintain so that I may solve my case." With that, he released the title transfer from one Thomas Banks to one Antonio Vásquez almost nine years before.

It fluttered back to the floor.

"And now if you will excuse me, Admiral, I have a training session I must attend. Good day." It was only through years of his own training that he was able to force his body to turn, to move and head for the door.

"It's been canceled."

TJ stopped. But he did not turn back. "I beg your pardon?"

"The infection-control class—it's been canceled. And before you suspect me of interfering, let me assure you I didn't. The nurse who was supposed to give it went into labor last night. It'll be rescheduled. You can—" He stopped, as if suddenly aware that he was rattling on.

Nerves.

Finally the man displays his nerves.

TJ could not even find satisfaction enough for a smile. He did, however, find one last nod—and he used it. *"Gracias."*

There was no response as he retrieved his helmet and bag and opened the door, just the soft click as he closed it firmly behind him. Then his boots, echoing down the deserted tiles. The walk was brief, and for this, he was grateful. For it allowed him to reach the elevator quickly, push the downward arrow and enter. The twin demons of memory and regret snaked through him as the doors closed, coiling themselves tightly about his mind and his heart, eager as always in their efforts to escort him to hell. For the first time, however, confusion did not accompany them.

The fight.

It made sense now.

Though he and Antonio had disagreed through the years, even argued upon occasion, they had never truly been at odds, but for that one time. He had been twenty-three, less than six months to the completion of his probation with the DEA. Antonio had come to him and told him it was time. Time to begin the search for his birth father. Time to greet and to know.

To forgive.

He had refused.

Antonio had pressed, most vocally. But as the days wore on and he had remained unyielding, Antonio had come to see the futility in his desire. He had always assumed Antonio had given up. Evidently not.

He drew his breath as the lift slowed, purging his mind of the memories, his heart of the ache. Antonio, his sire, his mother. They mattered not. He had his case and, more importantly, Karin to look after. Best he keep his mind focused upon this.

Unfortunately he had no class to attend.

The steel doors opened. He stepped free and turned down yet another antiseptic hall, nodding a return greeting to the pair of nurses he passed. The class. Now what? He was to have met the pharmacy chief after. It had taken him all of his morning break yesterday and lunch, as well, to befriend the man.

Chief Tassinger was new to the command, and like many sailors recent and not so recent to San Diego, looking for a good time south of the border. A few well-placed suggestions regarding clubs and a comment or two dropped about TJ's need to save money so that he might attend pharmacy school in the fall, and the chief was trading his slot serving drinks at Dr. Manning's party for the promise of a night full of tequila, women and song.

He could only pray the man had not been too hung over this morning to stand his duty today.

He nodded another greeting, this time to a doctor, before turning down the final hallway to the pharmacy. If he was lucky, the chief would be waiting and he would be able to get the information he needed before anyone realized he was even looking. But as he stopped before the outer door and peered through the glass, he stiffened. Luck was not with him this day, for at least one man had already beaten him to his goal.

Señor Callahan.

Was nothing to go in his favor?

Evidently not. For the moment he slipped back from view, a hand clamped onto his shoulder and spun him about.

Chapter 10

He was late.

Karin rearranged the silverware she'd laid out next to the plates on the breakfast bar for the fifteenth time in twenty minutes, trying desperately to ignore the steady, burning display of the clock on the back of the stove.

Dammit, he was fine. Held up, that was all.

Maybe the class ran over.

By two hours?

She slugged the demon down.

Stop. There were plenty of logical reasons why TJ could have been delayed. It was Saturday—he could have had trouble dropping off the prints he'd gotten from the papers in her desk, or he might have latched on to another lead and couldn't get to a phone. Hell, he could be flirting with every single female patient in the hospital for all she cared, but he was *not* staring down the wrong end of that damned gun.

The phone. She stiffened as its shrill pierced the air, snapping nerves all the way down her spine. Seconds later she'd spun about and hurried across the room to stand over the phone through two more equally piercing shrills.

You will let your machine pick up.

Though it nearly killed her, she obeyed.

She also prayed.

The machine finally switched on and her own voice filled the room. Then a short steady bleep…and another blasted *click*. That was the third hangup this morning. One more and she was going to smash that stupid thing into the wall. It was probably her mother. Between last night and this morning her mother had already left two messages. Her mom wasn't dumb. She had to know she was avoiding her by now.

Well, she was going to keep on avoiding her.

She'd followed the rest of TJ's instructions. She'd pack a bag. But she was not visiting her parents. The specter of her mother's meddling was bad enough, but Westin? Karin shuddered. She loved her stepfather dearly. But there was no way she was running to him now. He was worse than TJ. She'd deal with TJ's anger over Westin's "help" any day of the week. Especially if this morning's reaction was any indication.

TJ had to have been furious with her.

Hell, she knew he was. She'd seen it in his eyes before he'd turned. Not so much emotion as a complete lack of it. She never wanted to see that look again. But she did want to see him.

Now. Alive. And not in a professional capacity.

Once again the wound she'd stitched up two nights before flashed before her eyes. And then the gun.

Dammit, how much more of this torment could she take?

A shower.

Yes. Exactly what she needed. She hadn't taken one yet today. It would calm her nerves and clear her head. Most of all, it would give her something to do. Two minutes later steam was filling the master bathroom. She was about drop her worn terry robe when she remembered.

The chain.

TJ might not need a key to get through the lock, but she sincerely doubted he carried a pair of bolt cutters in that leather jacket of his. Karin headed for the front door. A minute later she'd unhooked the chain and was already back in her bedroom, closing the door. She entered the bathroom, sighing as the cloud of steam washed over her face.

Finally.

But as she went to drop the robe again, she heard it—or rather, him. Relief flooded her. She didn't even bother turning the shower off, just wrapped her robe tight and glanced at the clock as she threw open the bedroom door. 3:00 p.m. on the dot. About damned time.

But the living room was empty.

So was the kitchen.

Dammit, she'd heard him.

There, she heard him again. In her study. Another wave of relief and another sprint. She shoved the door open and plowed straight into someone. He was Hispanic. But it wasn't TJ.

And that wasn't TJ's fist.

A split second later it connected with her jaw.

Blinding pain, then another starburst as her head snapped back and smashed into the wall behind her.

And then nothing.

"¿Cariño? Por favor despiértate." A pause. *"Querida,* please, you must wake."

Why? Everything hurt. No, not everything.

Her head. Her head hurt. A lot.

Cold.

No, cool. A cloth. Someone was pressing a damp cloth to her forehead, smoothing it down her aching jaw.

"Querida, please. I beg you."

TJ.

The voice was low, broken, but it was definitely his.

She groaned. "Tomás?"

Good Lord, her voice was as hoarse as his.

And her head...

She swallowed thickly as the cloth disappeared and was immediately replaced by warm lips brushing the curls from her forehead. What sounded like fervent thanks to the Virgin Mother swirled into her ears.

There was something soft beneath her head. A pillow?

The shower, she could still hear it running.

She had to be in her bedroom, on her bed. TJ was pulling back to sit on the edge beside her as she forced her eyes open, his dark gaze searching.

"Wh-what...happened?"

"I was to ask this of you. You do not remember?"

"I..." She closed her eyes and willed the throbbing at the back of her skull to lessen. When it refused, she gave up and opened them again. "I don't... Wait. A man. I thought he was you." His fingers threaded into her hair, smoothing it back as she paused to swallow. "I was worried about you...decided to take a shower."

The time. How long had she been out?

She turned her head to the clock on her nightstand, relieved when her eyes focused immediately on the display.

Three minutes after three. Thank God.

He sighed. "The chain, you released it."

"Please, don't be mad at me." She couldn't handle his disappointment in her again. Not now.

He must have understood, because his lips were at her forehead again, soothing. "Ah, *Cariño,* do not worry. I cannot seem to stay angry with you."

He couldn't? She let out her breath slowly.

That was good to know.

Now if she could just get the back of her head and her jaw to stop screaming in concert. She sighed as TJ read her mind, cradling her close as he smoothed the cool cloth down her face.

"Besides, the fault does not lie with you. The pharmacy chief, he stopped me outside the door to warn me—" He broke off with a growl as he pulled back. "It matters not why. What matters is I should never have stayed so long. Never."

His eyes.

She'd never seen that look in them before. Raw, exposed. It went beyond pain. Whatever it was, she never wanted to see it again, and she sure as hell didn't want him feeling it.

She should say something.

Anything.

Except she couldn't get her lips to move, let alone force air past the lump that had lodged in her throat. Several moments passed before she managed to clear it. "So…do you, ah, think the break-in is connected to the note?"

"*Sí.*"

She blinked.

He seemed awfully certain.

"The guy could have been robbing—"

The equally firm shake of his head cut her off. "I found you just inside your study."

The look was back, even more intense than before. A second later he closed his eyes, as if willing the image away, and this time she responded without thinking. She smoothed her hands over his taut cheeks and stroked the tension from his jaw.

"Tomás, I'm fine."

He drew in his breath deeply before pressing his lips to her palm. Something primitive still lingered in the smoky depths of his eyes when he finally opened them. Another breath and then, "Whoever this man is, he would not break into this apartment to steal. Most especially on a Saturday afternoon. You live ten stories up, and you have a doorman downstairs. If this man came simply to rob, how would he carry his newfound possessions out of the building?"

"Well, you seem to be getting by Peter just fine."

He didn't miss a beat. "I have a badge, *querida*." An almost bitter smile twisted his lips. "You would be surprised at the places it lets me in—and how quickly."

Bedrooms included.

Stop it. TJ hadn't had a woman in six years.

Surely that meant something?

"What I do not understand, is how this man got past today. Peter was at the door when I arrived."

Saturday. That explained it. "Vince and Pete swap on Saturdays so Pete can spend the morning with his kids. He probably gave Vince a general description of you earlier this week. Vince probably assumed the guy was my new DEA friend."

The cloth fell away again and she took the opportunity to probe her jaw. Not bad. Still hurt like the devil, but it didn't seem to be swollen. Might even get off with a minor bruise.

She glanced up. TJ was staring at her hand, hard.

She pulled it down. "What is it?"

"Vince assumed this man was me? *Querida,* the man who struck you, was he Hispanic?"

She nodded. "I thought I mentioned that."

"You did not."

"Is it important?"

But he was still staring—at the cloth now. Concentrating. "Tomás?"

He blinked, his gaze clearing. "*Sí.* It may be very important. But first we must get you to the doctor and then to your mother's, and then I will set about finding out."

"No."

He didn't even bother arguing. He just folded the cloth and got up to return it to her bathroom.

Fine. Two could play this game.

She watched him through the mirror as she sat up gingerly, waiting until he turned his back to shut off the still-streaming shower, no doubt cold by now, before she stood.

Good. Balance was there. No nausea, no memory loss.

Nope, she remembered that fist quite clearly.

Heck, she wasn't even sleepy.

She threaded her fingers into the tangles at the back of her head, searching the whole of her skull. Sore, but no lumps, no broken skin. Even the throbbing seemed to have quieted to a dull ache. Her jaw still smarted, but that was to be expected. Other than a brief loss of consciousness, she was fine.

"What do you think you are doing?"

"Standing. And I'm doing a pretty good job of it, too. No, I don't need help. I'm going to the bathroom so I can get a look at my pupils."

He shadowed her, anyway.

Yikes.

There might not be a lump on her jaw, but if the yellow-and-purple bruise already appearing ripened to its fullest potential, she was going to look as if she'd absorbed the brunt of Muhammad Ali's right hook by morning.

TJ's gaze met hers in the mirror, those damned silent brows rising.

She shrugged. "So I bruise easily."

His brows reversed course as he frowned.

"Look—my pupils are fine." She turned around, pleased to be leaning against the lip of the sink because she wanted to, not because she had to. "I'm fine, and you can wipe that scowl off your face, because I'm not going to my mother's, either."

"You agreed—"

"No, you ordered. I simply kept the peace. I might be in the Navy, buster, but you do not look like my commanding officer."

Thank the Lord, because she'd have been slapped into the brig for fraternization—on her fantasies alone.

Besides, she'd only agreed to pack because TJ had looked too angry this morning for her to think she had a prayer of changing his mind. But since by his own admission, he couldn't stay mad at her... "I'll go to a hotel if you want, but I'm not going to my mother's."

"Why?"

Why? Wasn't it obvious? She sighed. "Tomás, I'm not a kid anymore. I don't go running home to Mommy."

He shook his head. "The real reason. And before you pretend ignorance, I see more in your eyes than pupils that are normal." He leaned close, resting his hands a fraction of an inch from her hips at the edge of the sink, trapping her. "Much more."

The hell with her eyes. It was what she saw in his that scared her. There was no mistaking the emotion searing from deep within that dark gaze.

Determination.

This wasn't Tijuana Jones breathing slowly but steadily three inches from her face. It wasn't even Tomás. This was Special Agent Vásquez. And something told her there was only one path to winning this particular argument with this particular man.

The truth.

She took a deep breath and spilled it. "Westin."

"Your stepfather?"

She nodded.

"What does he have to do with this?"

"Not a damned thing. And frankly I'd like to keep it that way. Don't get me wrong, Westin's a great guy. My mother's lucky to have him. *I'm* lucky to have him. He's just..." Oh, hell, how did she put this? She drew another breath. "He meddles."

"Meddles?"

"To put it mildly." She sighed. "The first time it happened I was in college. I graduated early from high school, so I was barely eighteen when it happened." She paused—and had to glance away from that probing gaze.

Lord, this was humiliating.

"When what happened?"

She kept her gaze on the wallpaper. The tiny ribboned baskets of wildflowers her mother would soon be plucking right off the walls if she couldn't figure out a way to stop her.

Damn, but she liked those flowers.

She tried to shift her gaze back to TJ's, but chickened out at the sight of his hair. She gave up and let her gaze linger on the thick glossy strands. "I was dating a classmate. He was ready. I wasn't."

"Ready? To have…"

"Yes, sex." She finally met his gaze. "He wanted to while away the study hours with his hand up my skirt, okay?"

TJ stiffened. Almost imperceptibly, but she could see it. She could also see the anger. Feel it. "You told him no."

"I told him no. I also told him why. Believe it or not, I actually thought he cared, that he'd understand. He didn't."

"And when you informed this boy you no longer wished to see him?"

"He harassed me. In class, during lab. The final straw was when he told his buddies and they started harassing me. Westin was guest-teaching two classes at the college. Eventually he got wind of it."

"And he meddled."

"Meddled, hell. He damn near wiped Steve out of existence. One minute the jerk was in my face, and the next he was gone. Totally. The official story was the guy dropped out to move to Boston. Right. Steve hated snow. Anyway, I knew what really happened, and so did everyone else. Can you imagine what Westin would do to Doug if he found out?"

"Perhaps Señor Callahan would deserve it, no?"

"I take it back. You're worse than Westin."

"I beg your pardon?"

"Never mind. The point is, I don't want my stepfather finding out. Ever. Understood? And while we're on the subject, I want you to swear to me you'll never tell Jade about this."

"I would never—"

"Not about Doug. She already knows about him. About my…that I haven't done it. Trust me, she'd never let me live it down. Not after what I put her through with Reese."

His brows shot up, definitely intrigued at that.

"No, I am not talking. And you're not asking or telling."

He appeared to give it some thought.

Too much thought.

"I mean it, Tomás. Swear it. Right now. No teasing little asides around her, no jokes, no references. Nothing."

He finally nodded solemnly. "On my honor, *querida,* I will not speak of this, nor tease you again—"

"Good."

"—should others be present. But when we are alone?" He shrugged and his lips quirked.

The rat.

But she'd give him that willingly. As long as he gave her the rest. "Then it's settled. I'll go call a hotel."

His smile faded.

She cut him off at the pass. "Look, if you're worried about my head, don't be. You got here right after it happened. I was out a minute, maybe two. Believe me, I know. I was watching the clock nonstop."

"*Querida,* you may have a concussion. You—"

"Excuse me, but which one of us is licensed to carry a gun?"

He frowned.

"And which one of us is licensed to practice medicine?"

His frown deepened. "Then do it correctly."

She threw up her hands. "Fine. I'll have the blasted bellhop phone me every hour to check up on me. I'll even leave instructions for him to call 911 if I don't answer. Will that make you happy?''

''What will make me happy is you at your mother's. And do not tell me you are avoiding your stepfather. You are not. You are avoiding a man, however. Your sire—and your mother.''

That's it.

She jerked up from the edge of the sink and shoved that damned imposing chest out of the way. But before she could cross the threshold into her bedroom, his hand clamped about her wrist and he tugged her back. She refused to meet his gaze, glaring at his T-shirt, instead.

It was the perfect color.

Black.

Right now her fury matched that scrap of snug fabric, and she was finally livid enough to ignore the sculpted steel beneath it. ''Let me go.''

''I cannot.''

''Dammit, Tomás, I mean it.''

He threaded his fingers into her hair and gently but insistently guided her head until she was forced to meet his gaze. ''*Cariño,* you must tell her. You should not avoid your mother so. It does not make you happy.''

''Since when are you the expert on me? I'll have you know I have a perfectly good relationship with my mother.''

''Why, then, can you not even tell her you do not like white?''

She flinched.

Damn him. ''You're a fine one to be lecturing me on family confrontation.''

It was his turn to flinch.

She had no business pressing the point home, but she did it, anyway. ''So when do you plan on scheduling your little one-on-one with your father?''

Silence.

It figured. So did the fire smoldering in his eyes.

She crossed her arms and stared up at him just as steadily as he was staring down at her. "I guess what we have here is a charming case of do as I say and not as I do, eh?"

More silence.

And more fire.

Didn't matter. She was not giving in. "I'm not going home."

Oddly enough, the fire cooled.

A moment later it had snuffed out altogether.

He nodded firmly. "Very well. If you will not go to the hospital or visit your mother, you have but one choice left. You must come home with me."

He was hovering.

As much as was humanly possible while simultaneously driving a Ford Explorer on a breathtaking cliffside ocean road in Baja California, but TJ was definitely hovering. If he asked her one more time how her head felt or, God forbid, if she needed to stop for air, she was going to scream. It had gotten so bad she almost wished he'd whip that damn cell phone out, call Joaquín and talk to his DEA buddy again.

In Spanish.

She hadn't bought his apologetic shrug for a second.

Those little portable gems were encrypted. At least his was. She'd learned that from Reese. The name Magdalena had come up again—several times. She was also dying to know what he'd done with the description of her attacker. Between questioning her and grilling poor Vince over the phone, she was pretty sure TJ had gotten a fairly solid description of the guy.

Thankfully, the doorman had gotten the better view, of course, so he'd won the ticket to visit the local cop shop and play Pictionary with their resident sketch artist. All she'd gotten was a blur—except for an excellent close-up of the guy's knuckles. Then again, they could always match the thug's fist to the bruise on her jaw. Nah, somehow, she didn't think TJ would be letting the man that close to her again.

Okay, so there were a few perks to his hovering.

She found another as TJ's right hand left the steering wheel and closed over hers on the seat. He squeezed gently. But then he spoke. "Your head, it feels okay?"

Don't do it. Don't scream.

Somehow she managed not to, even found her thirtieth cheery smile since they'd left San Diego thirty minutes before and followed it up with a crisp nod. His gaze probed hers, searching, measuring. He finally returned her nod and focused his attention back on the road, but he left his hand on hers.

She almost wished he hadn't.

His fingers had slipped between her index and thumb, curling beneath to whisper against her palm. Though subtle, the caress was gradually interfering with her concentration. Soon her palm began to ache, and it was all she could think about. Then the ache was spreading, consuming her hand, then her entire arm, spreading like brushfire until it had ignited her very core. He was driving a car for goodness' sake.

How could he just sit there and turn her on like this?

She didn't even think he was aware of what he was doing.

She was certain when he pulled his hand away to pass the neon green Bug intent on taking the scenic route at sub-snail speed. The moment they returned to their lane, his hand came back and so did that slow, seductive caress. He really had no clue that while he was busy hashing out his case in his head, she was sitting beside him, smoldering.

Hell, her palm had to be smoking by now.

Afraid to look, she whipped her gaze to the right, staring

out into the Pacific. If cold showers helped, a quick dip in
the ocean ought to work wonders. The man might even
realize what he was doing to her when the beachcombers
heard the sizzle—in Hawaii.

She was dimly aware of the Explorer turning off the
main highway and onto a smaller paved road. They'd left
the outskirts of Tijuana almost ten minutes ago and if she
remembered correctly from when she'd come down for
Reese and Jade's engagement party, it wasn't much further.
Another turn, and they were on gravel. One more, and it
changed to packed dirt. The roads weren't the best this far
off the beaten path, but the view was incredible. So much
so, houses had begun to crop up, each nested into the hill-
side with a breathtaking expanse of blue sky and even
deeper blue ocean. She might actually be able to enjoy it,
too.

If he'd stop stroking her blasted hand.

She slid her gaze to the floorboard, mentally reviewing
the contents of the black bag at her feet, wondering if there
was anything at all inside it she could use to vaccinate
herself from this intense desire that infected her whenever
this man was this close. Doubtful. Even if one existed, it
was too late.

Tomás was in her blood. She might as well face it.

Worrying about him all day had proven that if nothing
else.

The Explorer came to a stop.

"*¿Querida?*"

He finally removed his hand—and she could finally
breathe. She dragged her gaze from her bag. "Hmm?"

"We are home."

Home?

She stared at the sprawling hacienda TJ had restored to
its former glory. She hadn't even realized they were this
close, let alone that he'd already pulled into the semi-
circular drive and parked. The grounds and buildings of the

former estate had long since been sold and built up as well. TJ had told her last April he actually preferred it over the loss of privacy, for this way he had neighbors who were able to keep their eye on the place during the week and when he'd had to go deep undercover.

His hand touched her cheek. "Are you—"

"Yes, I'm fine. And, no, my head does not hurt. The blasted ibuprofen kicked in half an hour ago."

He frowned.

She flushed. "Sorry."

His smile was almost sheepish. It snapped the tension, sexual and otherwise, that had stretched between them during the trip. "I have been asking too much, no?"

"No, really. I just—"

His brow rose.

"Okay, you have. But I swear, I'm fine. My jaw doesn't even hurt anymore. In a few days, the bruise will fade, too. All right?"

He searched her eyes again, then finally nodded. "*Si.* Shall we go in then?"

She followed up his nod with one of her own, and leaned over to grab her purse and black bag from the floorboard as he bailed out of the cab. She was reaching for the handle to her door when it opened. Figures.

Impeccable manners to go with the charm.

Once again she mourned the loss of the man who'd raised him. She had a feeling she would have liked Antonio. As for Admiral Banks, TJ hadn't mentioned him since the night before, and she hadn't pressed. And she wouldn't.

For the time being.

She waited as he pulled her suitcase from the hatch and slung her tote on his shoulder, not bothering to help. She'd long since given up yelling at him for lifting. Her stitches seemed to be holding up despite the abuse he continually subjected them to. Not to mention the black look she'd earned for trying to heft them herself when they'd locked her place up. She did unlatch the iron gate leading to the stone courtyard and waited as he passed through. It was her turn to wait as he deactivated the alarm system and unlocked the door. And then, they were in.

He reactivated the system, then glanced down. "*Un momento,* I will put your bags in your room."

She nodded absently, trailing behind, staring, absorbing. Home.

Funny, he'd put it like that.

This place had felt like home from the moment she'd entered that first time eight months ago. From the red-tiled entryway to the central, open kitchen beyond, it was everything her parents' house—and now her own apartment—wasn't. Oh, it was just as elegant, but in an Old World, stately yet earthy way. Very Spanish and very sturdy. The open floor plan was warm and inviting with vibrant colors everywhere. Even the whitewash between the exposed beams in the ceiling and supporting the smoothly textured walls wasn't quite white, but more of a cozy weathered ivory.

According to Jade, Reese's mother had decorated the place after TJ had complimented the woman on what she'd done with her son's Spanish ranch in San Diego. Marian had done an excellent job in both places. Just enough throw rugs to soften the red tile and dark wood throughout, with oversized, overstuffed cream furniture brightened with pillows in deep reds and burnt orange. She'd also located several gorgeously intricate Mexican blankets and hung them on the walls for an effect that was, quite simply, stunning.

Maybe she could get Marian to give her mother lessons.

She swallowed the surge of guilt. It hit her stomach hard, dislodging several rude pains of another sort.

TJ chuckled softly behind her as the growls died out.

She spun back from the living room to find him standing beside the butcher block island in the middle of the kitchen.

"You are hungry, no?"

She smiled. "I'm fine."

His brow quirked along with his lips as her stomach betrayed her again, louder this time. "Come." He plucked her purse and her black bag and tossed them onto the ceramic counter next to the refrigerator, shrugging as he opened the side-by-side and stared inside. "I am afraid there is not much to work with. I have not been down in almost two weeks." He opened the bins and studied the contents. "Usually, I stop in Chula Vista to stock up, but I thought it best to bring you directly here."

In case they were followed.

He didn't have to say it. Just as he didn't have to tell her that if someone had been watching and really wanted to succeed—and had enough practice—it could be done. No one was that impervious. She wondered, not for the first time, how he and Reese could live so far out on the edge. Jade, too. She might be in the Navy, but danger wasn't exactly her thing. As far as she was concerned, she was there to clean up the mess, not create it.

TJ seemed to find a couple items to work with, as he put it—because he was stacking them into his arms. Obviously his idea of a bare fridge and hers were one-eighty out.

"What can I do to help?"

He turned back, that damned silent brow arching as he laid his vegetarian loot out on the counter and pulled a cutting board out from underneath. "You may rest. If you do not, I will tuck you into bed myself."

After that handholding session in the car, it didn't seem like a bad idea, until her stomach chimed in with yet another dissenting opinion. She got the message.

One craving at a time.

"Okay. I'll just, um, stand over here."

He turned back to the fridge and reached inside. "Ahhh…"

"What?"

"Yogurt."

"Vanilla?" She couldn't keep the prayer from her voice.

"*Sí.*" He reached into the drawer beside the fridge, smiling as he passed a spoon and, not one, but two cartons over.

Pay dirt.

By the time he'd plugged in the rice-cooker and filled it with water, she'd perched herself upon the island and had polished off the first and was well into the second. She could definitely get used to having Tomás around. The edge finally off her hunger, she set her gaze free, allowing it to roam over TJ's backside as he began chopping the vegetables on the counter across from her.

Lord, this man was hot.

Though his snug T-shirt and black jeans were doing their damnedest to hold her interest, she found herself yearning for a repeat of the striptease he'd given her two nights before in her bedroom. The show was bound to be more impressive in the full light of day—much more.

And what she wouldn't give for a nice long view of his front.

She sighed.

He turned and smiled that slow, sexy smile of his.

She'd long since finished the last of the yogurt but for some reason, she couldn't quite get her mouth to release the spoon.

"You need something, *Cariño*?"

Just you.

Her eyes must have said it out loud, because he took a step toward her, and then another. She panicked, slapping the spoon onto the island beside her—wincing as her hand hit something solid and smooth. Cold. Startled, she glanced down.

A candle?

It was one of those hefty, long-lasting ones. She picked up the glass jar. This one had been burned quite a bit too, because there was at most an inch-and-a-half of creamy wax left at the base. She uncorked the clear stopper, somehow knowing what scent it contained even before she sniffed.

Vanilla.

She loved vanilla. So much so, she'd packed her body wash and her shampoo in her suitcase. She glanced up. Did he—?

No, that was impossible.

But when he flushed, she knew it wasn't.

He'd bought it, and burned it, because of her.

Often.

He was less than a foot and a half away, staring into her eyes, and though he was definitely embarrassed over getting caught, it was equally obvious he wasn't in the least ashamed of the intense desire that had driven him to do it.

Desire for her.

God, what was she doing? Why had she fought this, fought him for so long? Why had she fought herself?

"*¿Querida?*"

She set the candle back on the counter, shaking her head as she smoothed the dark silk from the side of his face and then pressed her fingers to his lips. "Just kiss me."

He already was.

Those eyes.

His gaze flared hotter, brighter, searing. She could feel it skimming her fingers as he took her hand in his. Like he had that day in her office at the hospital, he brushed his lips lightly over her skin, but unlike that day, he did it again. Over and over, as his mouth moved slowly up her hand, pausing to turn her arm and press a kiss to the underside of her wrist. He dipped his head and feathered his lips down her forearm, stopping again when he reached the inside of her elbow.

She shivered as the tip of his tongue traced the crease.

Then he continued on.

He skipped the sleeve of her T-shirt, hovering at the curve of her neck, instead. But there, he didn't kiss.

He inhaled.

Slowly, deeply. And then he sighed.

His breath fanned her neck, then her cheek, as he straightened. He cupped his palms to her face and stared deep into her eyes, filling her gaze.

Filling her.

"*Cariño,* I have never known such beauty as you. Inside, as well as the out. I have dreamt of you since the day we met aboard your ship. My dreams now torture me all hours of the day as well as the night. I see your eyes, I hear your voice, I feel your skin. I smell your scent. Woman, you haunt me."

He brushed his thumbs beneath her eyes, catching the tears she hadn't even known had fallen, but he didn't kiss her.

God, what was he waiting for?

She wanted him, too. Surely he could see that?

"Tomás, please."

He shook his head gently, firmly. "I cannot. Please, do not ask this of me. You must not. I will have you in my home for as long as you would stay. Indeed, if called to do so, I would lay down my very life for you. You must know this. But, please, do not ask me to kiss you again. For if I do, I shall not be able to stop." He released her and stepped back.

She wanted desperately to pull him to her again, but his eyes stopped her. Her breath caught as she finally placed the darkest of emotions swirling in his gaze. How could she have missed it all this time? She'd seen the desire, yes, and a host of others as well. But not this.

He was in pain. No, he was in turmoil.

Because of her.

And then he was pulling the dish towel from his shoulder, turning away to lay it on the counter. She swore she could see his hand quaking as he curled his fingers down to his side. Then he was walking to the edge of the kitchen, stopping when he reached the entrance to the hallway beyond.

He didn't turn. But he did speak, "You will forgive me if I take a few moments to myself, *sí*?"

"Of course."

"*Gracias*." He nodded once, then headed down the hall, opening the door at the end softly, closing it behind himself just as softly, leaving her sitting on the counter, staring at the barrier.

Wondering.

Just what the hell was she supposed to do now?

Chapter 11

Karin sat on the kitchen island for close to eternity before she heard him again or, rather, it.

Running water.

TJ was taking a bath, not a shower, but a bath.

The reason was perfectly clear.

If he'd started the shower, she'd have known it. Two seconds later, she'd be in there, too. Yelling at him about his stitches again. It was ironic. In her own bathroom earlier today she'd told him he didn't know her. She'd been wrong.

He did know her.

Better than she knew herself, it seemed.

He knew she needed to make up her own mind in her own good time. And he was giving her the freedom to do it. Completely. The decision was hers and hers alone.

His door was not locked.

Neither was the one leading into the bathroom beyond.

She knew it just as surely as she could still feel the blood coursing through her body to pool deep inside her. All she had to do was open those doors and he would welcome her into his arms and into his bed. But if she chose not to climb down from this counter and follow him, he would finish his bath alone. And then he would dry off, dress and come back out.

Alone. No matter how much he wanted her.

Six years.

Tomás hadn't had a woman in six years. Surely that meant something? She'd asked herself the question often enough since last night and finally she had the answer.

It did mean something. To her.

It meant he was not like her father, and it was high time she recognized the difference.

Now.

She slid off the island and headed for the counter, reaching into her black bag for the single-sailor's shore packet. She'd handed out hundreds of condoms over the past two years. This time she took one for herself.

On second thought, she grabbed a handful.

Six years was an awfully long time, especially when she added it to twenty-seven. She didn't even bother stuffing them into the pocket of her jeans, just held on to them tightly as she took one step, then another. Before she knew it, she was at the end of the hall, standing in front of his door. A deep breath, and the door was open.

It wasn't hard at all.

She stepped inside, letting her eyes roam the room as she entered. Marian had followed the color scheme in here, as well. The four-poster bed was king-size—not a surprise given TJ's height—with the rest of the furniture dark and imposing, as well. Red pillows were scattered across the bronze comforter, but when Karin turned to lay the condoms on the nightstand, she came face-to-face with one accessory she knew Marian had not been responsible for.

Beside his wallet and his gun. It was a picture of her.

In TJ's arms.

It had been taken during the only dance she'd accepted

from him at the reception, mainly because as best man and maid of honor, she hadn't been able to get out of it.

She picked up the photo and studied it, studied him. Lord, did this man look good in a tux. Gorgeous. One hundred percent pure panther. Just like he had at Manning's party. Except his mane hadn't been pulled back at the wedding.

And his hands.

She could still feel his fingers stroking her back through the thin satin, flirting with the edges of her sleeveless blue dress. But as usual, it was his gaze that had done it.

Deep, smoldering.

Commanding.

One look into those eyes was all it had taken.

By the time she'd heard the shutter click, it was too late. The damage was done. She couldn't even claim she'd been framed. Because the camera had caught her in the act, exposing the very thing she'd been trying for months to hide from Tomás—and from herself. The evidence was right there in her gaze as she stared up into that smoke.

She loved him.

The wedding pictures had come back three days before their ship was deployed. Jade had offered a copy to her. At first she'd been too stunned to accept it and then, of course, too chicken.

Obviously TJ had not.

If there was any doubt left at all that she'd made the right decision, that picture erased it. She set the gilded frame back down next to his wallet and gun and stacked the condoms beside them, then turned to the bed and started to undress.

TJ stiffened as his straining ears finally picked up the faint but unmistakable sound of the bedroom door opening and then closing. His heart lurched, then began thundering so loudly he could hear naught else. He tried to slow it, to rein in his joy, but he could not.

Karin was in his room.

Unfortunately, this did not mean she would stay.

The photograph.

Sí. He had thought to remove it, lest its presence frighten her away. But why? Best she know now how deeply he cared. Perhaps the photo would calm her fears. It might even ease the doubts from her mind, soothe the shadows from her eyes. And if it did not, who was he to say her opening that door again and leaving was not for the best—for her?

He closed his eyes and forced his body to relax as he leaned back into the whirlpool. Coward that he was, he reached out and turned the jets on, in hopes the swirling bubbles would calm his pounding heart, as well as his fears.

They did not.

Perhaps he should not have bared his soul so soon.

He had told himself he would wait. And still, he would.

But from the moment the elevator doors had opened and he heard someone running down the hall near her apartment to slam the door to the stairwell beyond, everything had changed. He had changed. A moment later he was running. He would never forget the unspeakable terror that had surged through him upon finding her door unlocked, upon finding her.

His woman, his heart.

Lying there, not moving. No blood, no obvious wound save the mark on her jaw, and yet so very still. He had known then he could no longer pretend he did not feel what he did, even with her. She would accept him or not, but she must know.

Though he had hoped to settle her in her room first.

Had he spoken too soon?

She would not even trust in the love of her mother. A love he had seen with his own eyes. How could he ever hope she would trust in him? Her scars ran deep. He understood this perhaps too well. Just as he knew that making love with him would not heal those scars, much as he would like it to.

Indeed, in the end it might well destroy her.

He might destroy her.

His life was not an easy one. The danger, the waiting, the separations. Sometimes when he went undercover, he went weeks or more before he could contact his friends. And sometimes his fellow agents were women. Even in the depths of his despair he had never crossed that line, not even when he had been invited to do so. But would Karin believe this?

Could she?

He would rather cut his heart out here and now than slice hers open slowly, night after night, case after case.

Doubt after doubt.

Dios, what was taking so long?

Had she changed her mind?

He reached for the washcloth, determined to make use of the wait, but it fell to the water unnoticed as the door finally opened. She had come. His heart swelled painfully as she entered the room and closed the door. Her bruised chin high, her eyes burning bright and blue, she stared back at him, not at all shy.

And she wore his robe.

The black silk one piped in red that Jade had mailed three months before. Jade had also made certain he knew Karin had actually selected the garment while the two were shopping in Japan, though she swore Karin would never admit to this.

That his lady had chosen it pleased him greatly.

That she wore it now pleased him more.

She stepped to the edge of the tub and he swallowed, suddenly unsure. Did he stand? Would he frighten her? For part of him had already risen.

High.

In the end he glanced at the water swirling below his chest. "*Cariño,* I am not clothed."

She smiled softly, her slender fingers on the belt, un-knotting. And then they were not. "That makes two of us." The robe slipped slowly down her curves to pool at her feet.

And he stared.

She was a vision. *La perfección.*

Petite, but in no way a child. Creamy skin from her softly curving shoulders down to the valley between those en-chanting breasts. Their fullness did not surprise him, for he had weighed them in his palms in her kitchen the morning before and then in the hospital. But her nipples did. In sating his hunger, he had not noticed how wide nor how dark they were. The peaks already stiff, they begged for his touch.

He did not.

Instead, he simply stared.

He followed the creamy silk of her flat stomach down to that enchanting navel puckering at the center. Like the dim-ples that framed her smile, that dip drove him to distraction simply by being. He slid his gaze lower still—and smiled. Her womanly curls were of spun gold, also. He brought his hungry gaze back to her face and waited, for she, too, was looking her fill.

Those wide blue eyes finally left his chest and the ob-scuring froth at his waist and found his gaze again.

"Tomás?"

"*¿Sí, querida?*"

Her smile dipped deeply. "Make love to me."

"*Con todo mi corazón.*"

Her brow raised in question.

But he did not translate as he stood. While he loved her this day, he would tell her freely what he wished. And perhaps, when time allowed her to learn the meaning of his words, she would no longer doubt their truth. But there was one thing he would tell her that she must understand. "*Car-iño,* I have no protection. I can make it so it is not neces-sary, but if you wish, I can go—"

She opened her hand and relief flooded him.

She did want this, did want *him*.

He truly would have assured her pleasure without entering her if need be, had even thought it would perhaps be best this first time. But to know she wanted him inside her enough to come prepared—ay! His joy and excitement increased.

"Oh, my." Her gaze found his. "That night I, uh, stitched you up, were you this, uh…"

"Aroused?"

She nodded.

"Most definitely."

"Oh."

He felt her bravado waver along with her voice. He should not be surprised. If he was this nervous, how must she feel? And when he reached for the packet, he knew.

Her fingers trembled.

He set the packet beside the tub, his heart tightening as he turned back to her. Her fingers might be held loose at her thighs now, but they were also locked. Though she would never admit it, he suspected she was more than nervous. She covered her fears well, however, her dimples teasing him as she took his outstretched hand and allowed him to assist her into the tub. She even came willingly into his arms before he asked, but the feel of her full breasts and soft curls pressed so intimately to his flesh was nearly his undoing.

He sucked in his breath and brought his raging desire to heel as best he could. He must slow this now, or they would have no need of the protection she had provided. Or worse, he would take her here, now, in the tub. Given this was her first time, that would not be wise. For the position would no doubt prove too intense, too painful.

Somehow he managed to set her from him.

She frowned.

"Relax, *querida*. I will not be long, nor far." He turned to take a fresh cloth from the basket beside the tub, then dipped it into the bubbles swirling about her silken thighs, smiling as he added a squirt of soap and worked it into a lather. "You did not complete your shower today, *sí?*"

She shook her head mutely.

"Turn then. I shall bathe you."

Karin stared at TJ, thoroughly confused. But when he arched his brow and waited, she did as he requested.

A bath? She hadn't come in here to get clean. So why— Ahhh.

She sighed as Tomás rubbed the cloth across her shoulders, then worked it down her back. Okay, that did feel good. But even so, this wasn't exactly the way she thought he'd be touching her. True, she hadn't done this before, but that didn't mean she didn't know what she wanted. And it wasn't that damned cloth. Or a massage. Not matter how good it felt.

She wanted his hands.

All over her.

She wanted him to touch her the way he had in her dreams these past eight months. The way he'd been touching her before her mother walked in. But even as her mind grumbled, her body sighed. She took it back. The man did know what he was doing, because that cloth was working wonders on her nerves. Slowly, steadily, the tension was easing and, yes, even the fear that was coiled tightly along with her desire.

By the time Tomás reached around her for the copper pitcher and scooped it into the water surrounding them, she was completely through questioning his methods. She felt too darn good. He'd finished rinsing her back and was dipping the pitcher into the water again. She gave a start when he tipped her head back and soaked her hair, but the warm breath and soft words at her ear calmed her. More Spanish she couldn't understand.

She sighed, anyway. Then sucked in her breath.

Shampoo had followed the water. He was digging his fingers deep into the tangles on her head, massaging every inch of her scalp as he worked the lather in. She wasn't even aware she was groaning until he chuckled.

"This feels good, no?"

"Wonderful."

She didn't need to see the satisfaction in his smile—she could feel it. He continued to massage her scalp until she'd relaxed so much her head kept dropping back toward him. Then he filled the pitcher and rinsed. What now? Detangler?

Her favorite brand, no less?

She wouldn't put it past him. He knew her that well.

But it wasn't cream rinse. It was the washcloth again, this time at her thighs. She stiffened momentarily, then calmed as his voice caressed her ear once again.

Warm, gentle. Soothing.

His voice, the cloth.

But by the time the cloth made its way to her waist, the stroking had changed. He was still washing her. The rag still moving in slow circles over her skin, higher and higher—but then it was gone. He was massaging with the whole of his hands now. Palms and fingers splayed wide, strong and slick with soap, he kept up the same steady sweep, until he reached her breasts.

She pressed back against him, trying to rub her bottom against his erection, but she was too short. He groaned, sliding his hands down to grasp her pelvis and lift her so she could reach his shaft. His lips left her ear, trailed down her neck, nipping, tasting. He licked the water from her shoulders, then bit down gently.

She gasped as the erotic shock speared straight to her core and tried desperately to turn in his arms, but he wouldn't let her. "Tomás, I want—"

His mouth returned to her ear, soothing. "Shhh. You must trust me, *querida.*"

"I do."

Again she heard his smile. "Then be patient. In good time."

His hands slipped up her belly, still slick with soap. They reached her breasts, cupping, kneading, weighing. Teasing. His lips and his tongue resumed their torture, as well, this time at her ear as he lifted her to fit her rear to his groin. He drew the lobe of her ear in gently, worrying it between his teeth, his breathing turning harsh as her bottom began rubbing against him of its own accord, matching the torment he was plying with his fingers and his teeth stroke for stroke. His very breath was turning her on now.

And his voice. Dark, husky and so very seductive.

What on earth was he saying?

The sultry words swirled into her ears, but before she could ask what they meant, his hands parted company— one still caressing her breasts, plucking first one nipple, then the other, while his other hand slid low. Very low. Her breath caught as he skimmed her tuft of curls, but his hand continued down, sliding over her thighs, instead of skimming back up again.

She groaned, this time in frustration.

His soft chuckle washed over her. "This pleases you, no?"

"Yes—again."

"As you wish, *querida.*"

But when his hand returned, she didn't get quite what she'd asked for. She got more. His fingers were threading into the curls now, delving between the sensitive folds of her flesh, seeking, finding, filling. She arched back into his chest, gasping as she reached up to dig her hands into his hair, holding on for dear life as his fingers plundered freely and oh-so-firmly.

"You are so wet, *Cariño,* so very tight."

"Yes."

He shuddered as he withdrew his hand.

"No, I want—"

"It is time."

Before she realized what had happened, he'd swept her into his arms and was stepping out of the tub. How he got them through the bathroom door, she had no idea, but he did. The next thing she knew, she was lying beneath him on the bed she'd turned down, reveling in his weight as he pressed the length of his hard slick body into hers. And then he was kissing her.

Deeply.

Thoroughly.

She raked her fingers up the muscles of his arms and wound them into his thick silky hair. Moments later he was pushing his hands through her damp tangles, anchoring her as he ravaged her mouth, her neck, her shoulders and every inch of flesh in between. When he bent low to fasten his mouth to her breasts and suck each greedily in turn, she knew her opportunity had finally come. She reached between them, wrapped her hand around his solid shaft and squeezed.

He bucked, his shoulders flexing as he loomed over her, his dark gaze smoldering into hers.

"Please, I've been dreaming of this for months."

His gaze flared hotter at her confession, then molten as she stroked his shaft slowly, gradually working her way down to the base and then back up to the tip. She swore she could feel the blood surging through him as she squeezed again, firmly. She could definitely hear his breath hitch, then clog in his lungs. Driven to look, she tore her gaze from his and followed the black silk trailing below the taut quivering muscles of his waist and stared.

He was beautiful.

Thick and jutting and fully engorged.

No, not fully. Not quite yet. She could feel him thickening still, hardening beneath her sliding fingers as she watched his dusky satin turn duskier. She scraped her nails up his shaft, then smoothed the pads of her fingers over and around the blunt tip. He growled as she captured the telltale drop of fluid from his flesh, then choked as she brought it to her lips.

His hand shot up, wrapping around her wrist. His eyes

slammed shut as he fought for control. Moments later they opened, his gaze searing straight into her as he dragged her hands above her head and locked them together with one of his. "Woman, take care, lest you unman me before the deed is done."

She smiled.

And he got even.

His fingers found her curls again. He stroked them teasingly, probed intimately, laughing softly as she squirmed beneath him. She couldn't help it—soon her legs were parting shamelessly, inviting him farther. His breath filled her ear, hot and taunting. "What is it you want, *querida?* What else do you dream of? Have you not learned by now I can deny you nothing? You have but to ask and I will give it."

She moaned.

Another deep rumbling chuckle. "Perhaps you are not certain. Shall I help you decide? Tell me, is this what you want?" He slid first one firm finger deep inside her, then another, burying them to the hilt as he turned his hand slowly but surely, stretching her ever so gently. She sighed as he slid them out and then back in to do it again...and again.

"Yes, *that.*"

More sultry laughter. "You should not make up your mind so quickly, *querida,* for perhaps you would prefer this." He found the nub at her entrance and rubbed slowly, insistently, razing his mouth down her neck to incinerate the next moan right through the flesh of her throat.

Oh, yessss!

She shuddered as his fingers continued to knead gently, relentlessly, pulling her deeper and deeper into the sweltering haze. Soon she was drenched from within—but it had nothing to do with the bath they'd taken and everything to do with him.

And those magic hands.

If his intent was to hear her beg, he was going to get his wish any moment. She had no illusions. This man had enough experience to drive her to the brink of insanity and beyond if he wanted. She did not. But she could match him in one way.

In the only way she now knew mattered.

Love.

Tomás loved her as deeply and as desperately as she loved him. She could feel it inside every shudder racking his body, hear it in every ragged breath he took, every catch in his voice, every groan. And, most especially, in every fiery syllable he spoke as he continued to rub. She might not be able to understand a single word of Spanish—she didn't have to. She knew exactly what he was saying. Just as she knew exactly what he wanted. Because she wanted it, too.

Now.

She didn't think Tomás even realized he'd released her hands. He was too busy licking, tasting, consuming. Feeding his own hunger right along with hers as he nipped and sucked his way back down to her aching breasts. She reached blindly for the nightstand, knocking his gun and his wallet and probably the picture, as well, to the floor as she searched frantically for the condoms, sighing as she found one.

She blessed every single one of the times she'd been trapped into demonstrating how to don the damn things in front of a roomful of snickering sailors as she ripped the side of the packet down and tugged it out.

Finally.

He sucked in his breath as she reached between them, sheathing him in one smooth practiced sweep—but that was precisely where her expertise ran out.

It didn't matter.

Because he took over. Lifting, parting, nudging.

And then she was gasping.

He froze, staring deep into her eyes as he cupped her face. "*¿Querida?* If I have hurt you—"

"If you stop now, I'm going to hurt you."

The panic and concern vanished from his face. Sensual pleasure filled their place as he smiled. "As you wish."

And then he moved.

Slowly, steadily, incredibly.

There was no real pain, only minor burning, stretching, as he eased himself in and then out. And, of course, this exquisite erotic fullness.

He was watching her.

Gauging her every sigh, her every gasp, adjusting his pace as she adjusted to him. He filled her over and over, stopping ever so briefly each time he sheathed himself, just long enough to bend down and capture the soft moan that escaped her lips—and smile as he swallowed it whole. Then he would start over.

She wasn't exactly sure how he knew when it was time to pick up the pace, but he did. And by then, she welcomed it. Welcomed him. She was dimly aware of his stitches scraping into her shoulder as he began grinding in and out, again and again. She prayed the sutures could withstand the now-searing friction, because she did not want him to stop.

What she wanted was more.

Before she could even ask, he gave it. But it still wasn't enough. She wanted it all and she wanted it now.

She drove her nails into his shoulders, scored them down his back, digging them into his rear as Tomás gave her everything he had. Everything she'd ever wanted, let alone needed. Harder, faster, *deeper*. Until, suddenly, she couldn't stand it anymore. He had to end this.

Please.

His voice had turned harsh, thick, commanding.

But what did he want her to do?

And then she knew. Take it. Take him.

And so she did.

One moment she was locking her arms and her legs around his slick pounding body and the next she was a part of him, blending, merging, becoming one. And then they exploded, shattering into a billion blinding shards.

Together.

They hung there, suspended in heaven itself for a single glorious moment, and then they were raining down. Slowly, softly and surely, wrapped in each other's arms, sated and finally at peace.

Chapter 12

She was an angel.

A vision of spun gold, ivory skin and softly fanned lashes. His left wrist nearly numb, TJ propped himself onto his elbow so he could continue to watch Karin as she slept. Though he had experienced the miracle of their lovemaking himself, he still could not believe heaven had finally seen fit to bequeath to him this most precious of gifts. Yet here she was.

In his bed and in his arms.

He had given his body many times in the past—this was shamefully true. But until this woman, he had never given his heart. And this, he had learned, made all the difference.

He had found his paradise.

There was naught left for him to do but pray he was allowed to remain. He smoothed his fingers down her cheek, skirting the bruise shadowing her jaw to caress the curve of her neck. He trailed his fingers down her arm, then up, chuckling softly as he skimmed the edge of the sheet she had twisted about her breasts and waist. She had not even stirred as he touched her. It had been thus for the better part of an hour now.

Sí, his lady was truly an angel.

But she slept like the dead.

This alone would have worried him had she not turned in her sleep three times to twist the sheet more tightly about herself. These movements, combined with a comment Jade had once made about trying to wake Karin on the ship— and that she had slept deeply as he had carried her from her couch to her bed two nights past—had served to calm his fears. Praise to God, it was as Karin had said. There was no concussion.

TJ drew his gaze to the bruise marring her jaw.

Still, when he found the *bastardo* responsible for this mark, he sincerely hoped Joaquín was near, for he could not guarantee his own fists would not fly. The man who had dared to hurt his woman would pay—this he had already vowed.

Y pronto, if his suspicions panned out.

Joaquín should have phoned by now. That his fellow agent had not led TJ to believe the man had met with success in Karin's apartment. More reason why he should wake and feed her now. *Dios* knew she would not take the time to prepare a meal for herself if he was forced to leave her under Joaquín's protection. As for his fellow agent?

They would both likely suffer food poisoning.

It was decided, then.

He brushed the curls from her forehead. *"¿Cariño?"*

Nada.

He stroked her cheek, then clasped her shoulder and shook her gently. *"Querida,* it is time to wake."

Again, his efforts were for naught.

What was a man to do when faced with such a challenge?

He smiled. Because he knew.

And soon so would she.

Because she had curled into him so sweetly, he began at her ear, tracing the shell with the tip of his tongue until he reached the lobe. She sighed as he pulled it into his mouth and laved gently, but still she did not wake.

So he whispered his love in Spanish and moved on.

He pressed his lips to the satin of her shoulder next and nibbled. He found reward in another sigh as she turned onto her back, but her eyes remained closed. He had gained ground, however, because in shifting, she had loosened the sheet enough to allow him to draw it from those enchanting breasts and slide it past the dimple at her slender waist.

A difficult choice.

He decided in favor of her breasts.

And why not? He had not spent nearly as much time with them as he had wanted when he had loved her before, mostly because he had needed to keep her back to him in the tub in order to keep his wits about him. Having no such constraints now, he bent low and blew gently across the tips.

He smiled as they hardened and he bent lower.

Using first his fingers and then his lips and tongue, he flirted freely, paying particular attention to those charming pink tips. She moaned softly and arched into his hands and mouth, but incredibly, she still did not open those beautiful eyes.

Was he to take this to fruition before she awoke?

So be it.

Loath to leave her breasts just yet, he continued to suckle as he slid the sheet past her hips and slipped his fingers between her thighs. She moaned again as he reached those silky curls, seeking the spot that had brought her such pleasure earlier. By the time he had fitted his thumb and finger to the nub and begun to rub, he knew, he now had her complete and most wakeful attention. He had earned a deep gasp, as well.

"The nightstand. There's another—"

Still stroking, he broke his mouth from her breasts to seal his lips to her ear. "Hush, *mi amor.* I shall not need one. This is for you alone. Take what I give you."

He thought to return his mouth to her breasts, but found he could not. For he had seen the pleasure washing her face. Each time he rubbed, her lashes swept lower, until they were all but closed again. She was, however, most definitely awake, for she was writhing beneath his hand.

Her neck arched as another, deeper moan escaped.

He continued to stroke gently, leaning down to press his mouth to her throat, his own desire now raging hot and painfully hard as he caught the vibrations beneath his lips.

She was all he had dreamed she would be. And more.

He raised his head, drawn again to her face.

It was building.

Soon she would cry out for him as she had before. Already her limbs had begun to quiver, her flesh to dampen. Driven to taste her, he brought his mouth to her breasts and licked the salt from the valley between. He bowed to the craving again and consumed the remaining salt from the mounds themselves.

"Tomás, please. I want…I need…"

"*¿Sí, querida?* What is it you desire? Tell me."

How had his voice grown so hoarse? Why? He was not taking this time, merely giving. But when his gaze returned to her face and still she had not answered, he saw why.

She could not.

Her eyes.

They were wide with desire, darker than he had ever seen them. So deeply blue, he could see his face reflected within the shimmering pools. The sight was nearly his undoing.

As was the knowledge that came with it.

In giving so freely to this woman he loved, he was receiving a hundredfold. He stared into the growing fire in her eyes and only the fire, feeding it willingly as he rubbed her again and again. For how long he knew not. For his very existence had drawn down to this dark blue gaze and the sweet moisture flowing over his stroking fingers. Until suddenly, she stiffened, and then shuddered—and he watched her go blind.

But then *he* stiffened.

¡Pero, no—era imposible! He was not even touching himself, much less inside her.

But it was not impossible and it was happening.

He could not stop himself from locking his free hand to hers and pouring his love out beside her as she finished milking his fingers. He collapsed against her, so very grateful when her arms came up to wrap about him, pull him close and hold him tight—for he could not move.

She sighed into his neck. But then she groaned. "I take it back. I seem to have misdiagnosed myself."

He found the strength to move *immediately*. He jerked his head up to search her face, but swore he could find naught but contentment. Then what—

She nodded solemnly. "Concussion. I definitely have one." But then she was threading her fingers into his hair, her dimples winking impudently as she pushed the strands from his face. "I'm afraid I'll need to be woken every hour, on the hour, throughout the night. *Just like that.*"

Karin stared into the shock in Tomás's eyes and couldn't help it. The laughter just bubbled up and out. She was still chuckling as she watched the relief crash through the panic, shattering it instantly—and then she shrieked.

"Don't tickle me!"

Not only did Tomás refuse to listen, he dragged both her hands above her head and pinned them to the feather pillow with just one of his so he could torture her at will. She was gasping, damned near out of breath by the time he relented.

"Beast!"

The man hadn't even broken a sweat.

Now. But before…

She would never forget the look on his face as his release hit. How he had managed to look so stunned and so incredibly aroused at the same time, she'd never know. But she would treasure that expression for the rest of her life. She didn't need to ask if he'd ever been so involved that he'd just lost it before. She knew.

He hadn't.

She sighed as he finally freed her hands, looping her arms about his neck as he bent to nuzzle her throat. "Brute."

"Brute?" He dug his elbows into the bed on either side of her, chuckling as he levered the bulk of his dusky chest from hers. Though she missed the weight, she could at least find her breath. She promptly lost it again as his gaze smoldered anew. "Woman, I gave you plenty of warning in my kitchen. It is far too late to cry foul over the man you have received."

It sure as hell was.

Thank God.

She smiled. "Okay, I'll give you that. But you made another promise in that kitchen. One for food. And you've yet to make good on it."

"I admit, I am guilty. For this, I humbly beg your forgiveness."

Ha! He didn't look humble.

What he looked was sated.

Like the proverbial panther in the sun. Any moment now she expected to hear a deep purr rumbling from his chest. He sighed, instead—smugly. "However, in my own defense I must add that I tried to satisfy the one appetite before the other, but you simply would not wake. *Querida,* you sleep like the—"

"I know—you don't have to say it. In fact, please don't say it. I had to listen to my mother make that same complaint every single morning as I got ready for school growing up."

She took advantage of TJ's lazy stretch and wriggled out from beneath him, pulling the sheet to her breasts as she sat up.

Not that it did any good.

Between his wandering lips and fingers, the man was doing his damnedest to see if he could get that first hunger to override the second again. She slapped his nimble fingers as they drifted beneath the sheet, almost succeeding.

"Are you going to feed me or not?"

He sighed his defeat and jackknifed off the bed to retrieve the folded jeans he'd stacked neatly on his dresser. Hers, of course, were crumpled on the floor somewhere. Guilt fled in favor of hedonistic delight as she was finally treated to a reverse replay of the night he'd stripped in her room.

She sighed as he tucked himself inside and zipped up.

He smiled and arched that teasing brow.

As if on cue, her stomach rumbled.

"Very well, I shall try. But I must warn you, a decent meal may prove difficult as we left what little we did possess sitting on the counter—" He retrieved his watch from the dresser and glanced at the face as he strapped the leather band to his wrist. "Nearly two hours ago."

"I have faith."

"*Gracias.* But even I must have food in order to cook it."

She shrugged. "So make me a list. I'll go shopping while you get started."

He chuckled. "I think not."

"Excuse me? You think I can't get by south of the border?" She crossed her arms over the sheet. "I'm sure I can find one or two bilingual men willing to use English around me."

He had the nerve to add a smile to his shrug. "You will learn."

"And I can start right now—and don't try to use what happened today to stop me. If someone had followed us, they'd have made their move by now." She swung her legs to the floor, determined to nip this latest he-man episode in the bud. Unfortunately her man was looming over her, bracing his hands about her on either side of the bed, trapping her before she could get her arms uncrossed, let alone get into the T-shirt he'd dropped next to her.

He did not look happy with this latest challenge to his authority, either.

Too bad. She was through giving in. "Tomás, I have a degree in medicine. I know my way around the human body. Surely I can find my way around the outskirts of a city—even a Mexican one."

He sighed. "*Cariño,* you do not understand. Furthermore, this has naught to do with the case. You must not leave my house unattended, even after it is solved. Surely you can see this?"

"I'm afraid I can't."

"Woman, have you no idea the temptation you present?"

She stiffened.

Dammit, she no longer cared how Tomás had been raised, or where. If they had any hope for a relationship, he was going to need a remedial course in equality.

American equality.

"That attitude is completely chauvinistic—"

"As is this entire country. And do not bother to lecture me on what I can see in your face. You think to bring your rules and your laws down with you and expect my countrymen to comply? It will not happen. And I will not have my woman harassed because she is too stubborn to accept what is best for her. *¿Entiendes?*"

My woman?

And that tone.

A split second before her temper reached liftoff, she managed to short-circuit the switch. He wanted to play lord of the jungle? Fine with her. She'd let him beat his chest and roar. And then she'd do what she damn well pleased.

In the meantime she managed a nod. "I understand."

He nodded and raised her a teasing smile. "You see, you begin to learn the language already."

No, what she'd learned was that this man had the manners of a snorting bull when thwarted. Not to mention the testosterone level to go with it. My woman, her ass. No matter. She continued to bite her tongue, her bottom lip along with it.

Sit here and take it.

Unfortunately he saw right through her.

And changed his tactics.

He lifted one of his hands and trailed his fingers beneath her jaw, urging it up until she was forced to meet his gaze. "Please, you must trust me on this. That border you crossed, it is more than a line drawn across a piece of paper. It is a line drawn between cultures. When it comes to *los hombres y las mujeres,* most of my countrymen believe in the difference, not the equality. If you persist, you may find yourself the object of unwanted attention—or worse." He moved to intercept her evading glance. "Is this what you want? To win your argument at the expense of my fear— and perhaps your own safety?"

Arrgh, why did he have to put it like that?

She closed her eyes. "No."

"Then you will not leave unless I am able to escort you, *sí?*" He stroked his thumb across her bottom lip.

She knew exactly what he was doing.

And, dammit, it was working.

The Tarzan tactics she could handle. She could turn her back on them in two seconds flat. But not this overpowering concern. And not that bottomless gaze. How did he manage to get those eyes to command and plead at the same time?

His thumb found her mouth again. *"¿Querida?"*

She sighed. "Oh, all right. I won't leave without you."

"Bien."

He didn't have to look so damned happy about it.

Or relieved.

He lowered himself to the bed, threading the fingers of one hand into hers as he stroked the bruise along her jaw with the other. "I promise to take you shopping in Tijuana or even to Ensenada once I have found the man responsible for this. We will shop and I will prepare a feast, *sí?* Whatever you wish. For you and for your parents. And if Reese and Jade have returned—''

She stiffened. "Excuse me?"

Parents? The man just couldn't stop, could he?

He shook his head. "What?"

"You're doing it again, Tomás. You're planning my life for me. And you're meddling."

It was his turned to stiffen. "I beg your pardon?"

"Uh-uh, I'm not falling for it this time. You don't want me to run to the store, fine. I'll give in. But not about this. I told you, I don't want to discuss the past with my mother. And that's exactly what you're trying to get me to do. Oh, it was smooth, but it was there."

She knew she'd nailed him. She could tell by his eyes.

But she certainly didn't feel victorious about it. All she felt was the sting of defeat. "Please, you've got to stop trying to force me into things. Especially that."

"Cariño—"

"Karin, and I admit, you know a lot about me. But you don't know everything. My relationship with my mother is fine. What happened—or rather, what didn't—between my father and me is over and done with. The man is gone, Tomás, and he's not ever coming back. So there's no point in—"

"He is not."

It was said so quietly, so firmly, she froze.

And then she blinked. "I beg your pardon?"

"I said, he is not."

"I caught that. What exactly is that cryptic comment supposed to mean? I know your long-lost father just showed up, but trust me, mine isn't next."

He took her hand and squeezed it gently. *"Querida,* your father does not need to return, because he has never left."

Okay, now she was really confused, especially when he cupped her cheek. And those eyes. Why the hell did he look so sad? "What are you trying to say?"

"Your father, he is right here between us. He has been

since the day we met. This man, he colors everything in your life. No, he drains the color from it, from you. Just as he drains your soul. And he will continue to do so until you speak about this to your mother. You must tell her what happened. It will free you.''

First the Tarzan routine, now Dr. Freud.

She didn't care how much she loved this man, it had to stop. Now. ''You don't know what you're talking about.''

''What about Consuela?''

''Your cousin?''

''Sí, mi prima.''

She wasn't confused anymore. She was livid.

She managed to work off some of her fury by shooting off the bed and stalking across the room. She grabbed her underpants from the floor and yanked them on.

But it didn't help.

''Consuela. That's rich. I catch you with your tongue down her throat, and I'm the one who has problems dealing with the past?''

''I told you what you saw.''

''Ha!'' She grabbed her bra next and jerked it into place. ''I'm supposed to take *your* word for it?'' Even as she finished throwing the punch, she knew it had landed well below the belt.

But she was too ticked off to care.

And, damn him, he just sat there.

However, he wasn't as calm as he wanted her to believe. The fire in his eyes gave him away, as did the steel in his voice. ''Woman, I have never lied to you, not one time. But I see you do not believe me. This is not what worries me, for this trust will come in time. What truly terrifies me is you did not have the courage to confront me months ago when this happened. You could have screamed at me, struck at me—anything. Instead, you break our date with not so much as an explanation and then run and hide from me like a child.''

That was it. She'd had enough.

Hell, she'd heard enough.

She yanked her T-shirt over her head and snatched her jeans off the floor. Where the devil were her shoes?

Screw 'em. It wasn't cold.

The hell with this man and his whole damned country. She'd walk to the border in her bare feet if she had to, and God help the latter-day Neanderthal who got in the way of *her* club. She stalked to the door and slapped her hand on the knob. Tomás finally vaulted to his feet as she jerked it open.

"*Cariño,* please. Do not—"

She whirled around, focusing all her fury into one glare. "It's *Karin.* I've told you and I've told you. My name is *Karin.*"

"This, I know! Just as I know you are running away *again.*" He raked his hands thorough his hair and locked them together at the back of his neck, but he didn't move from the side of the bed. "Now tell me something. Tell me, where is the woman who stands and fights for her patients when she is at the hospital? Where is the woman who still fights to keep Señor Callahan from grinding her name into the dirt? Where is this woman who fought to pull me back from my despair this past night? And where is she who battled her deepest fears just this day so she might come to me and make love with me, despite them? I want this woman. Give her back to me—and tell this frightened child to leave for good!"

"*Damn you.*"

He stood there, just staring.

Then he sighed. Deeply.

And nodded. "I am. I see this most clearly now. I thought I had entered paradise today. I was wrong—I have entered hell. For I love a woman who does not love herself."

TJ held his breath as he waited for Karin's response, praying as he had never prayed before. Not even when he had held Antonio in his arms as the man hovered on the brink of death had he prayed so hard. In the end it mattered not.

God had already answered.

And as with Antonio, He had answered no.

This golden angel was not his, nor would she be staying—for she did not wish to stay. He clenched his fingers into the back of his neck so fiercely he was stunned he did not draw blood. Perhaps he should not have been surprised. It merely meant the bleeding in his heart had already drained his soul.

She turned to leave.

And gasped.

Until that moment, he had not noticed, either.

Joaquín.

His fellow agent and friend appeared as frozen as they amid the chilling silence of the still open door. Joaquín finally held up the manila file in his right hand. "I have it."

The case.

Like a wooden puppet, TJ jerked his nod. Karin, too, stared at the file. It seemed he had been granted a reprieve.

But at what cost?

Enough.

Though he could not save his heart, he would save her life. He reached the door as she turned back to him, staring blindly into his eyes, seeing what, he did not know.

Nor did he wish to know.

"Wh-what does he have?"

TJ picked up her jeans from where they had fallen at her feet and carefully folded them over her arm as he guided her back to the bed. He did not need to see Joaquín turn and depart to know he had. He knew his friend well. "Clothe yourself. We will talk when you have finished, *sí?*"

A stiff nod.

And then he left, closing the door behind him to afford her privacy.

TJ found his friend in the kitchen, attempting to tidy the mess. He smiled grimly, for though they were alike in many ways, appearance included, desire for an uncluttered kitchen was not one of them. The information he had chosen to carry south in place of phoning must be weighty indeed.

He cleared his throat.

Joaquín dumped the cutting board and wilted vegetables into the sink and turned, by tacit agreement, beginning in their native tongue. "I should have knocked. But the door, she opened it, and then…" He sighed. "I am sorry."

TJ shrugged.

First her mother, now his friend. Although his most intimate moments of late seemed to come with interruption, this time he was forced to acknowledge the relief that had come, as well. At least to himself.

Joaquín held up his key.

TJ shook his head.

There was no need to alter the alarm codes, either.

"But next time I should knock, yes?"

In the end, it was less painful to nod. "Perhaps you should."

"Agreed." His friend slipped the key back into his pocket as he cocked his head to the hallway beyond. "Your lady, does she know?"

"So, what have you boys been keeping from me?"

Karin.

They whirled about together.

They had been conversing in Spanish, had they not? How could she have understood? Then he knew.

A guess. An excellent one at that.

It seemed her wits had survived their confrontation more firmly intact than his, for he could not even remember what language he spoke. But his mind was not so dulled that he failed to notice how she kept the kitchen island between them or the schooled steadiness to her gaze.

They had truly come full circle, then.

The wariness, the mistrust. It was back.

As surely as the rest was gone. Or perhaps it had not really been there at all. Had it been his imagination?

"Well, are you going to tell me or not?"

It seemed he had little choice. He nodded from one to the other. "Special Agent Joaquín Cortez, Dr. Karin Scott."

"Please, call me Joe. It is a pleasure to finally meet you, Doctor." TJ averted his gaze as Joaquín kissed her hand.

Because her smile had been real.

"Karin. But I think we've already met. You were at Dr. Manning's party, weren't you? Serving drinks?"

Joaquín turned to include TJ in his answering grin. "You were right, *mi amigo.* She is quick. *Sí,* I was there, and may I again apologize for my clumsiness?" His smile faded. "And also for my interruption?"

Her smile wavered, then faded also. "Yes, well...as I remember it, I was the one who bumped into you at the party. And I did open the door." A deep breath. "So now that the introductions are complete, perhaps one of you would kindly tell me what's going on?"

Joaquín turned to TJ again, this time to slide the file across the island. "You will not believe the results, Tomás. I, myself, checked three times to be sure."

TJ retrieved the folder. "You have a match, then?"

"Not from the apartment nor the intruder, though we did get several excellent sets to work with from the study. However, it was when—"

"Just a damn minute."

Carajó. He had hoped it would not come to this.

Especially now.

At least the fire had found its way back into her gaze. Unfortunately it was directed at him. "You had my apartment dusted for prints, didn't you?"

Joaquín coughed. "If you will excuse me a moment, I seem to have left my notebook in my truck."

TJ offered no response, as none was expected. But perhaps the slam of the front door was overdone. He would thank his friend later, regardless. For now he had another to answer to.

He turned to her.

"You could have asked."

"Would it have changed the outcome?"

"You could have asked."

"*Sí,* I could have. But you had just been injured. You would not go to your mother's. How was I to know you would not have insisted on remaining until they had finished?"

"Dammit, you didn't even *ask.*"

"No, I did not. I did what I thought was best for you—"

She slammed her palms on the island. "That's exactly my point. Listen to yourself. You did what you thought was best for me. What am I—some brainless twit who can't put one foot in front of the other without a man around to steady me?"

"*Cariñ—*Karin. Please. You must listen to me. I was concerned. I was worried you were still in immediate danger. You would not even go to the doctor—"

"I am a doctor!"

Madre de Dios, how had he screwed this up so thoroughly?

He took a deep breath.

But before he could decide how best to approach her again, she reached across the island and snatched up the folder Joaquín had left and opened it.

"Wh-what?"

"*Qué es?*"

She seemed unable to move, so he came around the counter to her. She blinked up at him. "I...I don't understand. How...?"

Neither did he.

TJ pulled the file closer and studied the latent prints the technician had lifted from the note in Karin's box and compared them to the print card the coroner had prepared for one Jane Doe, now dubbed Magdalena.

They matched.

But surely this was impossible.

Class twos are walking.

What would a prostitute know of medicine? How would she know to phrase it just so, in the correct lingo? And how would she know of the theft in any hospital, let alone a naval one? Like Joaquín, he studied the prints again.

They did match.

"Tomás, I don't understand. Doug, Eric, Magdalena, Shelley—what possible connection could they all have?"

"You."

"But I don't even know any Mexican girls that young. Hell, I've been out of the country for the past six months."

He cupped her shoulders and squeezed gently. "Think, *querida.* This girl, you must have crossed paths somehow. The envelope had your name on it. This could not have been unintentional. You must have been selected for a reason."

She glanced at the open file. "Do you have a picture?"

Sí. Joaquín was thorough. The photograph would be there. But it would not be pleasant. What he would have given to spare her this. But as she had pointed out, she was a doctor. And she had been most clear on her feelings on his meddling. Above all, it was necessary.

He shifted his right hand to keep it at her shoulder as she faced the file, then reached down with his left to flip the cards, exposing the photo of the corpse.

She shook her head slowly. "I've never seen her before."

That whisper.

It sliced through him as even her fury could not.

He closed the file and waited until she turned back to him. She was so very pale. "You are certain you have not seen this girl?"

She nodded. But she still would not look at him, would not speak.

"The pharmacy chief, when I was at the hospital this morning, I spoke to him. I was to meet him after the infection-control class, but when my father told me the class was postponed, I—"

Her gaze shot up, wide. "Your father? You saw him again?"

He nearly groaned at the slip. Now what?

He could not lie. Not to her. Never to her.

"This morning. He found me searching your office."

She gasped. "Oh, my God—your cover. You'll be fired by Monday, if you aren't already."

"*Querida,* my cover is gone." He smoothed his fingers down her bruised jaw to make his point.

"Oh."

"It matters not. The man knew already. He claims to have been searching for me."

"And?"

And what? Tell her Antonio knew?

He could scarcely believe it himself. Besides, it did not matter. He could not let it matter, would not. There was too much weighing on his mind as it was. Her safety, his case.

"So what did your father have to say?"

"It does not matter."

"You didn't even hear him out, did you?"

He did not answer.

"You didn't. Why should you? Once again, the omnipotent Tomás Vásquez gets to decide what should be discussed and who gets to discuss it." She shook her head as she laughed sharply. "Why am I even surprised?"

"Do you want to know what happened with the pharmacy chief or not?"

"You mean you actually plan on telling me?"

He sighed, more at her tone than her answer. Perhaps he deserved this—but how it stung. "The chief tells me Señor

Callahan was furious to learn I was called to clean up the fentanyl. Is it possible Señor Callahan also knew this girl?''

''I have no idea who Doug knows. But if she's underage and around drugs, he shouldn't have been within fifty miles of her.'' She shrugged. ''Hell, what do I know? Fentanyl should never have been found in her system. The other two girls', either.''

Joaquín chose that moment to reopen the front door.

Loudly.

As he entered the kitchen he brandished a battered red notebook TJ had not seen before. ''I found it.'' He slapped it on the counter. ''So, I may bring in my bag?''

He had forgotten to tell her the plan.

He prayed she would overlook the slight.

But of course, she did not. ''Let me guess. Tomás asked you to keep an eye on me while he heads back to San Diego to do the manly work, right?''

Evidently Joaquín could not lie to this woman any easier than he, for his friend managed to evade her piercing gaze for all of five seconds before he nodded reluctantly.

''I see. I tell you what, Joe. Why don't you do me a favor and get my bags and bring them out here while I call a cab? Then you can move into my room.''

Joaquín looked to him.

''*Cariñ*—''

She stabbed him with the unholiest of glares as Joaquín retreated to do her bidding. The man knew full well she could not be held against her will.

He, however, did not care. ''Have you no sense, woman?'' He tapped her jaw. ''Did this teach you nothing? You think these men are not serious? They most certainly are. They would do to you what they have done to Magdalena before your precious bellhop can even lift the phone to call the police.''

She said nothing. She simply turned away from him to round the island and pluck her black bag and purse from the counter. Then she walked to the foyer.

Calmly.

"You are not leaving."

She ignored him still, leaving him naught to do but grab her arm to haul her back. She spun around, jerking her body to the wall as she glared up at him.

"Get your hands off me!"

"*Querida,* I beg you."

"Now."

He was aware of Joaquín setting the bags down in the kitchen and passing behind him to escape through the front door as he shook his head slowly, firmly. "I cannot let you leave."

"You can't stop me."

"I can and I am."

"Fine, hold me here—now. Illegally. But tell me, Tomás, how are you going to get to sleep tonight knowing the second your eyes are closed, I'm gone. Or are you going to chain me to the bed with your handcuffs? Is that what this has come to? Do you need to run my life that badly? Or do you just want me to hate you? Because if that's all it is, let me save you the trouble—I'm already halfway there."

He closed his eyes. Absorbed the ache.

She was correct. In the end there was naught he could do.

Joaquín. His friend would help him.

He must.

TJ drew a deep breath and prepared himself.

He was ready. He could do this.

He released her and stepped back. "Go."

"What?"

"Now. Leave me. Do what you will."

"Is this a trick?"

He laughed curtly. "No trick. But you do me this one favor, *sí?* When you look back on this day, you remember—I did not abandon you, *Cariño. You* left me."

Those beautiful blue eyes.

He stared into them, praying she had heard the true message in his words. But she had not. The ghost of her father was too strong. Perhaps his spirit always would be.

It mattered not.

For she picked up her bags and left.

He turned away from the door as it closed softly and stared into his home. His sanctuary these five years past, this pile of stucco and tile was now his curse. She was everywhere. In this kitchen where he had spent so many hours. In the water he had yet to drain from his tub and in the sheets he would soon be forced to strip from his bed. In the photo that stood beside it.

And in that cursed candle.

He picked it up and uncorked the stopper, inhaling as he had so many times these past months her ship was away.

It was not right.

But then, it never had been.

Though this cold wax carried the scent of vanilla, it had never carried her essence. That part of her that clung to her flesh after he had washed the manmade fragrance from her. He had long since wondered what she smelled like without the perfume mingling within her own true scent.

Now he knew.

And he wished to *Dios* he did not.

He hefted the candle and hurled it across the room with all his might, welcoming the shatter splintering the air as it smashed into the sink.

It was done.

The waiting was truly over.

It had lasted eight months and fourteen days. And though at times it had pained him greatly, he had just discovered a far deeper wound. For the ache of waiting for Karin Marie Scott was nothing compared to the agony of letting her go.

Chapter 13

She still couldn't believe it.

He'd let her go.

Tomás had actually let her walk out of his house, put her own bags into the hatch of Joe's truck, opened her own door and just left. If she and Joe weren't stuck in this blasted parking lot of a border crossing, she'd swear she'd dreamed it. The noxious carbon-monoxide fumes helped, too.

And the lack of conversation.

She finally sighed.

"Did you need something?"

"Just a word." Or two.

"Ah…" He glanced over. "I thought perhaps you would appreciate the quiet."

Quiet, yes. This oppressive silence, no.

Even amid the endless sea of honking cars and steady supply of bronzed vendors hawking everything from food to piñatas, blankets and pottery, she could feel it.

Stark. Heavy.

Stifling.

They'd been gone all of fifteen minutes, and it was already weighing on her shoulders—right along with TJ's absence.

She sighed. "How long do we have before you're supposed to check in with him?"

"*Cómo?*"

She actually managed a smile as she swallowed the lump in her throat. The same husky roll to his *r*'s. The same glossy hair. The same proud features. Except for the twin dimples and the small emerald earring, they were a pretty damn good match. No wonder Tomás had filled in for him. "Joe, did anyone ever tell you that you and Tomás look a lot alike?"

He grinned. "But I am more handsome, no?"

She laughed.

Yeah, there were differences. For one thing, Joe's grin carried a hell of a lot more pirate than panther.

Funny, she'd always been partial to cats.

"So whose prints were you hoping to find at my place?"

Yet another boy of ten or twelve slipped between the cars stalled beside them and squirted washer fluid over the windshield before Joe could wave him off. They were trapped into waiting as the boy, grinning and whistling, worked the suds across the glass. She couldn't help but be reminded of another boy on another street—and she had no doubt he hadn't been smiling.

"Tomás was not certain."

She stiffened and swung her gaze across the cab. She hadn't really expected Joe to answer. Apparently there were internal differences, as well.

"The man who struck you, he was Hispanic, no?"

"Yes."

He nodded. "Tomás realized one of your doctor friends may have easily met this man who struck you—and perhaps Magdalena, as well—if the doctor had been reduced at some time to scoring his fentanyl on the streets as China

White. Hence, this man who struck you should be able to identify the doctor we are seeking. And if this man has a criminal record—"

Understanding dawned. "His prints would be on file."

"*Sí.*"

"Are they?"

"So far, no hits."

"Oh." Disappointed, she fell silent.

The boy finished the windshield and spread his palms to show it off. Joe rolled the window down and passed a dollar through. He murmured something in Spanish, then turned to her as the boy bobbed his head and took off. "He will get the back and sides for another."

She knew as well as he did the glass was already sparkling.

"Tell me, Karin. Why do you not ask me what you really wish to know?"

Oh, God, where had she heard that before?

Then again, why not—at this rate, the snails would beat them home. "Does he always need to make the decisions?"

"You are here, are you not?"

"With an escort—and don't bother telling me you plan to drop me off at the curb and wave as you drive away."

"I will not. But if I heard your wish correctly, you asked to leave his house and for Tomás not to follow. Is this not what you have received?"

She wondered not for the first time what else this man had heard. "Yes, but—"

"So you wish for him to care so little he would allow you to endanger yourself?"

"It's *my* self."

"Indeed it is. Tell me, what would you do if I were to tell you I planned to press my foot on this gas pedal and crush that elderly man selling those blankets over there?"

Startled, she followed his finger. "You wouldn't."

"Ah, but if I did, would you stop to tell him, or would you simply push him out of the way?"

"I'd push. But that's different and you know it."

"Is it? You know this man?"

"No." But she was already feeling the bite of the trap.

"And yet you care what happens and would risk your life to save his?"

The boy was back at the window, chattering and gesturing to the back of the cab. Joe passed several dollars through the window, then rolled it up as the boy grinned and scampered off.

"Are you always this philosophical?"

"At times. I studied from my friend. I believe the two of you have met, no? And now may I ask a question of you?"

Something told her this setup was going to be worse than the last. She nodded, anyway—warily.

"Do you remember the first time our mutual friend called you *Cariño?*"

"Just how much did you hear of that fight?"

"Enough. Now do you remember?"

How could she not? It was at the wedding. He'd trapped her into that dance, melted her with that smoldering gaze and rolled her name over his tongue like she'd never heard it before and then refused to pronounce it correctly again—until tonight.

Joe chuckled. "I see you do remember. This is good, for you now know the first time my friend told you he loved you."

"What?"

That grin really did belong on the high seas. "Tomás was right. We must teach you Spanish, and soon. Lesson one—without the qualifier *'mi', Cariño*—not Karin—means love of my life, my heart. Though I suppose to Tomás, the two are interchangeable. As for lesson two, I suspect you may have heard a host of other words this afternoon that need translating as well. But you will forgive me if I decline, no? I do value my life, you know."

The *wedding?*

Tomás had known he loved her since the wedding?

I did not abandon you, Cariño. You left me.

He wasn't her father.

That was what he'd been telling her. She'd just been too pigheaded—and too scared—to listen. Sure, he could have used the words, but why? Her father had used them. So did her mother and her stepfather. One left and the other two *smothered.* Tomás was trying to tell her that he would meet her in the middle. He would take only what she offered and no more. And he would force nothing on her in return.

Funny, she'd always thought of love as black and white. It wasn't.

She saw now that love was black and white—and every color in between. It was steady and it was consistent, and if she gave it half a chance—if she gave him half a chance—it would even leave her room to breathe.

"Joe?"

"Sí?"

"Is there any way you can get us out of this parking lot faster than you got us in?"

That wide grin was back, a wink tagging close behind. *"Sí*…and, Karin?"

"Yes?"

"I never told you what that meant."

She smiled as he rolled down the window and reached under his seat to pull out a portable police siren and slap it on the roof. *"Sí,* you never did."

She was not coming back.

Why could he not accept this?

Go drain the tub, change the sheets. Burn them, if that is what it takes.

He would.

TJ tore his gaze from the sink and strode down the hall to his barren room. He would face the tub first, then the glass from the candle, and then the sheets. Perhaps then he would not be so tempted to call Joaquín on his cellular phone and demand an update before they had even crossed the border.

He reached the door to his room, took a deep breath and shoved it open. One down, one more to go. Avoiding the bed, he headed to the bathroom.

Madre de Dios.

The security alarm. He had yet to reset it.

He started to turn—and froze.

In front of the dresser.

Behind him.

But even as he heard the man's heavy breathing and smelled the distinctive cloying scent of hydrocarbon fumes, it was too late. The cloth was already clamped about his nose and his mouth, and then there was nothing but burning as the sevoflurane seared into his lungs amid the screaming claxon in his brain.

Karin.

And then, as the darkness crowded in, the prayer he had never thought to pray. Please to God, do not let her return now.

His car was gone.

Karin glanced at Joe as he pulled the truck into the drive.

His quick smile didn't fool her for a second. There was more grit than grin to that sudden twist of lips. "Wait here."

"I will not."

"You will do as I say. *¿Entiendes?*"

Good Lord, he was worse than Tomás.

She opened her mouth to argue as he shot across her to open the glove box—but the gun he withdrew crammed the words right back down her throat.

Panic slammed into their place.

But she didn't get a chance to voice that, either, because a split second later Joe was locking her into the cab and then he was gone, slipping around the side of the Spanish ranch with the deadly looking thing clamped within the hand he'd tucked behind his back. And then, she was alone in the silence.

For eternity.

Tomás claimed he'd found hell.

She no longer doubted him, because she'd found it, too.

But for her, hell was different. For her, it was counting her heartbeats as she sat in a dark-blue truck waiting to know if the man she loved was dead or alive. It was feeling each breath sear into her lungs as she wondered if he was taking his last. It was listening to every tweet and chirp of a blasted bird's song and wishing the damn thing would just shut up so she wouldn't miss the shot.

As if she could.

The front door opened.

Joe.

Alone.

She was fumbling for the handle to the truck door even before his hand came up to wave her into the house. The next thing she knew he was tugging her inside, closing the front door and reassuring her. Yes, the alarm had been off and Tomás was gone, but so were his keys, his wallet and his gun.

He was safe.

Maybe even stocking up before the grocery store closed. *Thank you, God.*

She slumped against the foyer wall as relief burned through the panic. And then she started shaking.

Great—delayed nerves.

"You are okay?"

She managed a jerky nod. "I think I'll just get s-some water." God, even her teeth were chattering. She searched for the professional calm she'd worked so hard to perfect over the past few years but discovered it, too, had fled in the face of this thoroughly unexpected bout of extremely personal panic.

"I will get it."

"No, I'll do it." She needed something to do. After all,

the second bout of panic had already set in. When TJ got back, she was going to have to face him. She drew a deep breath and headed for the sink, but stopped a good five feet away, jerking her gaze to the floor as something solid crunched between the soles of her tennis shoes.

Glass.

Once she really looked at the ceramic tiles, she could see the tiny shards everywhere. She kept on walking, inexplicably drawn to the sink. More glass. The remains of the candle. He'd smashed it. The discovery was comforting in an odd sort of way.

But the mess?

That was not.

"Karin?"

She ignored Joe as she turned and passed him at the entrance to the hallway and kept on walking.

He followed. "You are sure you are okay?"

She might be, if she could just make it to the bedroom. *One foot in front of the other* and she was there.

Facing the tangled sheets on the bed Tomás would never have left unmade. Hell, even she wouldn't have been able to handle them. Not after what had happened.

She forced herself to keep walking across the room, to bend down and bypass the wedding photo that had fallen to the floor as she'd searched frantically for the condom— until she was reaching blindly between the nightstand and the bed. Even before her hand brushed past the soft leather of his wallet to close over the cold smooth steel beyond, she knew—

Tomás had not left voluntarily.

And he did not have his gun.

"Relax. They will be there."

Unable to obey Joe any better than she'd been able to obey Tomás, Karin twisted her hands in her lap and picked up the longest prayer of her life right where she'd left off. She'd been praying for half an hour now, though it felt like half the day. Car after car slowed and veered to the right of the freeway, bailing out of the truck's path as they streaked past.

Like gleaming eyes, those brake lights leered.

Red. Taunting.

The steady siren atop their truck screamed at her, as well. All with the same message.

Why? Why hadn't she listened to him?

Tomás was right. She had been running.

Whenever anyone had gotten too close or asked too much, she just left. Sometimes calmly, sometimes loudly. Sometimes physically and sometimes just mentally. But it all boiled down to the same thing. She ran. But she'd never run so hard and so fast in all her life as she was running now.

And this time it was to someone.

To him.

But what if she couldn't find him? Or worse, what if she did—and it was too late? Joe was certain they had time. How much, he couldn't say. But he was positive whoever had taken Tomás was the same man who'd struck her. The morning hangups on her answering machine only added to his theory. Her presence in the apartment must have spooked the thug. Though obviously, the man had recovered enough to wait outside and follow them south. Only there, he hadn't been confronted with a distracted doorman he could slip past. He'd faced an alarm.

Until Joe disengaged it.

Once Joe entered the house, the thug had made his move through the master-bedroom window. The tool marks at the lock and on the sill were faint and fine enough to be professional, but they were there. Once inside, the man had simply waited again. And then she'd left, selfishly leaving Tomás behind—too angry, too hurt and too worried to think clearly.

That candle.

Joe was wrong. This wasn't his fault.

It was hers.

What if he was wrong about the rest?

"They *will* be there." He was repeating himself.

She wondered if he even knew.

When Joe reached out and locked his hand over hers, squeezing so hard her knuckles popped, she knew—he didn't. She turned her hand into his, locking on just as tight.

"Are you sure?"

Joe kept his gaze welded to the road as he slowed the truck to sub-light speed. Their freeway exit finally, mercifully, loomed ahead. "I am sure. I spoke to Admiral Banks myself, remember? He gave his word. He swore to me he would locate them all and have them there."

Tomás's father.

If Tomás wasn't dead, he was going to kill her.

Too bad. She hadn't known what else to do. Admiral Banks was one of a handful of men who had the authority to track down Doug, Shelley, the pharmacy chief and even Eric Hunter and throw them all into the same room. And the fact that Banks had tried to confront his son just this morning guaranteed he'd move heaven and earth to make it happen. Before she realized it, they were off the freeway, and Joe's right hand was back on the wheel.

Thank God he was driving.

She never would have been able to handle her own car, let alone Joe's truck, at this speed down these roads, and taking these turns. Dammit, couldn't he go any faster?

And then, suddenly, they were there.

The Naval Medical Center was looming ahead, the familiar sprawling mix of white concrete and glass growing larger and larger until all she saw were the main doors. She was vaulting out of the truck along with Joe, and by the time they'd slammed through the glass doors and made a beeline for the stairs, she wasn't sure who was dragging who anymore. It didn't matter, because they were both out of breath as they reached the outer door to the chief of staff's office.

It was already open.

And someone was already yelling.

"Goddamn it, I want answers, and I want them now!"

"*Jesucristo.* He has blown this for certain."

A second later they were in the room. With the skill an ER doctor would give his malpractice insurance for, Joe had quickly and calmly lanced the admiral's tirade and triaged the situation. Shelley and the pharmacy chief were separated and escorted out by the three camouflaged Shore Patrol and two civilian cops the admiral had used to pluck them from their Saturday-evening lives, leaving Doug Callahan behind. The two remaining Shore Patrol flanked him, and he did not look happy.

In fact, he looked downright ill.

And he was looking at her.

Right then, she knew—Doug *knew*.

She advanced on him, trapping him between the secretary's desk and the row of file cabinets. *"Where is he?"*

His color bled down to match the white T-shirt tucked into his faded jeans. "I d-don't know."

"The hell you don't. You nearly lost your dinner when you saw me. You're sweating, your pupils are dilated, and if I timed the pulse throbbing in your neck, I swear you'd break—"

"Karin."

She stiffened as hands as firm as that voice clamped down on her shoulders.

Joe.

He pulled her back several steps and turned her around to face him. "You are not helping. Please, if you cannot remain quiet, I must ask you to leave."

"But…" Her argument died as she looked into that dark steady gaze. If anyone could handle Doug right now, it was Joe.

Hell, she couldn't even stop shaking.

"Okay."

Another set of hands took over as Joe turned back to Doug.

She was dimly aware of being led through the doorway into the chief of staff's office. It was only after she'd been pressed down into a chair that she realized the man who'd led her was the Chief-of-Staff himself. "Admiral."

He shook his head wearily. "Thomas. I think we're well beyond rank here, wouldn't you say?"

She jerked a nod. "Yes, sir—Thomas. Oh, God, what if—"

His arms banded around her. "Shhh, he's going to be okay. I didn't search eight damn years just to lose him now. They'll find him. We'll find him. You hold on to that— and that's an order, Lieutenant. You got that?"

She actually smiled at his contradiction, then winced as she pulled away, getting her first really good look at Thomas Banks since the party. This wasn't a naval admiral sitting two feet away clenching his hands to hers. It wasn't even a doctor.

This was a father.

Tomás was wrong. His father loved him.

Desperately.

If he could see the man now, he'd know it was true.

Grief and worry had taken a hellish toll on the confident handsome guest of honor of Dr. Manning's party. Bloodshot eyes, ravaged cheeks and a five-o'clock shadow she'd bet Admiral Banks hadn't sported in thirty years scuffed his jaw. The stubble was gray and getting grayer before her very eyes.

She squeezed his hands back. "He's fine. I know it."

But what if he wasn't?

Don't go there. Don't even think it.

Talk. "Did you get anything out of them?"

He nodded. "But not much. Ryder admits she let Callahan cover up her fentanyl loss."

"What?"

The admiral nodded grimly. "Yup. She says she misplaced her narcotic supply for a four-way heart bypass Friday morning. Her career's over. So is Callahan's. He admits he extracted sex from her in exchange for the favor, but he's still swearing up and down he had nothing to do with my son's disappearance.''

That explained Shelley's mood when they'd run into each other. The woman had needed drugs all right, just not for a fix. She'd needed them to save her career. It made sense. Shelley wasn't the type to look for sex outside a happy marriage, let alone with someone like Doug Callahan.

Sex?

Good God, why hadn't she thought of it before?

''Sex.''

Another nod. ''I heard. Any mention of the incident with Lt. Callahan will be stricken from your record. I'll make sure of it.''

The hell with her record—and her career.

Magdalena.

She shot to her feet.

''What is it?''

''Let's go.'' She was barreling through the door before he could argue, stalking up between the Shore Patrol and slamming Doug back into the secretary's chair before Joe could grab her. ''You son of a bitch.''

''Karin!''

She whirled on Joe. ''Ask the bastard who else he's been sleeping with—and how *old* she was.''

All eyes turned to Doug.

He swallowed. Hard.

And then he broke. Sobbed, really. Blubbered.

It was disgusting. He was disgusting.

And she was going to be sick.

''Eric set it up. I swear to God, I didn't know. By the time I found out she was jailbait, it was too late. He's addicted. He knew I'd find out eventually. So he set me up.''

"You didn't have to sleep with her."

"*Karin.*" Joe.

She swung her gaze to his. "She was a kid, dammit. I saw her picture. She was just a kid."

"Who killed her?" Again, Joe.

"Eric. I swear I had nothing to do with it. I didn't even know. She was staying at my place. When I heard about the two girls that had OD'd, I flipped out. God, he was sharing the damned fentanyl, giving it away. Magdalena overheard us arguing. She actually threatened me. Told me she knew some PI south of the border she could call if she ever got in a jam. I blew it off. Hell, why not? She was sleeping with me. Like she really had friends in high places. But then I caught her at the hospital, and I freaked. She said she'd come to visit me, but I knew better. The next day *José* shows—and he's poking around."

"The note."

Doug whipped his stare back to her. "What?"

"She sent me a note."

Class twos are walking. At least now they knew why Magdalena had phrased it correctly. She'd just written down what she'd heard, exactly as she'd heard it. "But I still don't understand why she sent the note to me. I didn't even know her."

Doug sighed. "But she knew of you. Eric told her. How else would they know enough to set me up?"

"Set you up? They didn't set you up. You did that all by yourself. You're a sleaze, Doug. A parasite. Don't you get it? You were the adult. You were the responsible one. You knew better. And you sure as hell better know where Tomás is."

"I told you, I don't."

"You're lying. I saw your face when I walked in. You looked like you'd seen a ghost—" She gasped as pure blinding terror ripped through her. "Oh, my God, is he already dead?"

Doug raked his hands through his hair. "I don't know.

All I know is Eric was supposed to do you two together. Make it look like a private party that got out of hand. The deaths didn't start till your ship got back in port, so they'd think it was you."

"*Where?*" Joe.

"Jesus, I keep telling you. I don't know!"

Before her eyes, calm, cool, collected Joe just snapped. He launched himself at Doug, roaring with fury as he wrapped his hands about the man's throat, pressing his thumbs into Doug's windpipe, damn near severing it before the Shore Patrol could stop him. "If you do not tell me where he is, I swear on my mother's grave I will strangle you here and now."

Doug choked, gasped, turned blue. Terror streaked through his eyes, turning them black.

She grabbed Joe's hands, pulled at them, but he wouldn't budge. "Joe, please, back off."

He did—barely.

Doug hacked and wheezed. "T-Tijuana. S-some m-motel. That's all I know. I swear. He didn't trust me with the rest."

Joe slammed Doug's gagging form back into the chair and left him there as he spun to her. "Karin, get what you will need. We leave now."

"You know where he is?"

"I do not. But we leave regardless. And we pray."

Why could he not move?

This darkness, this fog. This heaviness of limbs he simply could not seem to overcome. Nor even find the desire to try.

This was wrong.

He did not sleep thus. He had never slept thus. Not as a boy sleeping on dirt waiting for the next cuff from his mother's latest companion nor as a special agent waiting for the phone, his beeper, even the alarm clock. Unlike Karin, he had always been able to rouse himself.

Karin.

She was gone.

He was gone. Drugged. *Sí*—the cloth.

He remembered now.

Karin. He must find her. Protect her.

He drew strength from the need, gathered the fragments of his disembodied thoughts and drew them together, forcing them to coalesce as he began to claw his way through the mist.

There. His eyes were open now, though barely.

The room was dim.

He was sitting, perhaps reclining, and his hands, his arms—why could he still not feel them? He studied them.

Heplock.

The IV port was embedded in one of the veins on the back of his left hand, the short tubing already taped down, the taunting rubber stopper already awaiting more of…what? What was this drug that embraced him within its seductive thrall?

Fentanyl?

And from whom had he received it?

TJ forced his lids to raise farther, waiting patiently for the room to take shape.

A hotel?

Sí. The poorly plastered walls, the threadbare coverlet on the bed, the nightstand with its single lamp, the stained carpet beneath his boots. The scarred legs of his chair.

He was sitting. And…someone was standing.

He concentrated all his energies, all of his senses, and forced his gaze up. Focused it.

A man. At the dresser.

Tall, blond, digging into a bag not unlike the one Karin had brought into his home.

Eric Hunter.

He turned and smiled. "Hey there, José. Looks like you made it back, after all. I was starting to wonder. Hell, I was half-afraid you wouldn't need another hit."

TJ worked his throat and mouth, both parched. Despite this, he managed to force sound through. "Hit?"

The grin grew.

"Fentanyl. Well, you've got a bit of ketamine in you, too. Call it a bonus. How's it feel? Damn sweet stuff, isn't it?"

Hunter *used.*

"Why?" Still hoarse, but audible.

A shrug. "Why not? At any rate, it doesn't matter—not to you, good buddy. Not anymore." He turned to the bag and resumed his rummaging. "Ah…"

Carajó, a syringe.

And then, an ampule.

For himself?

No, not this one. TJ was sure of it. Hunter's hands were shaking. This one was for the good doctor himself.

TJ studied Hunter as he prepared the injection. Watched him remove the cap from the syringe, break off the tip of the glass ampule and slide the needle inside to draw the fentanyl into the syringe. The man would not inject beneath the band of his watch. Too risky, given his profession.

No, he would go lower.

Hunter proved him right as he unzipped his jeans, dropping them low to trace his fingers up his inner thigh, finding his own femoral vein with an ease that bespoke of a rich and lengthy affair with this drug. He sighed as the needle pierced the skin, then closed his eyes briefly, smiling as he emptied the syringe and withdrew the needle. This was more in anticipation, TJ knew. For even injected directly into the vein like so, it would still take several minutes for the drug to take effect.

Excellent. Hunter would no doubt wish to savor his high.

This meant he had time.

Time to fight this siren singing in his own blood.

He dropped his gaze to the heplock. Most clever. Evidently Hunter had learned from his mistakes. He would wager there was no puncture in his upper arm as there had been with Magdalena to suggest he had been subdued. And since the sevoflurane he had inhaled had long since been excreted from his system, the tox screen would not even show it. But if he was still in Mexico, as he suspected, the screen would not even be run. But perhaps Hunter's cleverness was overshadowed by his self-confidence.

For Hunter had misjudged the dose.

Already TJ could feel his mind and body breaking free. His wits were not nearly so dulled, nor his breathing so depressed. Indeed, he could feel his heart rate increasing, as well. Soon he would find the strength to stand and fight, to search for Karin. But as Hunter turned with yet another syringe and ampule in hand, he knew there would be no more time, for this injection was his. And from the amount Hunter was drawing into that syringe, it was clear. This was to be his last.

The fentanyl would take him quickly.

He would have five minutes, ten at most.

This was it, then. He would simply stop breathing. For who carried the antidote in their pocket?

Not even Karin.

And she did not even know he was missing.

"Relax, buddy. Don't look so down. We're not ready for you to take the full ride yet. I'm just gonna give you a little lift so you'll be nice and happy when your girlfriend shows."

"Girlfriend?"

The man chuckled as he dumped the empty ampule into his bag. "Come on, let's not play stupid. I know what you really are. Just like I know who you've been screwing. I had Karin watched. In fact, I have to be honest with you—I'm a little pissed you got to her first." He shrugged as he withdrew an alcohol swipe from the bag. "But don't worry, I'll take my turn, anyway. Usually I like a bit more participation, but what the hell. I won't get another chance, will I? Then again—" another chuckle "—neither will you."

TJ stared into that obscene grin as it drew closer.

He must act now or it would be too late.

True, he had no weapon save his head and his bare hands, and the latter were useless right now. It mattered not. For he also possessed the one emotion he had never been able to direct at Karin for long. Anger. And it was in roiling abundance at this moment. He had no problem drawing on it freely for this man, feeding it as he stared into Hunter's leering face.

The bridge of that arrogant nose.

It was his only hope.

TJ studied the still-trembling hands swiping the alcohol pad over the rubber stopper on his heplock—out of habit, no doubt—and pictured again those same hands on his beloved.

The bruise on her jaw.

The blinding anguish of lifting her precious body, yet feeling nothing but lifeless weight in his arms. The memories stoked his fury, his rage. He held to it fiercely, forcing himself to wait until Hunter reached for the syringe and bent low to inject it.

Ahora.

He reared his head up, then jerked it down with all his might, slamming his forehead into the man's face. He himself did not feel the pain—a gift of the ketamine, no doubt.

But Hunter did.

"Son of a bitch!" His free hand came up, cupping his face as the blood poured down. "You broke my goddamn nose!"

TJ did not give him time to recover as he vaulted to his feet and launched his body into the still-cursing man. They went down together—but Hunter did not get up.

Why?

TJ rolled away from the man's limp body and slowly worked to convince his own hands to cooperate. And then, he knew why. There was blood seeping from a gash at the rear of Hunter's skull. The Virgin Mother must have helped him with his aim, for the man had struck the dresser on his way to the floor.

Hunter was out cold.

Now. He must move, and quickly.

But…he could not.

He dragged himself to his feet slowly and tried to shake the growing fog from his brain and from his limbs. Why was the lethargy worsening? This was more than exhaustion.

And his mind—it was floating again, images taking shape that should not be. Not here. Karin—she was not with him.

Why then, could he see her?

She was so real. So warm, so welcoming.

No, this was not right. She was angry with him.

He knew this. *Fight* this. He staggered to the mirror and stared at himself to convince himself she was not beside him. And there, reflected in the cracked glass, he saw it.

The syringe.

He forced his gaze down from the glass and stared at the needle that was embedded into his upper arm. He could not even lift his hands to remove it. He stared back into the mirror, searching. *Sí*, his *Cariño* was a mirage, but this syringe was not.

And it was empty.

He did not remember floating back to the floor. Perhaps this was but a hallucination, as well. He knew not.

Once more, he found he no longer cared.

The siren, she was calling to him sweetly now. And the shape she took was not one he could resist.

So this was dying.

Most curious. He had always thought to go by way of the gun or even the knife. But perhaps this was for the best, for this drug allowed his lady to be at his side, to hold him and to caress him as he drifted to the end.

Chapter 14

She'd revised her definition of hell.

It was a Mexican city by the name of Tijuana. More specifically, it was the side roads, back alleys and slums of that city. It was each and every damned crowded motel parking lot they'd driven in, around and then right back out of as they searched for Tomás's Explorer. It was the wait.

"He's amazing, you know," the Admiral said.

Karin pulled her gaze from the bumper of the last car of the lot they'd just finished searching and followed the hoarse whisper across the rear seat of the Mexican police cruiser she, Admiral Banks and Joe had dived into at the border ten minutes ago.

She couldn't remember the driver's name.

Hell, she couldn't remember her own name right now.

The Admiral swallowed hard. "It was an accident. One I take full responsibility for. One that was never supposed to happen. My wife and I'd had a fight. She'd left me. I used to think it was a mistake. Especially after we made up. But when Tomás showed up at my door eight years ago and then left before I even got to see his face, I knew. It might have been an accident, but it was no mistake. *He* was not a mistake.''

"No, he's not."

"I love him, you know? I can't explain it. Hell, I'll be the first to admit I don't even know him. But I love him."

"I know."

Oh, God, did she ever.

It had take her long enough to figure it out, but she definitely knew. Because she loved Tomás, too. But what if she never got to tell him? What if she never got to look into those dark smoldering eyes again and just say it. What if—

"He's fine, Karin. He has to be. You and I—and Joe, too—we'd all know it if he wasn't. We would."

She nodded numbly as the cruiser turned into yet another motel lot crammed with Saturday-night collegiate and sailor mobiles. The sorority neon-pink-and-yellow Jeeps were easy to spot. The military cars and pickups with their alternating blue-and-white officer and red-and-white enlisted Department of Defense stickers were not far behind.

Five sport utility vehicles in all.

Three Ford Explorers—two were even black.

Neither was his.

She scrubbed back a fresh bout of tears as they left yet another motel lot behind—and then jerked her gaze to the front of the Mexican cruiser as Joe wrenched the bleating cell phone off the dash and sealed it to his ear.

A stream of fiery Spanish filled the car. Before he'd even finished speaking, their driver had slammed on the brakes, thrown the transmission into reverse and peeled back down the side street they'd just driven up. An intersection and a one-eighty turn later, Joe was tossing the phone back to the dash.

He turned. "They found the car. Ten blocks, two minutes."

They made it in one.

Seconds later she and the admiral had vaulted from the cruiser, black bags in hand. Joe and the driver were already at the door, joining the other two Mexican cops smashing through the wood. The cheap slab splintered, then gave way altogether. A split second later so did the cops—as she and the admiral catapulted through. And then all she saw was him.

Tomás.

Please, God, no!

He was lying on the floor on his side, two feet from a chair, a bed and Eric Hunter's body. His eyes were closed, and his skin was gray. She jumped over Eric and slammed to her knees beside the man she loved more than life itself, turning him to his back and fitting her fingers to his carotid artery as the admiral took the airway.

"He's not breathing."

Goddamn it—pull yourself together!

She purged the panic from her brain as the admiral started mouth-to-mouth on his own son and forced herself to fuse her frantic stare to her watch. Her own heart nearly stopped as she timed the excruciatingly slow beats beneath her fingers.

Oh God.

"His pulse is thirty—I'm going in."

She ripped her fingers from his neck and tore into her black bag, not bothering to wait for a response as the Mexican cops dragged Eric's moaning carcass from the room. The admiral wouldn't be free to do a damn thing except breathe until they were done—one way or the other. She caught sight of Tomás's face as she grabbed the precious vial of Narcan and the needle she'd need to inject it with from her bag.

Eyes closed. Skin beyond gray now, damn near blue.

Lifeless.

No, don't look. Don't think.

Act.

She tore her gaze from his face and dumped the capped

needle and drug next to her knees on the filthy carpet, then plowed through her bag again, yanking out a rubber tourniquet, tape, alcohol swipes and the IV catheter and port she'd need to form a new heplock. She'd already seen the one Eric had inserted, but the vein had blown. It was useless now.

She shivered as she stretched Tomás's right arm to her knees. Dead weight.

"I need light, dammit!"

The heavens parted on cue, even concentrating the rays for her as they burned down from above. Flashlight.

Joe, no doubt.

She could hear him breathing, feel him praying two inches behind her back as she wrapped the rubber tourniquet just above Tomás's elbow and snapped it into place. She left his veins to cook as she tore off a section of tape and tacked it to her own forearm, before pulling the cap from the syringe. Plunging the needle deep into the vial of Narcan, she drew up four precious milligrams of the narcotic antagonist.

"Hold."

Joe grabbed the syringe from her hand a split second before she lowered her fingers to tap them to the underside of Tomás's arm. Her latest prayer was answered in the form of his weak—but definitely there—anticubital vein.

Thank you, God.

"Pulse is twenty." His father, and still breathing.

Screw sterilization.

Karin bypassed the alcohol swipe and went straight for the catheter, pulling the cap off the end with her teeth to spit it out. A second later she was piercing skin, then the spurting scarlet flash as Tomás's dark beautiful blood flooded the end chamber.

"I'm in."

And the needle was out, leaving the thin catheter embedded within the vein. She tore the tape from her arm and used it to anchor the end of the catheter, then grabbed the

threaded IV port to pull and spit its cap with her teeth, as
well. A quarter twist and the port was locked into place,
the heplock complete. She unsnapped the rubber tourniquet
with one hand and pushed the saline flush with the other,
before detaching and pitching that needle, as well.

"Syringe."

It was in her hand before she raised it, cap already gone.
Then the Narcan was shooting through the IV port, heading
straight for the neuroreceptors in Tomás's brain.

And now the wait.

Narcan had been nicknamed "Jesus Christ" for good
reason. If they'd made it in time, the drug would literally
raise Tomás from the dead. Within two minutes they'd either get all of him back—or none.

She fought the panic slamming back into her with yet
another round of prayers as she finally caved in to the need
to touch this man, the way she wanted to be touching him.
Not as a doctor, but as a woman. She didn't even care that
his father was still breathing for him. She took her snatches
where she could, stroking the side of his handsome face,
smoothing the silk from his forehead, leaning closer to
press a kiss to his cheek between breaths and *beg* him to
come back to her.

His color was better, a result of his father's breathing.

But still, those gorgeous eyes would not open.

Please, God, *please.*

If Tomás got up off this floor and walked out of her life
after she'd pushed him away, she'd find a way to handle
it. She would. But she had to see that smoldering gaze one
more time. She had to know this incredibly precious man
would live.

Dammit, she couldn't take it any longer.

She grabbed the penlight from her bag and eased his
right eyelid up, wiping back her tears as she stared into
reality. She didn't even need to turn the blasted light on.

His pupils were still pinpoints.

Tomás was still hovering on the other side.

A hand closed over her shoulder, squeezed.

His father.

The admiral was blinking back his own tears as she met his tortured gaze. "It's too soon, honey. Another minute."

Another breath.

She nodded numbly, lowering her lips to his dusky temple as the admiral completed the breath. "Please, Tomás, I'll call my mother, I swear it. Just please don't leave me. I love you too much. I need you." Unable to stop herself, she lifted his lids again, and this time the tears started pouring from her eyes, rolling down to splash onto his cheeks. Because those beautiful black pupils were dilating right before her very eyes, returning to normal.

And then he blinked.

And smiled.

The smolder was even back as he slowly lifted his hand to wipe the tears from her cheeks. It didn't help.

They were still raining down.

"If this is but another *ilusión, Cariño,* I care not. For I do not wish it to end."

"It's not. I'm here."

He was here.

His smile grew. "Then I will answer. *Yo lo amo y yo lo necesito también, querida.* I love you, and I need you, as well."

The dam broke then, and the tears gushed forth.

By the time she'd gotten them under control, she was so far downstream she had to turn to his father to ask him to complete the neural checks…but the admiral was gone.

And so was Joe.

That was when she heard the Life-Flight chopper Joe had had standing by. Good Lord, how could she have missed that noise? The damn thing sounded as if it was right outside the room. The blades were still rotating. Twenty minutes and she'd have this man exactly where he'd been trying to get her all day.

The hospital.

And she'd never been happier in her entire life.

Tomás reached for her hand and squeezed it, snapping her attention back to his beautiful face and the neural checks she still needed to make.

"Smile for me again."

He did.

Gorgeous and—more importantly—even.

No brain damage evident in his facial muscles.

"Just relax, okay? I need to check your eyes." She lifted the lid to his left, flashing the penlight into it as she studied the pupil of his right, shooting yet another round of gratitude heavenward as it contracted.

"Tomás."

He chuckled, ignoring the scold as he slid his wandering hands up the rest of her body to wrap his arms about her neck and draw her closer. *"Sí, Cariño?"*

She smoothed his hair from his face. "I still need to check your vitals and the rest of your reflexes."

He tugged her closer until her lips were hovering a fraction of an inch from his, his warm steady breath spiriting hers away as the devil slipped into his smile. "Ah, *querida,* my reflexes are working just fine. Every last one of them."

She couldn't argue with that.

Nor could she argue with his kiss.

It was well past midnight, but the testing was complete. She'd finally convinced Joe it was safe to leave. Frankly she suspected the man was off to pay Eric a little late-night visit at his new digs—a steel cage in the Navy brig. Joe had refused to say. She also suspected Eric was going to wish he'd gone the way of Magdalena by the time Joe was done with him.

Too bad.

Karin closed the cover to Tomás's chart containing his latest blood workup and laid it back on the counter at the nurses' station.

"Thank you."

The nurse nodded as she retrieved it. "No problem, Doctor. I assume you'll be staying the night?"

"Yes."

"Would you like an extra pillow and—"

She shook her head. "That won't be necessary."

She doubted she'd get much sleep watching Tomás sleep, anyway. Even if she did nod off, she'd prefer to do it upright, so she'd wake if he stirred. Besides, despite the hour, she had something she still needed to take care of.

Before she chickened out.

Karin waited just long enough for the nurse to round the counter and busy herself sorting the next scheduled distribution of meds before she picked up the phone. She took a deep breath, her hand not quite steady as she punched out the number she'd been avoiding all week.

One and a half rings was all it took.

Given the hour, it wasn't surprising.

"Hello?"

"Mom?"

"Karin? Honey, what's wrong? I've been trying to call you all—"

"I know. I'm sorry, Mom. Look, I know it's late, but I've been really tied up today and I wanted to return your calls. And I wanted…I wanted to tell you I love you."

"Oh, honey. I love you, too."

She could hear the tears in her mother's voice. Hell, she could feel them in hers. Another deep breath. "Anyway, I'd like to know if you can get together this week. I'm on leave until next Monday and, well…" Her breath came out in a rush. "There are some things I'd like to talk to you about." There, that wasn't nearly as hard as she'd thought it would be.

"You just name the time and I'll be there."

"How about tomorrow? Around noon? You could meet me at the hospital cafeteria."

"I'll be there."

"And, Mom?" She twisted the cord about her hand, then

took another breath as she unwound it. "Do you think Westin can make it, too? When we're done, there's someone I'd like you both to meet."

"Does he have long dark hair and gorgeous bedroom eyes?"

Karin laughed. "Yeah, he does."

"We're looking forward to it. Good night, honey."

"Good night."

Karin stared at the receiver as she clicked it into place.

Bedroom eyes.

It was a pretty good description.

Whenever she looked into those smoky eyes, that was exactly where she wished she and Tomás were. But despite his arguments to the contrary, he wasn't getting her there for another day, perhaps two. Not until she'd made sure the side effects of the ketamine were completely gone from his system. She turned away from the counter and headed back to his room. Nope, no more hallucinations for Tomás. Not even the ones he'd confessed to her while they were waiting for the CAT scan results from his liver and kidneys.

She blushed just thinking about one in particular.

The next time he was doing *that* to her, she was damn sure going to be around to feel it—and feel him.

In the end he'd agreed.

Karin reached the private room at the end of the hall and pushed the door open and froze.

His father.

She tried to back out again, but both men had already turned their heads. Tomás was sitting up in bed, the white gown he'd grumbled over having to don plastered to a chest that was much too healthy to be within fifty miles of this place. And standing next to Tomás was an equally handsome—smiling—man. This close together, they looked a lot alike.

Lord, he was going to age well.

"I didn't mean to interrupt. I'll just wait out—"

Tomás shook his head, smiling as he stretched out his

arm. "Come." He took her hand in his as she reached his side and kissed it. "*Querida,* I would like you to meet my father, Thomas Banks." He turned to his father. "Thomas, I am honored to present Karin Scott, my beloved and someday—if she will have me—my wife."

Tomás held his breath as he waited for Karin's response.

But unlike these past eight months, there was no need.

Her deep blue gaze widened, then softened, then shimmered, bright with unshed tears. He dearly hoped they would not fall—at least not until his father left, for surely her joy would cause his own to spill down as well.

A throat cleared.

Whose, he could not have said.

And then his father spoke. "I should be getting home."

Tomás nodded. "I understand. Perhaps, if you have the time, you would stop by tomorrow and we will speak again, no?"

A blinding smile.

Yes, the tears were to come for certain.

"I'll be here."

He managed another nod as Karin squeezed his hand. "*Bien.* And then perhaps when this woman releases me from this place, you will come to my home. There is this motorcycle I would show you. It was a gift from both my fathers, though I did not know this until today."

A stiff nod, no doubt from the effort to keep the tears Tomás could also see in his father's eyes from falling, then a handshake.

His father turned and left the room.

Tomàs wondered briefly if this feeling he had of Antonio smiling and leaving, as well, was real or merely another *ilusión.* He decided it mattered not as Karin's soft hands found his again. He sighed as she leaned down to press her lips to his.

"I love you."

He smiled. "*Sí,* this I know. But what I am not so certain of is whether or not you will have a man who tends to meddle in your life—and though he will try to curtail this flaw, he will most likely slip and do so again.''

''Does this mean I can call my mother back and rescind my lunch invitation?''

He blinked.

She smiled softly. ''No, I haven't told her. I thought I'd save that for tomorrow. But only if I can bring her up here afterward and introduce her to her future son-in-law.''

Dios mío.

The tears had finally come and there was no stopping them. He did not even try. He merely lifted his hands to caress those cheeks of ivory silk and stare into the most beautiful blue eyes he had ever seen. As she stroked his jaw, he turned his face into her hand and breathed deeply.

Such sweet perfume.

Even here, in this place, with these smells.

''Tomás?''

''*Sí, Cariño?*''

''How long would you have waited?''

He threaded his fingers into those golden curls and drew his lady close, sighing as her arms slipped about his neck to guide him the rest of his way home.

''Forever.''

* * * * *

Spines will tingle…mysteries await…
and dangerous passion lurks in the night
as Silhouette presents

DREAM SCAPES!

Thrills and chills abound in these four romances
welcoming readers to the dark side of love.
Available May 2001 at your favorite retail outlet:

IMMINENT THUNDER
by Rachel Lee

STRANGER IN THE MIST
by Lee Karr

FLASHBACK
by Terri Herrington

NOW AND FOREVER
by Kimberly Raye

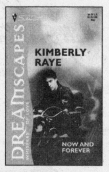

SILHOUETTE®
MAKES YOU
A STAR!

Look in the back pages of
all June Silhouette series books to find an
exciting new contest with fabulous prizes!
Available exclusively through Silhouette.

Don't miss it!

Silhouette®
Where love comes alive™

P.S. Watch for details on how you can meet
your favorite Silhouette author.

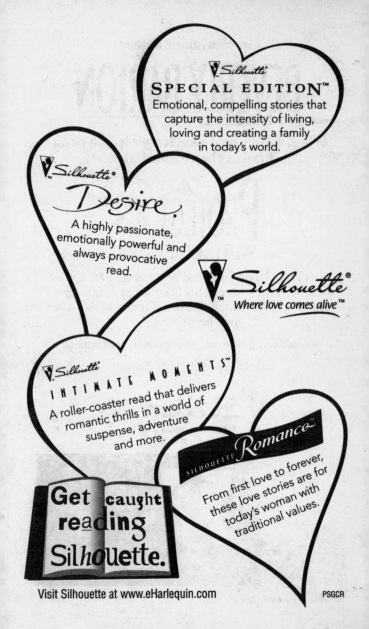